the women of hearts book four

MARCI BOLDEN
SECRET HEARTS

ISBN-13: 978-1-950348-41-1

SECRET HEARTS

MARCI BOLDEN

PINK
SAND
PRESS

PROLOGUE

"God damn it, Eliza," Quinn Stanton muttered under his breath. He checked his phone for the twentieth time, but no matter how many times he looked, there was no reply from his ex-wife. *Again.* They'd been divorced for long enough that Quinn knew her pattern. Eliza met a new guy, immersed herself in his life, and started ignoring Quinn's calls and texts. He understood why she'd ignore questions about *how* she was, *where* she was. But when it came to their son...

When Eliza didn't show to pick up Danny, Quinn had loaded the boy in his car, grabbed a fast food kid's meal for dinner, and headed out toward his ex's house. Eliza was supposed to pick up Danny—per their custody agreement. Since she'd started dating before the divorce was even final, she'd said that having Quinn come back and forth to their old house made her feel vulnerable—and even watched. She wanted to know that she could have the privacy to date, and be free, during those precious few hours a week when Danny was with his dad. Eliza was probably snuggled up with the flavor of the month on the couch, making out, watching a movie, oblivious to the fact that it was Sunday evening and Quinn's weekend visitation with Danny had ended—three hours ago.

As Quinn pulled into the driveway of the house he and Eliza used to share, he peered in the rearview mirror at his six-year-old son. Danny was sound asleep in the back seat. Quinn cut the engine on his SUV and sighed. The living room lights were on, and by the flickering images he could make out through the curtains, he could tell the TV was on too. So Quinn hesitated in the driveway before getting out of the car. He knew Eliza would be pissed he'd showed up. She'd make accusations. Maybe make a scene. If one of the cops from work she was so fond of dating was over at the house, then... Well, Quinn expected to end up in cuffs. Or worse. But it was a Sunday night, and Danny was supposed to be back home with his mom. It wasn't his fault if Eliza had her head too far up some dude's ass to tell time.

Quinn checked his watch and decided to try one last time. He stepped quietly out of the car so he didn't wake his son. He closed the car door softly and paced halfway up the drive while dialing Eliza's phone. He squinted to try to see movement or shapes or anything beyond the privacy curtains hanging in the living room. Nothing seemed to move or change as he listened to her phone ring and ring and ring.

"Come on, Li-li," Quinn grumbled. "Answer the phone, damnit."

Quinn tossed a glance back at the car to assure himself Danny was still asleep. His stomach clenched in a knot as he looked at the front door of his former house. Memories flooded back as he fought the highlight reel in his brain. Putting out the holiday doormat monogrammed with the letter S for Stanton. Hanging bunny wreaths at Easter. Shoveling a path to the car when Danny was just coming home from the hospital, born six weeks premature.

Quinn sighed. If he'd known then what he knew now... Danny and Eliza had come through an incredibly complicated pregnancy, but nearly losing her life and their son had changed Eliza. She came home from the hospital angry, afraid, defensive. She seemed to see every fault Quinn had before fatherhood as ten times bigger after. If he was disorganized before, he was an absolute train wreck after the baby. Losing his keys or misplacing the remote was no longer an annoyance—these were reasons to bail on the marriage.

They separated when Danny was only six months old. The kid had never known what it was like to have two parents tuck him in at night. To have a mother and father peer over the bathtub and laugh at a pile of bubbles that he'd piled on his face like a beard. To wake up on Christmas morning to parents who had stayed up late to plant gifts "from Santa" before making love quietly and falling asleep way too late on Christmas Eve. Quinn shoved away the could-have-beens. The past was the past now, and what mattered was getting along with Eliza for the good of their son. And if that meant interrupting Eliza on a date, when she didn't have the decency to show up for her son when she was supposed to, then...

Quinn braced himself. If Eliza was dating another cop from work, then he might end up with a fat lip or a bruised ego. But he was Danny's dad, and it was his job to get the kid home, in bed on a school night, and back where he belonged. With his mom.

After a last glance toward the car to ensure that Danny was still sleeping, Quinn walked quickly up the front walk. He still had keys to the house—in case of an emergency—but Eliza had warned him that if he ever just let himself back into their house, she would call the police. He was to ring the bell and wait like any other invited guest. That was another reason why she normally picked up Danny. Eliminate the temptation of Quinn forgetting that he wasn't really welcome here anymore. That this had ceased to be his home six years ago.

But Quinn thought this—parental abandonment of their child—constituted an emergency. He checked his keychain and confirmed the house key was there. If she didn't answer the door, he'd let himself in and shout at the top of his voice from the entryway. And pray to God no one inside shot first and asked questions later.

But Quinn didn't need to let himself in. As soon as he approached the front step, he could see that the heavy, varnished front door was not fully closed. It wasn't ajar, but the catch hadn't fastened. Anyone who passed by could have nudged it and just walked in. The anxious twist in Quinn's gut turned to something more like dread. The cops Eliza normally dated would never leave the front door open like that. Eliza had lived alone with Danny for years—she would never *not* lock the door...leave it open and unsecured like that. *Never*.

Quinn pushed the door open and called out tentatively.

"Eliza?" He listened for any sounds of her shuffling feet, her high-pitched laugh. Or her all-too familiar yell. But all he heard was the tinny, canned sound of a commercial on TV echoing back at him.

"Eliza? Are you home? It's Quinn! I'm back with Danny!" He stepped inside the doorway, leaving the front door open behind him so he could keep one eye on his son— and the other braced for Eliza's boyfriend. But still, nothing. No response, no sounds. Nothing but the overly loud volume of the TV.

Quinn scanned the familiar layout of their first floor. From the front hallway, he could see the TV mounted above the fireplace. There were lamps on in the living room, and the kitchen lights were on too. Her purse sat on the kitchen table, and while he didn't see her cell phone, on a whim, he dialed it again. Maybe she hadn't heard it ringing over the sounds of the TV?

Quinn waited for the ring of Eliza's phone as he stepped carefully into the house. If he turned off that damn TV, maybe Eliza would hear him calling her—or calling out to her. He headed toward the living room in search of the remote. If he could shut off the damn TV... But before he made it past the foyer, he heard the telltale ringtone of Eliza's cell not on the other end of his call but from inside the house.

"What the hell?" he asked. He cocked his head in confusion. It sounded like Eliza's phone was in the living room. He followed the sound and walked through the open floor plan toward the well-worn sectional sofa Li-li loved so much. By the time her phone went to voice mail, Quinn had dropped to his knees on the carpet.

"Oh my God, no! Eliza!" he screamed.

Quinn jammed his phone in his pocket and ran to the front door. The streetlights illuminated the back seat of his SUV. His son was still buckled in and sleeping. Quinn stifled a wave of nausea and rubbed a hand over his mouth and then pulled his cell phone from the back pocket of his jeans. His brother picked up on the first ring.

"Keith," Quinn said, his voice shaking. "I need your help."

1

PRIVATE INVESTIGATOR RENE SCHWARTZ leaned forward in her chair and rested her forearms on the cool surface of the conference room table. She studied the man sitting across from her. The potential client continually ran his hand over his face and sucked in breaths of air like a drowning man breaking the surface of choppy water.

"So you called your brother *before* you called 9-1-1?" Rene asked. Keeping her voice neutral in an interrogation was second nature, although this was not an interrogation. This was a prospective client intake-interview—one of the more unusual ones they'd had. Rene flicked an almost imperceptible glance at Holly Austin, founder and lead investigator of HEARTS Investigative Services. Rene and Holly often partnered up on the intake of the more complex cases that presented to HEARTS. Cheating spouses and parents who suspected their kids were on drugs—those cases were simple enough. Those were the bread-and-butter of the PI business. Even Sam, the gossip-magazine obsessed receptionist-slash-hacker, could complete that kind of assessment. But this case was different. Quinn Stanton's ex-wife had been murdered. He'd been alone when he found her after she failed to pick up their son per their formal custody agreement. Nearly four months later, the case had gone completely cold.

"Yes," Quinn replied, meeting Rene's gaze. "My twin brother Keith is a cop. I knew he'd want to know immediately that Eliza was dead. I called 9-1-1 less than fifteen seconds after I hung up with him."

As weary as the man seemed, he had quickly and consistently answered every question they'd asked. But this wasn't Rene's first rodeo—nor was it Holly's. Rene had always been excellent at reading people. Since joining HEARTS, she spent a good amount of her time proving people were liars and cheats. But before becoming a private investigator, Rene had worked as a U.S. Marshal for the Witness Security Program—the department most people knew as Witness Protection. After years of hiding people, who themselves were hiding secrets, Rene knew how to read people. Though the man sitting directly across from her didn't set off any of the usual alarm bells, she couldn't help but question his story.

Holly intervened, but more gently than she normally did in these situations. "Mr. Stanton," she said, absently twisting the diamond engagement ring on her finger. Rene knew that was something Holly did when she wanted to attract the attention of a witness or client. When Holly was really lost in thought, she touched the simple silver heart charm on her necklace—a token that reminded her of her departed mother.

The ring was different. Intentional. Rene knew too well that fidgeting with the glittery ring from her fiancé, Detective Jakeem "Jack" Tarek, was simply a tiny movement meant to disrupt the train of thought of someone who might be working really hard to keep his story straight. "You realize," Holly continued, "that placing the 9-1-1 call second, not first... That alone is unusual. *Highly* unusual. Most people's instincts in that situation would be to call 9-1-1."

Rene watched the quick flicker of Quinn's eyes around the conference table. The light purple shadows under his eyes testified to his lack of sleep. But Rene was focused on the man's posture. His slumped shoulders and inability to stop sighing suggesting something deeper—something he probably hadn't admitted to even himself yet.

Rene smoothed the lapels of her charcoal-gray blazer and picked up where Holly left off. Being able to partner in these meetings was what made working at HEARTS so fulfilling for Rene. She might not have been on the same kind of team as she was with WITSEC, but HEARTS gave her a chance to flex her muscles in a satisfying way.

"You know, Mr. Stanton, some people might say that the twin brother of a police officer would know better. We're trained as children to call 9-1-1 in an emergency. I'm sure you considered how that call might look...maybe even before you placed it?"

"Yes. I did. And I do know," Quinn said, nodding. "I explained all of that to the police. My brother knew Eliza—knew her well."

"Romantically?" Rene interrupted. She didn't know yet if Quinn was lying. The only way to test him was to push him—break up his train of thought, trigger his emotions. Quinn's ex-wife, Eliza Stanton, had been found dead in her home four months ago. By Quinn. Within minutes of that discovery he became the only suspect in his ex-wife's suspicious demise, on top of going from divorced dad with visitation to full-time caregiver for a grieving six-year old. A dead ex, a brother who received the first call after the body was found... The police may have cleared Quinn as a suspect, but in Rene's experience, that sure as hell didn't mean he was innocent.

"We're sorry, Mr. Stanton." Holly charged ahead with their familiar 'good cop' routine. "That may seem like an insensitive question given the circumstances."

Other than the quiet hum of the heater circulating air through the vents, the conference room was quiet. Quinn looked past Holly and Rene and seemed to skim the whiteboard panels on the wall behind them. Rene knew he wasn't seeing any vital or confidential information on the cases the HEARTS team had been working up on those boards. Whenever one of the investigators wasn't staring at notes trying to tie evidence together, they rolled two privacy panels over the photos and notes. Right now, Quinn was looking at nothing more than a highly polished surface—a not-quite mirror reflection of himself and the backs of Holly's and Rene's heads.

"No. I mean when I say he knew her well, I didn't mean that," he said thoughtfully. "Romantically? Eliza and Keith? Not my brother." He hesitated. Curiosity wasn't drawing his attention to the wall. He was avoiding Rene's hard stare as he considered the question she'd just asked.

Rene knew she'd pressed a button. And she intended to press harder.

"What can you tell us about the relationship between your twin brother and your ex-wife?" Rene asked.

He shrugged his broad shoulders, the wool cardigan stretching with the movement. "I can't," he said as he looked at her, his eyes dark. "I can't really say much about it. Keith and I are incredibly close, but my marriage to Eliza was a short one."

He sighed again, one of those long, shuddering sighs. Rene hadn't yet decided who he was feeling sorry for—Eliza, his brother, or himself.

"Eliza and I split when Danny was just a baby," Quinn explained. "We'd only been married about two years We'd been dating a year when we found out she was expecting Danny." He looked at Rene. "He wasn't planned, but I was happy about it. I was ready to be a husband and father—or so I thought."

Rene allowed herself the slightest smile. At the mention of his son, if she didn't show a little warmth, she might lose any rapport she was building with this man. Not that she didn't love kids. The adorable Danny was down the hall playing in Alexa's office. And if she knew her teammate, the boy was eating a meal home-cooked by Alexa's *abuela* herself.

"Eliza worked at the police station," Quinn explained. He looked down at the conference table. "And she had a tendency to date cops."

"Cops plural?" Rene asked. "Do you know anything about who your wife was dating before she died?"

Quinn looked at her with slightly bloodshot eyes. The question seemed to cause him pain—but exactly why, she couldn't yet be sure.

"Well, not Keith," he said resolutely. "My brother has been dating a detective for about two years. They're solid. But not only was Eliza my ex-wife and Danny's mom, I know Keith knew her from work."

Suddenly, with that small admission, something in Quinn's demeanor changed. He seemed to be begging her to hear what he was saying. To make sense of the pieces that he'd tried—and clearly failed—to connect.

"I don't get it," Quinn said quietly. "Why would anyone want Eliza dead?"

Rene had seen the desperate look on his face a thousand times in her line of work. People who'd lost something big. Sometimes the losses felt so senseless, so huge, that the world itself no longer made sense. Gravity and sunshine and the rules of law—nothing changed in the day-to-day lives of most of the world, but after a horrific loss like this... What he needed was what everyone in this situation needed. He needed answers. To be understood. To believe that the incomprehensible madness of the loss of the magnitude Quinn and Danny had suffered would somehow make sense. He needed what anyone in his situation needed. To be validated by someone, *anyone*. Right now, Quinn Stanton was looking to HEARTS for that confirmation. And as much as Rene may have wanted to give it to him, she wasn't sure yet how much of his pain was grief...as opposed to guilt.

"Can we talk about that a little more?" Holly opened the manila file folder that Quinn had brought in when he'd made the appointment. "So the medical examiner deter-mined that Eliza had been gone about two days when you found her?"

Quinn visibly winced. He looked like he was remem-bering the scene and seeing Eliza like that all over again.

"Yeah," he said. "She'd been...strangled..." He looked a little sick as he said the word. "No signs of a struggle. No signs of forced entry."

"You said Eliza worked at the police station," Rene said, trying to keep the conversation going. She smoothed back a lock of walnut-brown hair that had fallen loose from her bun and watched as Quinn's eyes followed her hand.

"Yeah," Quinn confirmed. "Several of them, actually. She was a forensic artist."

"A sketch artist?" Rene asked. "And was she based here in town?"

The muscles in his square jaw flexed. He pressed his lips together as he stared at her for several long seconds. "Sort of." His tone was weary, as if he'd been asking her to help him carry the weight of the world and had just realized she wasn't interested in his burden. "She was a floater. The local PD didn't have the budget for a full-time artist. She was part of a pool of regional artists who could be called up by any of the PDs in the state." He allowed himself a sad, weak smile. "She was really talented. Very much in demand. She trav-elled to different law enforcement facilities throughout the region almost every week. But she made it a point to get home almost every night for Danny."

"Was there one particular station she worked at the most?" Holly asked. She would be the one to ultimately determine if HEARTS would take the case. If they agreed there was a case. So far, they had a distraught ex-husband and a cold case. That wasn't much to go on.

"I don't doubt the last months have been traumatizing for you and for Danny," Rene said softly. "But everything you can think to tell us about Eliza's life and work might help us understand her death."

He seemed even more distraught by her statement. "I know that," he snapped. "That's the goddamn problem. I don't know anything. I didn't know who she was dating—only that she definitely had a thing for cops." He ran a frustrated hand through his hair again. "I don't know how many people she was seeing or even where she was half the time. I feel like the world's biggest asshole."

He looked up at Rene, a glimmer of tears in his eyes. The look on his face—the press of his lips together—made Rene think he was not just frustrated or sad—he was ashamed.

"Eliza never loved me," he said. "And I guess when she left, I just thought we'd somehow stay close for Danny. But the opposite happened. She shut me out completely." Quinn leaned back in the chair. He looked directly at Rene. "There is so much I don't know and can't answer. But I did know Eliza. And in the weeks before she died, she'd been acting unusual."

"Unusual how?" Holly interrupted.

Quinn took out a piece of paper from the pocket of his jeans. "I made a list. This is the same list I gave to the police when they questioned me." He unfolded it. "Twice she was late to pick up Danny." He looked up at Holly. "Not including the...that last night." He swallowed hard. "The tone of her text messages changed. They were more curt—like all business. Not even *hi, Quinn,* just *'I'm here. Send Danny out.'* And a couple of times when I called her, a guy answered her phone. It was almost like she was seeing someone who didn't trust her and he'd started checking her phone and screening her calls."

Rene nodded, encouraging him. "Did you ever have a conversation with your—with Eliza—about the changes in her behavior?" Rene watched Quinn closely as she asked that question. She'd intentionally nearly slipped and called Eliza his wife—just to see his reaction.

He hadn't flinched at all but looked steadily at Rene. "No," he admitted. "I didn't ask Eliza." His shoulders tensed as he looked from Holly to Rene. "But I did ask my brother."

Holly gave Quinn an understanding smile. "Mr. Stanton—"

"You can just call me Quinn," he stated as he dragged his hand over his face. When he looked at Rene again, his eyes seemed to reflect a sense of defeat. "If you're going to call me crazy, at least use my first name."

"Nobody is calling you crazy," Rene offered.

Holly nodded. "We're not doubting your version of events, Quinn. We're trying to piece together any details you have to complete the picture as best we can." She smiled. "So if you think Eliza was seeing someone who had issues with you—or your relationship with your ex-wife—that doesn't sound crazy to us."

"What did you ask your brother?" Rene stood and took that opportunity to walk to the side table. She engrossed herself in pouring two glasses of water and then set one on the table in front of Quinn. It gave her the opportunity to get a little closer to him. Invade his personal space just a bit while he considered his answer to the question. While Quinn might not have been a suspect in the murder of Eliza, if he'd come to HEARTS for help, he felt he needed protection. Or answers. Or maybe something else altogether. They couldn't be too careful, and Rene studied the man's hands as she offered him the water. She picked up the vague scent of a musky, masculine fragrance rising from his body. Heat and sweat revealed a lot about a person—especially a person under stress.

Quinn passed the test. He met Rene's eyes with a look of warmth and appreciation. "Thank you," he said, immediately picking up the water glass. His hand passed close to hers as he reached for it, and Rene noticed he didn't shrink back from their near contact. He took a quick sip and set the glass back on the table. "The last few months have been such a nightmare, such a blur." He sank back in his chair as his posture faded into what seemed like complete disillusionment. "I do my best to make sure Danny is okay, but sometimes I forget about myself. I didn't even realize I was thirsty." He took another quick sip and cleared his throat. "So about two weeks ago, I asked my brother if he'd seen anything around the station that made him think Eliza was in trouble. Heard anything about who she was dating maybe."

"And what did your brother say?" Holly asked.

"Nothing," Quinn said. "Keith is a beat cop and he knew Eliza, but it's not like he worked much with her. We never really had family get-togethers when she and I were married, so they didn't spend any time together. Not really, you know? And at work, I mean... I can't say for sure, but I never got the impression from either of them that they socialized."

"Okay," Rene pressed. "So your brother didn't know whether Eliza's demeanor had changed? Or he didn't know if she was maybe dating someone who was making her feel unsafe?"

"Both," he said. "I mean neither. He didn't know if she was dating, and he didn't know whether she'd seemed any different lately either."

Holly picked up the questioning. "And Eliza never mentioned anything to you? Is it possible she was in some kind of trouble at work—related to a case? Or maybe she didn't feel unsafe in her relationship and didn't realize she might be in some kind of danger?"

"Anything is possible. I really don't know." Quinn sighed again. "I wish I had answers. Anything. I'm as useless as the cops are right now."

Rene tilted her head to one side and narrowed her eyes at Quinn. He was an attractive man—tall, broad-shouldered —with a sexy stubble on his chin she imagined meant he hadn't spent the last six years since his divorce alone. "What about you, Quinn? Are you dating anyone who might have had a problem with Eliza?"

Quinn shook his head. "No," he admitted. "I mean, I date—I've dated off and on since we split. But there's no one right now and nothing that's lasted. Frankly, it's been a while."

Holly gave Quinn a smile. "How do you think we can help, Quinn? The case is still open, yes?"

Quinn leaned forward and clasped his hands together. "Yeah," he said. "But it's gone cold. They have no leads, no suspects. My son's mother is...*gone*..." His voice trailed off. "Killed. Just like that. And no one can do anything about it."

"She worked with the police," Holly pointed out. "I'm sure no one is giving up on her case."

He frowned. "That's why I'm here. I think they *are* giving up on her case." Frustration colored his tone. "Since Eliza and I weren't married, once I was cleared as a suspect, they stopped telling me anything. They can't talk about an ongoing investigation. The case is still open. Even my brother has said to just leave it alone."

"That's not unusual," Rene said. "But that doesn't mean they aren't doing everything they can to find out who is responsible for this."

Quinn looked at his hands. He let out a long, slow breath as his shoulders drooped even more. "There's more," he admitted.

Rene waited, trading the quickest of glances with Holly. She watched the man visibly tense.

He exhaled loudly. "My son." Quinn's voice trembled just a bit as he mentioned Danny. "He's been having terrible nightmares. Waking up screaming at all hours. I've got him in therapy, but he's terrified. Like what happened to his mom at her house will happen to us in ours."

"That's perfectly normal, Quinn," Holly said, her voice even. "We can talk to Danny. Make sure he knows that there is nothing to be afraid of."

"Can you have that same talk with me?" He paused for a moment and looked a little sheepish. Embarrassed almost.

"I'm sure Eliza was dating a cop. I know I'm going to sound like a jealous ex or a hung-up, paranoid lover..." He met Rene's eyes with a steady, calm expression. "I'm not," he said. "I'm really not. But I feel like someone has been coming in and out of my house." Quinn sighed. "It's just a feeling I have. Maybe it's having Danny around all the time now, you know? Nothing seems to stay in the same place I left it. But I can't shake this feeling that when we're not around, someone has been there. Snooping around. And then I start thinking. If a cop did this to Eliza and covered it up..." He rubbed his face roughly. "I might be the only one who cares enough to push this. Bring the fucker to justice. And maybe there's more to the story? If someone is casing my house? Checking up on Danny?" He took a deep breath. "Can you help me? I don't know what that involves, what the costs are. But I owe it to my son to try to find his mother's killer. At least to make sure that while this case is unsolved, my son and I are safe."

Rene glanced at Holly. As Rene expected, Holly's hand worried the silver heart charm at her neck. Holly's mother had been murdered in front of Holly when she was just a child. The person responsible had never been brought to justice. While Rene knew that every woman at HEARTS had decided to work in private investigation because of some past work or personal trauma, she also knew that the team Holly had assembled were among the strongest, most intelligent, and capable, women she'd ever known. If Holly felt Quinn had a case, she'd take it—regardless of how close to home the facts of this murder might have hit.

"Have you mentioned your suspicions to your brother?"

Rene pressed, refocusing her attention on their potential client. "Is he aware you feel you might be in danger?"

Quinn nodded. "Yeah, but he keeps saying not to over-think things. To let the police do their job."

"Does that feel genuine to you, Quinn?" Rene's stomach sank even as she asked the question. If Quinn had come to them for help—after asking his twin brother—then he certainly must have felt something nagging at him to do so.

"Yeah, of course," Quinn said. "I trust my brother with my life. But I'd feel better if I knew there was someone who would talk to me. Give me answers. If there are any to be found."

"We understand what you're going through right now." Holly motioned toward Rene. "We all do. We've handled these cases and experienced the same kind of losses our clients have. It's human nature to try to connect dots that don't always connect, especially when we are under extreme stress like you've been."

In a matter of seconds, he went from looking determined to broken. "Wait... Are you saying you can't help me? You won't take my case?"

"We didn't say that." Rene nodded toward Holly.

Holly stood and held her hand out to Quinn for him to shake. "Take Rene's card. She'll be your point of contact from now on. I'm going to have Sam set up a new client profile for you. We'll make sure we have your contact information, and we'll agree on an initial plan to see if we can help. We can't make any promises about solving Eliza's case, Quinn. But we'll start with taking a look at your house. Maybe we can help you feel a little more safe with your son."

"Thank you," Quinn said. He stood and watched Holly leave the conference room. After Holly left the room, he faced Rene. "I'm starting to feel a little foolish. Like I'm asking you to check for monsters under my bed."

Rene laughed at that. "Please don't." She picked up the file he'd brought. It didn't contain anything they couldn't access through their resources, so she handed it back to him. "You can keep this for now. And don't feel silly. Believe me when I tell you this isn't even close to the craziest thing we'll hear today."

He returned her smile, but the motion was obviously forced.

"Can I make another suggestion?" Rene asked, but she didn't wait for him to respond. "Is there a grandparent or close family friend you can leave Danny with for a day? Part of the weekend, even? You clearly need time to sleep, drink, scream, yell, or whatever it is that you do to unwind. You've had a hell of a time, Quinn. You obviously need to work through this without putting Danny's needs first. Even if it's just for a few hours or the weekend."

He held her gaze for so long she thought he was going to tell her to go to hell for telling him how to grieve. Instead, he chuckled. It was the first time she'd heard the sound since he walked through their door. The sound was self-deprecating and sincere. "Shit," he said. "Do I look that bad? And here I thought I was holding myself together pretty well."

"You're doing great," she assured him. "But every now and then we all need a break from being the strong one." Rene pushed herself from her chair and headed for the conference room door. She led him to Alexa's office, where Danny had been hanging out during their meeting.

Alexa held two playing cards close to her chest, as if they held some great truth as she stared down at them.

Finally Danny asked, "Do you have a four?"

Alexa groaned before handing over a card. "You win," she said. "*Again*." Alexa started gathering the cards in front of her. "I don't know how you keep beating me. I was the Go Fish champ in my first-grade class for the entire school year."

"For real?" The little guy's hair was messed in the front. Rene guessed he tugged on his hair, like his dad did, when he was stressed. And Danny had the same expressive, chocolate-brown eyes as his father. He was like an adorable miniature version of Quinn...right down to their matched worried expressions.

"For real. Nobody could beat me. Until you!" Alexa gestured toward the door where Rene and Quinn were standing. "Looks like your dad is all done."

Danny hopped off the chair and headed slowly toward his father. He seemed like a weary child, so much youthful innocence muted by the burdens he carried. Parents divorced when he was an infant and now a mother gone far too soon. Danny brightened only slightly when he stood beside Quinn. "I won five of the games we played, Dad. And she didn't let me win like you do. I won fair and square."

Quinn ruffled the boy's already mussed hair and then pulled him into a half hug. "I only let you win sometimes, buddy. Ready to go home?"

"I guess," the child said.

"We're gonna be okay," Quinn said. "These women are

our friends, Danny. They want to help us feel safe at home and make sure we're both okay after losing Mom. They know how hard things have been."

Rene bent down enough to look the boy in the eye. "Danny, if it's okay with you, I'm going to come over to your house. I want you to feel super safe there. And I'm an expert in safety."

"You're a girl," Danny pointed out.

"Hey," Quinn said as he tugged Danny's hand slightly. "Girls are as tough as boys—most of the time women are more tough. Mom was a girl. A very strong one too."

Danny looked up with a grimace. "But Mom *died*."

It felt as though the air left the room in an instant, creating a tense vacuum. Danny, however, seemed oblivious as he pulled away from Quinn and ran toward the lobby. Rene stood and watched the look of defeat on Quinn's face deepen as he watched his son run away. He offered her a little shrug.

"He's still processing it all," he said after a few tense seconds.

"Grief takes time," Rene said. "You can't blame him for saying what he thinks."

"Yeah." Quinn looked at Alexa. "Thank you for entertaining him. Alexa, is it?"

"Yes, and you're welcome," Alexa said, tucking the deck of cards back into her desk drawer. "My pleasure. That's a sweet little man you've got there."

Alexa shook Quinn's hand and followed his back with her eyes as he left her office.

"Is he okay?" Alexa whispered after Quinn followed his son toward the lobby.

Rene shook her head. "Not sure about that. I think he's gonna snap if he doesn't get some rest."

"We took the case, then?"

Rene nodded. "There are definitely some avenues to explore. Maybe not a case, but we're going to see what we can do to help." She left Alexa and made sure she had a couple of business cards in the pocket of her blazer. She found Quinn and Danny shrugging into their coats in the lobby near Sam's desk.

"I want to go on the field trip tomorrow," Danny was saying. "It's science, Dad! Please!"

"It's not a good idea right now, bud," Quinn countered. "I'll stay home from work, and we'll spend some time together, okay?"

Danny zipped his coat. "That's lame."

Quinn sighed and put his hand on Danny's head as he focused on Rene. "Apparently a lot of the new rules with Dad are lame. Can I get with you on that security check later? I'd like to get him home."

"Of course. Just give me a call when it's convenient for you." She handed him a couple of her business cards and smiled at Danny. "I'll see you soon, Danny. When I stop by the house, I'll give you some of my secrets to winning Go Fish."

"You have secrets for winning?" Danny widened his eyes and stared at Rene with wonder.

She kneeled on the floor beside him, the black, rubber-soled boots she wore squeaking softly against the highly polished tile. "I sure do," she said. "He won't even have to let you win anymore."

"Yes!" Danny held up his hand and offered her a high-five. Rene clapped against his hand with hers and grinned. For that brief moment, the heaviness covering over his youth faded away. He grabbed his dad's hand and tugged him toward the door. "Come on, Dad. You promised I could get a candy bar after this, right? Can I get chocolate?"

"Yes, okay," Quinn said, allowing his son to lead him toward the door. "But something small." He turned back to Rene as they reached the glass doors. "Thank you. I'll be in touch."

Rene nodded and watched as the man tried to slow his running son to a manageable walk through the parking lot.

"He was a cute one," Sam murmured from behind the enormous monitor on her desk. "Single dad, puppy-dog eyes..."

Rene shook her head. "And a dead ex-wife, Sam. Not every living. breathing male who walks through here is a potential mate."

"Potential mate?" Sam repeated, clucking her tongue and raising a perfectly shaped brow at Rene. "What are you, ninety?" She tapped her nails against her ergonomic keyboard and lowered her voice. "If you all would just leave your love lives in my hands, you all could be as happily blissed out and sexed up as Holly and Jack."

Rene rolled her eyes. Sam believed that her job wasn't just receptionist/technology intelligence. She single-handedly wanted to pair up each of the lonely hearts on the HEARTS team. She'd have taken credit for Jack and Holly's romance if anyone would have let her, but Jack was smitten with Holly from the first time he walked through the office doors to consult with her on a case.

"This is an investigative agency, Sam, not a dating service," Rene said, humor underlying her comment. She loved Sam and her obsession with all things colorful, sexy, and fun. She might have been the only one of the HEARTS who didn't bring trauma and tragedy to her work. But that wasn't always a good thing—sometimes Sam's playful attitude straddled the line a little too closely. "Back to work," Rene said.

She sighed and thought back over the details Quinn had provided about Eliza's murder. There were a few questions she hadn't asked Quinn—things she'd wanted to research so she had some facts before she put him too much deeper under the microscope. The man may have been completely innocent and in no way involved with his ex-wife's murder, but that didn't mean that he wasn't in danger. And before she knew how seriously to take his fears, she needed more intel.

"Can you send his intake form to my email when it's done?" Rene asked, turning on her heel and heading back toward her office. "And let Holly know I need to have a quick chat with her fiancé, Detective Tarek—in an official capacity."

2

QUINN FROWNED at the enormous treat clenched in his son's hand. His *oh-no-you-don't* expression was enough to make Danny dramatically throw his head back as he accepted that he was going to have to return the king-sized candy bar to the convenience store shelf.

"I never get anything good," Danny said.

"Because you have the world's worst dad," Quinn joked. "Come on, buddy. I actually care about your teeth being healthy and you not having a tummy ache. Can you find something else?" Quinn gave the boy a nod. "You can get something sweet, but let's not grab the biggest thing you can find. Okay?"

"Okay." Danny jammed his hands in the pocket of his jacket and hung his head.

Quinn grinned as he ruffled Danny's shaggy brown hair. He wasn't quite sure where his son had learned to sigh, roll his eyes, and drop his head back like he was completely exasperated from dealing with the fools around him, but the kid's talent for that ran deep. Eliza had always been a no-nonsense straight shooter. She had very little tolerance for dramatics— which was what made her so effective in her work. She was calm, thoughtful, and demanding. And now...she was gone. A pang of paternal concern clenched Quinn's heart as he reconsidered the king-sized candy. The kid had been through so much... Maybe a damn chocolate bar would soothe some of the inequities life had thrown at him.

Not life, Quinn thought. *His mom and I did this...* That old familiar guilt surged as he thought of how hard and unsteady life had been for Danny so far. Divorced parents, splitting his time between two houses, two rooms. Two single parents, neither of whom had much in the way of supportive family to offer. What kind of life would Danny have now? Growing up without a mom, a whole new schedule and home with his dad... The kid had spent most of his time with Eliza—Quinn had been the every-other-weekend and once-a-week-on-Wednesdays parent. He looked into his son's expressive eyes that were mirror reflections of his own. But there were hints of Eliza there too. If they'd done this to their son, they'd also created him, given him life together. And that was something he could never be sorry for.

And in that brief moment he corralled his resolve. What Danny needed was a strong father. Loving and clear. A parent who could be both mother and father—not just because he needed to but because that's what Danny deserved. Quinn nudged his son and watched the boy reluctantly set the candy bar back in its place. *His mom and I got us here,* Quinn thought again, *but I can make it right. I have to.* He may not have been the man Eliza needed, but he damned well could be the father his son needed now more than ever.

"Hey Dan-o," Quinn called. His son looked up, and Quinn gave him a huge smile as he met Danny in the candy aisle. "What do you think of this? We'll each get one, huh?" Quinn selected a protein bar that had chocolate chips and peanut butter. It was the brand he often got for himself— sweet enough to satisfy but healthy-ish. Quinn held it out to Danny. He knew what the boy's reaction would be before the boy had a chance to scrunch his nose up and twist his lips into a surprised smile.

"*Dad!*" Danny nearly shouted. "You never let me get those! Really?"

"Yeah," Quinn said, softening. "Bars like this have a lot of vitamins, so they are good for grown-ups. You can't eat more than one a day, but I think you're responsible enough to try these now. What do you think?"

Danny's face lit up for the first time in what seemed like months. "Thanks, Dad!" He threw himself against Quinn's leg, and Quinn reached down to hold his son's small frame.

"You're welcome, son," Quinn whispered, holding back a sudden rush of emotion for his boy. "Let's grab some milk and get home."

They picked out a couple of items and headed to the cashier. As Quinn waited behind a woman buying what seemed like one hundred lottery tickets, he rolled his conversation with Rene Schwartz and Holly Austin through his mind again. He wasn't certain whether they'd be able to do anything to help him get to the bottom of Eliza's murder, and considering what even the police hadn't accomplished so far, he wouldn't blame them if they didn't dig up anything of use. But his instincts told him there was something going on, some unseen threat to him and Danny, and he didn't know where else to turn. He'd rather have tried and failed than not have tried at all.

As soon as they were in the car, Quinn asked what game they should play after dinner. A nightly game was part of the new routine Danny's therapist had recommended. Ever since Eliza had passed, Quinn had made sure his son had weekly therapy sessions. Quinn used the time to see a therapist himself. Scheduling concurrent sessions didn't always line up. Sometimes Quinn had to take a virtual session from his office in the middle of the day, but he was committed to doing anything and everything he needed to do to create the right kind of stability for his son—no matter how costly or inconvenient. One of the recommendations of the counselor was that Quinn give Danny new routines. Quinn had to provide a new kind of stability for Danny, a new reality that he could count on. A reality that didn't depend on the habits that Eliza had established when she was alive.

So they debated between card games and board games until Quinn pulled into the driveway of the two-story brick home that he bought not long after moving out of the home he'd shared with Eliza during the brief tenure of their marriage. Initially after Eliza died, he'd considered moving into Eliza's house so he could keep Danny in the place that the majority of the time had been his home. But after some tears and soul-searching, he decided that despite the familiar surroundings, they would simply never be able to overcome the fact that Eliza's body was found in the living room.

While Danny hadn't seen his mother that night...knowing that she'd been there was something Quinn could hardly overcome, let alone guide Danny through. So they'd moved all of Danny's things into his room at his dad's house and put a For Sale sign out front at Eliza's.

Once they pulled into the driveway of Quinn's house, Danny unbuckled his child safety seat on his own and jumped from the car.

"Hold up, buddy. Wait for me." As Danny darted toward the front door, Quinn grabbed his messenger bag and the plastic bag of snacks from the convenience store while fumbling for his phone and house keys.

"Candyland takes longer," Danny said, "so I want to play the longer game!"

"Of course you do," Quinn chuckled. "Well then, bath before game!" he negotiated.

"Ugh, I hate baths. Can't I skip just one night?" Danny groaned.

"I know, being clean is so lame." Quinn chuckled as he unlocked the front door. "Trust me, you'll thank me in a few years." Once inside, he reached for the alarm panel. He was millimeters from waving the fob on his key ring in front of the sensor before he realized the alarm wasn't beeping. He normally had fifteen seconds to wave the fob in front of the alarm and disarm it while the high-pitched tone chirped a countdown. But tonight, there was no telltale beep. No chirp to alert him that the passing of time was being tracked until emergency services would be called. There was nothing. Silence. That meant either the alarm wasn't on or it had been disabled.

Quinn squinted as a momentary flash of concern struck him. Had he forgotten to set the alarm when they'd left that morning? He couldn't believe that he'd been so careless. Not with everything that had happened over the last few months. But what other explanation could there have been for the alarm not beeping—other than it hadn't been set? Silently chastising himself, he set his bags down and toed off his shoes.

"We're having meatloaf tonight, so let's save the treats for dessert," Quinn called as Danny ran toward the kitchen. He was always running, and Quinn was always reminding him to slow down. This time, however, Quinn was too focused on the alarm to pay attention to Danny's pace.

He inspected the display screen mounted on the wall and tapped it, as if that would somehow explain how he'd forgotten to set the alarm. "I could have sworn I—" Quinn's train of thought was immediately derailed by a high-pitched scream from the kitchen.

"*Dad!*"

Startled but immediately reacting, Quinn spun in time to see a dark figure emerge from the kitchen. The man headed right for him as Quinn planted his sock-covered feet on the entryway tiles and dropped his left shoulder forward, crouching to brace himself for impact.

The intruder crashed into him as hard as Quinn had anticipated, and they slammed back against the closed front door. Quinn grunted as he was pinned between the wood panel and the shoulder of the man attacking him.

"Don't hurt my dad!" Danny cried out.

"Stay back," Quinn warned his son. He managed to get the words out moments before the stranger rammed a fist into Quinn's ribs. At the impact, the breath rushed out of him, but instinct also kicked in. Quinn clung to the man and tried to pull him closer so he couldn't get enough leverage to land another blow to Quinn's side. His blood ran cold and his heart thudded in his chest. Even though he was short of breath from the punch, his adrenaline spiked. There was no way he was going to go down without the fight of his life. With his son just feet away, Quinn frantically tried to land a disabling blow anywhere—the intruder's nose, face. But all his attempts failed. After the intruder landed a second assault to his ribcage, Quinn released his hold on the attacker, gusted air from his lips, and dropped to the floor in pain.

The man dressed head-to-toe in black leaped past Quinn's prone form and reached for the door. Quinn squinted after the man, hoping to spot any details to help identify the man later, but before he could get a good look, the figure disappeared outside. Quinn picked himself up and called out to his son.

"It's okay, Danny! Stay where you are!" His eyes on the crying boy, he hobbled to the door, shut it, and turned the deadbolt. He took a steadying breath and tried to minimize the outward expression of his pain. He hoped like hell nothing was fractured.

"We're okay, Danny. I'm okay. Don't be scared now." He dug his hand in his pocket, seeking out his cell phone, but Danny's sniffling distracted Quinn. He looked up and rushed toward his son, pulling him close even though the contact stung his sore ribs. "It's okay, buddy. He's gone. We're safe now. Come here."

Danny's body shuddered as the terrified kid threw his body against Quinn's legs.

Agonized at being in this position yet again, Quinn looked down at his phone. He considered who to call first. Keith? 9-1-1? After a beat, he narrowed his eyes. He pulled the card Rene Schwartz had handed him from his pocket and dialed her number instead.

RENE PARKED HER CAR AT THE CURB IN FRONT OF Quinn's home. The neighborhood was quiet—the kind of quiet that gave people a false sense of security. Autumn had finally taken hold. The trees scattered their orange, red, and yellow leaves in the front yards of the small but well-maintained homes. To Rene's eyes, the scene was freaking picturesque. Flags from colleges and universities hung proudly from front porches. Seasonal wreaths and mono-grammed welcome mats created a sense of pride and community. She half expected to see a bespectacled grandmother rocking in a porch swing with a cat in her lap! No wonder Quinn was shaken. Crime didn't seem to fit into this idyllic, well-composed picture. But Rene knew all too well that evil existed in even the prettiest places. Anything could happen anywhere—anytime. And in her experience, it did.

However, she was still struggling to fully comprehend what he had explained on the phone. He said the man who had attacked him may have disabled his alarm...knew his code... something. The man had been in Quinn's house and didn't seem to have expected them home. Her first question was whether he'd called his brother or 9-1-1. When he'd admitted his first call this time had been to her, she'd jumped in her vehicle and headed immediately over. Once she got him calmed down, she would ask why he'd called her and neither his police officer brother nor the police dispatch. She assumed he had his reasons. Rene watched Alexa park her vehicle across the street and climb out with Eva. She'd brought two of her teammates to help assess the situation and provide backup while she secured Quinn and Danny and took a look inside the house.

"The intruder was in the house when they came in," she said to Eva and Alexa when they joined her in Quinn's driveway. "Quinn thinks the man may have disabled his alarm or possibly knew his security code."

"The twin?" Eva asked as they headed toward the front door.

Rene shot her a glance. "We can't rule it out. But until we talk to Quinn, I'd avoid making the suggestion. For now, we don't even know for sure there was an intruder."

Eva nodded. "Do you think there's a chance he's setting this up?"

Alexa frowned. "Do you think he would do that? With poor little Danny right there? His kid saw the whole thing... Quinn didn't strike me as the kind of man who would put his son intentionally in harm's way."

Rene nodded sadly. Her instincts told her that Quinn would never do anything to hurt his son and that Quinn was not involved in whatever was going on. But she knew from her time at WITSEC that even sweet, bubbly PTA moms could be vicious killers. She'd seen it all—people sacrificed their spouses when their own futures were on the line. Mothers against children, husbands against wives... She trusted her gut, but she'd learned the hard way that she could never, ever, afford to be too cautious. "I think we'll know soon enough if Quinn is a victim or if something else altogether is happening. I'll take the lead with Quinn, okay?" She motioned toward her teammate. "Alexa, you got the little one?"

"Yes, of course! That poor baby. No matter what's going on...he's lost his mama. As if he hasn't been through enough!" Alexa said.

With her teammates close behind, Rene knocked and called out to Quinn to let him know who was at his door. A few moments later, the deadbolt disengaged and the door opened. Rene did a quick visual analysis of the man who opened the door. Quinn was pale but seemed to be holding up okay. Danny, however, was clinging to him, his head buried in his dad's neck, clearly shaken.

"Hey, guys," she said lightly as they all moved inside. She focused on Danny. "Nice to see you again. I hear you had a big scare, huh?"

He nodded and tucked even closer into Quinn's side.

"It's okay," she reassured him. "I'm here to make sure nothing else happens." She looked at Quinn. "Did you get packed?"

"I managed to get Danny packed. I still need to get my things." He put his hand on the little boy's head. "Been a bit of a struggle. I haven't put him down since I called you."

"Danny," Alexa said, walking behind Quinn's back to meet the boy's eyes. "Can you stay with me for a few minutes so your dad and Rene can get some things? We'll stay right here and wait for them. I promise they will be right back."

Danny hesitated before releasing his dad's neck. Rene watched as Quinn lowered his son to the ground, a pained expression on his face. He pressed his lips together, and he winced but set his son onto his feet and looked the boy in the eyes.

"I'll be right upstairs, son," Quinn said, his voice tense. "And Alexa will be right here with you the whole time." When Danny accepted Alexa's hand, Quinn turned to Rene. "This way."

Rene followed Quinn up the carpeted steps, acutely aware of his slow, labored steps and the way he held his shoulders stiffly, as if every movement and breath was an effort. His body language and demeanor seemed sincere—he looked like a man who'd taken a beating and was trying to tough through it. Once they made it to the top of the carpeted stairs, Rene looked toward each door as they passed them. Each was open, allowing Rene a view into every room.

"Did you check the house, Quinn?" she asked. The last thing anyone needed was another surprise.

Quinn tried to turn his head to look back at her but instead huffed a groan and turned his entire body to face her. "Yeah," he said. "But I had Danny with me, so it was quick. I opened all the doors and checked the closets. I couldn't bend down to check under the beds."

"Let's hope no monsters got in," she said, reminding Quinn of his joke from earlier that day.

He winced and smiled. "God, I hope not. But if you're up for looking under the beds, my ego couldn't be any more bruised than my ribs. Do you want to check?" he asked, a new look of concern on his face.

"I think we're okay," Rene said. "I'll take a look as we walk through, but I don't think a full search is necessary. My teammates are downstairs with your son, and with all the commotion, I think a second intruder would have made himself known by now."

As she walked through the hallway, she peered quickly into each room. In the office, she could make out a desk and comfortable-looking chair. Next was a powder room. She suppressed a smile at the baseball-themed décor in the bathroom and noted the shower curtain on the bathtub was pushed aside.

"No bogeymen there," she assured Quinn.

They traded a look, and Rene headed over to Danny's room. She deduced it was Danny's room based on the colorful signs and stickers Quinn had allowed the boy to hang on the door itself. After a quick peek inside, she could tell that the racecar bed frame was too close to the floor to allow enough room for anyone to hide beneath. She spotted the open closet door and again noted that everything seemed exposed and in view. As far as she could see, there was no place for someone to hide and ambush them. Or ambush her.

Finally, Quinn walked into the master bedroom and released an agonized breath. He walked into his room and gripped his thigh with one hand.

"Fuck," he said. He quickly looked up and met Rene's eyes. "Pardon my language, but that fucking hurts. Guy got me pretty good."

"Your ribs?" Rene raised her brows in concern at the grimace on Quinn's face. "You may need medical attention, Quinn. Alexa and Eva are with Danny. He's okay. They'll keep him safe." She stepped closer to Quinn. "May I?"

He nodded, his face still unnaturally white. "What do you need to do?"

"Just stand still," she said. "Where did he hit you?"

Quinn motioned toward the right side of his ribcage. "Asshole knew just how to hit, too."

"I'm just going to see if they're broken, okay?" She mentally made a note that if the intruder struck Quinn on the right side, that might reveal something about him. Nothing definite or concrete, but she made a note to remember the detail. She gently rested a hand against the front of his shirt to see if she could feel any obvious injuries. "Does that hurt?" she asked.

"Define hurt," Quinn chuckled. "I'm not going to cry, but..."

Rene smiled. "Okay, can you take a deep breath for me?"

He complied but released the breath with a sputter. "Fuck." He met Rene's eyes with a defeated look. "Can you fix this sudden cursing problem? I'd really like to not drop F-bombs every time I take a deep breath in front of my son."

"Sit, Quinn," Rene said. She motioned toward the king-sized bed and offered her hand. "Come on."

"Thanks," he said. "I'm embarrassed to say my room isn't exactly fit for female company." He took her hand and held it firmly as he eased himself onto the simple navy-blue comforter. "Not that I've had any of that in a while."

She couldn't help but catch the note in Quinn's voice. Was this another self-deprecating dad moment? Or was the look in Quinn's eye a little flirtatious? A little teasing? Rene looked at the single pair of discarded socks, flannel pajama pants, and a T-shirt that had been casually tossed on the bed and redirected the undercurrent between them into something lighthearted. "All this?" She gave him a reassuring grin. "If this is as bad as it gets, I don't know many women who'd be all that offended. Single dad didn't put his PJs in the hamper." She set a hand on his shoulder. "Not exactly front-page news, Quinn. Now, can you twist for me? Just a little. I want to see how bad the pain is when you move your torso."

Quinn raised his brows at Rene. "Okay," he agreed, "but if I curse or cry, I'm holding you responsible." He took a shallow breath and tried to rotate his shoulders.

"Try to move your ribs a bit, from here." Rene put two fingers on the lower end of Quinn's ribcage. The warmth of his skin radiated through the Henley-style shirt he was wearing. "Good," she encouraged. "That's really good."

Quinn grimaced. "I'm not sure good is the word I'd use, but it's not worse. Just sore."

"Okay, Quinn." Rene lightly touched his shoulder. Whether or not the attack was staged, she felt even more certain his injuries were authentic. Quinn had been hurt, and it seemed highly unlikely the man would expose his son to a horrific attack in his own home. More confident in her client, she dropped her reserve a bit more and gave him a warm look. "I'm not a doctor, but this looks like a case of badly bruised ribs. Let's get you packed and out of here. If you start having trouble breathing or if the pain gets worse, tell me right away. I've got anti-inflammatories packed, and we'll get you more comfortable once we've got you out of here. Got it?"

"Got it," he said, nodding. He stood from the bed and puffed out a breath over a pained moan.

"Here," Rene said. "I'll help. Do you have a duffel bag or a suitcase?"

As Quinn pointed toward his closet, he shuffled over to his chest of drawers. "If you could grab the duffel, I'll toss stuff in. I have a small gym bag, but do you see the larger bag? Yep, that's the one."

Rene grabbed both the small gym bag and the larger travel duffel. She kneeled on the floor and asked if he wanted an extra pair of shoes.

"You think we'll be gone long enough for me to need a change of shoes?" He searched her face as he tossed a handful of paired socks into the bag.

"Might as well take what you can while we're here," she said. She knew too well how these things went. Planning for a night in hiding turned into days, weeks... If Quinn was in real danger, there was no telling when he might be back home. She didn't tell him that now but reminded him, "If there are things you wouldn't leave behind for a week away from home, bring them. It's easier to carry more now than it may be to come back later."

She scanned his room while he rummaged through his underwear drawer for boxer briefs. The light green walls gave off a soft, cozy feel. There were a few pictures hung on the walls. Across from the bed was a framed dinosaur that Danny had drawn, and beside the bed in a simple frame was a portrait of Quinn holding his son when Danny must have been just a few weeks old. Rene noticed the titles of the books on the bedside table and couldn't help grinning at Quinn's choice of reading material. She knew from the intake form that Quinn was an accountant. He worked with small businesses mostly and had a small firm of his own. But his bedside reading revealed another side of him.

"Travel much, Quinn?" Rene asked, pointing to the colorful, well-worn travel books. "Bali?" she asked.

Quinn's face fully relaxed for the first time since she'd walked through the door. This seemed like a nice home. Small but well-maintained and cozy. Small personal touches like partially burned candles on the dresser reminded Rene that this was a place of intimacy. Of rest, of sleep, of love. She could imagine Quinn alone, tucked away in this picture-perfect neighborhood where nothing bad ever seemed to happen. Now, his ex-wife was dead...and he and his son seemed to be in danger. A nagging sense of loss tugged at Rene's heart. She wasn't nearly as embittered about life as some of her teammates. Holly's mother had been murdered, and Alexa's sister had vanished without a trace. Their realities had been harsh, but so had hers—in a different way. Rene had grown up in Brooklyn, New York. Every day her life was rough and uncertain. Danger lurked everywhere. She'd gone into law enforcement, in part, as a way to control the chaos that she'd hated growing up. The bad guys were everywhere, and only if she was smarter, and a little bit better prepared, than they were could she breathe a little easier. She hated that Quinn and Danny seemed to have learned that lesson the hard way. Not only when they lost Eliza but when they realized they weren't even safe in their own home.

"I don't travel, actually," he said wistfully. "I'd always hoped Eliza and I could take Danny on some great trips, but after he was born premature...and then our marriage..." He gave a resigned grin. "I experience the world through books these days."

Rene nodded. She understood that experience all too well. "Tell me more about what happened here tonight, Quinn," Rene said.

He was silent for a few moments. "I could have sworn I set the alarm when we left this morning, but it didn't go off when I came home. That countdown when you enter the house," he said, looking at Rene to see if she understood. "That never started. But when I checked the alarm itself, it was still set. It just didn't go off for some reason."

Rene sighed. "That's not surprising. Any criminal worth his salt knows to buy a jammer. They are pretty cheap online and will bypass a wireless alarm's signals." She studied his movements as he stuffed T-shirts into the bag. "Did you notice anything else about the man who attacked you? His height, approximately? Weight?"

"Just that he was about my height and weight," Quinn said. "As unhelpful as I know that is..." Quinn motioned toward his body with a hand. "I always wanted to be special —" he quirked up the corner of his mouth "—but I'm absolutely average in nearly every way. Average height, weight..."

Rene considered him thoughtfully. "But you do have a twin."

Quinn grew quiet and sighed. "Yeah. I guess that makes me special. Or makes *us* special."

"I don't suppose you recognized who tackled you?" Rene asked the question directly. There was no point tiptoeing around the obvious. "Do you think you know who did this?"

He shook his head. "No, Rene. I really don't know. Maybe it's because my adrenaline was running and Danny was screaming... I didn't get a good look at him. He was about my size, but I only know that because I was close enough to grab him when he punched me. That's all I can tell you. He was dressed in black and had on a mask. I don't remember anything. I don't even think I looked the guy in the eyes, you know?" He looked defeated again and rubbed a hand over his brow. "Goddamn," he whispered. "I didn't even think, Rene. I'm not trained for this shit. I'm so beat up and broken by everything—Eliza, Danny. Six months ago, maybe if I'd come upon someone in my house, I would have had more in me to fight back with. I fucking hate who I've become."

"Okay, Quinn," she said, not wanting to push him harder on the attack. Once she got him someplace he could relax, she'd ask more questions. For now, she didn't want to press too much. He was going down a dark path, and Rene knew all too well how hard it was to bring back the light once it went out. "You're blaming yourself for things you can't possibly control." She stepped a little closer to him and put a hand on his forearm. "Why do you think professionals train and train, over and over? Because normal human instincts don't give us the tools we need in an emergency. Fight or flight, yes. But you can't be expected to have gotten the eye color, shoe size, and blood type of the intruder you felt was threatening your safety." She gave him a smile. "With your son in the house...you did exactly the right thing. You two are safe, and that's literally all that matters right now, okay?"

He sighed but nodded. "Thanks, Rene." He studied her face for a moment and then said, "I meant what I said to my son earlier in your office. I've always believed that women are strong. I can tell you've been through a lot yourself. I'm glad we're on the same side." He pointed toward the en-suite bathroom. "I'm going to grab toiletries."

She took another look around Quinn's room while he rummaged through his medicine cabinet. When he came back out with a small travel bag in hand, he stopped.

"Rene," he asked. "Do you have a plan? I called you, but God. I don't know what to do. I don't know what comes next. I can't go to Eliza's house. I'm not safe in my own home..." The man looked lost. "How the hell do I keep my son safe?"

Rene hefted Quinn's duffel bag over her shoulder. "Let me worry about that, Quinn. Hiding people was my job for a long time. I'm going to protect you and Danny for as long as you need it."

"I hope so," he said seriously. Then he nodded toward the bag. "I'm not even going to fight you for that right now. I'll take the tiny bag with my toothbrush and hobble down the stairs with what's left of my ego."

She grinned at him. "Come on. When you're healed up, I'll let you carry all the heavy stuff you'd like." She turned off the lights in his room and took a final look around to make sure they'd grabbed everything before heading back downstairs. "Quinn," she said. "Hold up. Do you mind if my team puts security cameras around your property? With the defect in the alarm system, it might be good to have video. Just in case someone comes back."

"Do whatever you have to do," he said. Again, she heard the exhaustion in his voice. "Whatever you think is best. Just please...help me end this before something else happens that puts Danny even more at risk."

"Hey." She grabbed his elbow before he could pass her on the stairs but then quickly released him. She knew better than to make promises. She'd learned the hard way that she couldn't control every situation. And she sure as hell couldn't control every outcome. Promises—as tempting as they were to make—were no longer part of her vocabulary. Still, something about Quinn and his vulnerable son tugged at her. She felt compelled to say something. Not a promise, but something. "We'll do absolutely everything we can, Quinn. To protect Danny and you too."

"Thank you," Quinn said. This time, he reached for her. The touch was grateful, sincere, just the lightest brush of his hand on her forearm and then it was over, his hand fallen slack at his side. "I know you'll do everything you can. And please don't take offense. I just wish that made me feel better."

"I know," she said. "It's not a promise. I don't make those anymore. But it's the best I can do."

Quinn let out a long, slow breath as the stress seemed to immediately return. The welcome sound of a small laugh from Danny echoing from downstairs broke the tension.

Their eyes met, and for a moment, Quinn looked hopeful. Rene felt resolved.

"Alexa and Eva are going to stay behind. They'll lock up and secure the house when they're done." Rene didn't break eye contact with Quinn, and she felt a stir at the steadiness of his gaze. "Come on," she said. "Let's get out of here."

"You and me? Staying overnight together?" Quinn asked as Rene turned into the HEARTS parking lot. In the few hours since he'd called her, the HEARTS team had shown up at his home, packed for him and his son, and coordinated a plan to hide them. He'd hardly been able to think past the pain in his ribcage, but the team of women had mobilized like a well-oiled machine. But the one thing he hadn't counted on, when he'd reached out for help, was personalized service. He couldn't believe the woman beside him was going to pose as his wife.

"It's the best way," Rene assured him. She flicked her eyes to the rearview mirror for what seemed like the hundredth time since they left him house. "Don't worry," she said in a low voice. He noticed her eyes flicking toward Danny. They'd moved his child safety seat to Rene's car, and Danny was buckled up and playing with action figures, seemingly oblivious to the conversation in the front seat. "We're not being followed. I've been watching for a tail."

Without thinking, Quinn tried to look behind them but thought the better of it when his ribs protested. He hadn't even considered someone might be following them. He was more concerned with... Hell, he didn't even know what he was concerned with. Everything. Everything seemed to be compounding his worries. Everything except the woman beside him, who seemed calm, collected, and—oddly—in her element.

"You're going to be safer with me than alone," Rene said.

Even though she reassured him, Quinn didn't miss the fact that she pulled through the parking lot and around the building. She guided her car down an alley and parked next to a commercial dumpster with the name of a property management company painted on the front and a warning against illegal dumping and fines a violator would face.

Rene released her seat belt. "Stay put until I get the door open, okay?"

"Yeah," he said.

She climbed out and scanned the area, obviously checking the alley and their surroundings, before closing her door and heading toward the building.

"Let's get ready to go in, buddy," he said to Danny.

Rene pressed some buttons on a panel next to the door and then pulled the back door open. As soon as she waved for Quinn and Danny to join her, they hopped out and rushed toward the open door. For once, Quinn was happy Danny was so prone to running instead of walking. He didn't have to urge him to hurry, which might have caused Danny some concern. The little guy was more than happy to rush along, his action figures gripped tightly in his hand.

They entered the building through a dimly lit hallway. Rene put her hand up, silently telling Quinn to stay before she opened a door and went into the office area.

"What are we doing?" Danny whispered.

"Hanging out until we're invited in," Quinn answered. His uneasiness increased with every heartbeat. This morning, he'd woken up stressed and worried. But having Rene actively being so cautious about their safety suddenly made Quinn realize that he and Danny might be in real danger. There really could be someone willing to hurt them. If the same person who'd hurt Eliza wanted something from them... He couldn't consider that now. He just had to focus on the moment. Looking, listening, and trusting Rene and her plan.

A few seconds later, Rene opened the door. With a sweeping motion of her hand, she said as calmly as if they had just knocked on her front door, "Come on in, guys. Let me show you to my office."

Quinn and Danny followed her to a little space with a dark desk. A comfortable leather desk chair sat on one side, and facing it were two cloth-covered guest chairs. The office wasn't large, but it was cozy.

"Quinn, can you take a look at this? I'll need you to read it, and if you don't have any questions, sign." She set a contract on her desk and then turned her attention to Danny. "Hey, buddy. Want to play with your action figures for a few minutes? I can get you some markers or a pencil if you want to draw."

"I can play," he said and plopped down on the carpeted floor.

Quinn turned to ask Rene what she was planning, but she was gone. While Danny occupied himself with his toys, Quinn eased into the chair next to him and scanned the contract. He was too tired to actually read the small print. Rather than squint until his dry eyes could focus, he flipped to the page with the little purple tab and jotted his name on the line. After setting the contract on her desk, he focused his attention on Rene's office. The last time they were at HEARTS, Quinn had been led to the conference room. He hadn't seen Rene's private space until now. Her desk was immaculate, unlike Alexa's office. He remembered when they'd picked up Danny, she had piles of papers and small index cards everywhere. Books and travel coffee mugs stacked two and three deep.

But Rene's desk looked as if she didn't even work there. The surface was pristine and clutter-free. She even had a can of disinfecting wipes right on the desk. As an accountant who tended toward the A-type of organization as well, he appreciated that. Behind her desk was a shelf with a few reference books, a framed private investigator license, and a plant that looked like it could use some water. What caught his attention, though, was the photo of Rene with the other women who made up her team. HEARTS was made up of Holly, Eva, Alexa, Rene, Tika, and Sam. It was an acronym honoring the women whose backgrounds and skills brought them together to form the team. In the picture they were all clearly celebrating something, smiling and holding up glasses of champagne. He walked over to the shelf and picked up the frame. He looked over each face. The women looked more like girlfriends out partying than the team of private investigators someone in trouble would hire for protection.

He recognized the women he'd met so far. Holly with her sandy blond hair and wary but beautiful smile. Alexa's natural warmth practically leaped off the print. Eva was smirking in the photo much like he'd seen in the few moments' contact he'd had with her so far. Sam, the woman who worked the front desk, looked like the lightest of all of them, bubbly energy and playfulness making her seem almost like a little sister and not a part of the team. There was a woman in the photo he hadn't met yet. But his eyes kept tracking back to Rene.

Though he had seen the softer side of her more serious personality when she addressed Danny, the relaxed version of the woman in the photo highlighted aspects of her that he hadn't really noticed before. Simply put, Rene was stunningly beautiful. He took in the way her poker straight dark hair was curled in the photo and fell just above her shoulders. The waves softened the angle of her sharp, square jawline. Today Rene seemed not to be wearing makeup at all, but in the photo, her red lipstick looked bright against her tan skin. The little black dress clung to her curves in a way the somber suit definitely did not. In that photo, the women of HEARTS didn't look like private investigators who could kick someone's ass. But Quinn could tell good looks were just part of the package. Not just the team—but specifically Rene. He could already tell how capable she was. He somehow felt safer with her at his side—even if on some level that was an unusual feeling to have.

He focused on Rene's face again. She appeared at ease

on the surface, but even in the photo, Quinn thought her eyes looked haunted. He could only imagine the things she'd seen in the line of work she'd chosen. And since she was no longer with WITSEC...he had to wonder what happened to make her leave that work behind. He knew from his brother and Eliza that working in any capacity in law enforcement was a calling, a life commitment. He suspected her secrets were heavier than most.

At the sound of Rene's boots approaching, Quinn put the picture back on her desk.

"We need someplace secluded," she was saying in her phone as she walked back into her office. "We don't have the manpower to hide them in plain sight. We need to be able to control the area."

Quinn's heart dropped to his stomach. Once again that sensation hit him—everything was becoming more real with each passing second. They really were in trouble. Big trouble. The kind of trouble that could get them hurt. Or killed. He ruffled Danny's hair and smiled when the kid looked at him. Danny gave him a flat smile and then returned his attention to his toys.

Rene set a camera bag next to the photo Quinn had just replaced and started releasing the clips that held it closed. "Sam is getting me some more cash, but I really don't want us holed up in a hotel too long," she continued into the phone. "Too many people coming and going. Excuse me one sec." She pulled a camera out of the bag, removed the lens cap, and pushed a button that made the camera come to life. "Quinn, can you stand against the wall for me please?" she asked.

He did as she asked while she pinned her cell phone between her ear and her shoulder. Then she held the camera out in both hands and snapped three photos before resuming her conversation. She took the camera, the bag, and her phone with her as she disappeared again.

From where he sat in her office, Quinn could hear a whirlwind of activity down the hall. He was curious but waited. This was Rene's turf. She knew what to do, and he was relieved to sit for a minute, let his son play, and wait. While he sat, his spine rigid, taking care not to lean into his ribs, he rolled the attack through his mind. As if replaying the events for the thousandth time would bring any more clarity. The only thing that became more clear was that someone was prowling around his house. But why? What could the man have been after? Whether or not the guy had been there a long time, as far as he could tell, nothing had been taken or disturbed. It was like the man was in his house...just for the sake of being there. Which made absolutely no sense at all.

The thoughts rolled through his mind in an endless loop until Rene returned. He leaned back as he took in her appearance. Her crisp slacks and white blouse had been replaced with nondescript gray yoga pants and a zipped-up hooded sweatshirt. Her dark hair was hidden under a baseball cap, with her long ponytail tucked through the back. She looked like she was ready for a round of kickboxing at the gym.

"You...uh...changed," he pointed out.

She smiled and held out a manila envelope to him. "Sure

did. Now I look like any other person on a road trip checking into a hotel for the night."

He couldn't argue with the fact that she was dressed like any other traveler—all she needed was a travel mug of coffee and an oversized tote to finish off the Midwestern mom look —but he thought she was probably underestimating her ability to go unnoticed. Even without makeup, her face was striking. "I can't imagine you ever really blend in," Quinn said before he could stop himself.

Her thin brow slightly arched at the compliment underlying his words, but she didn't respond. "Take this," she said, pushing her hand closer to him.

He accepted her offering and peered into the envelope. Along with some cash and a cheap phone, there was a small laminated card. He pulled that out and looked at his picture —the one she'd taken just few minutes before—on a driver's license with someone else's name and address. His jaw dropped. "You made me a fake ID?"

"That's a prepaid phone and some emergency cash," she explained as she pulled a backpack from beneath her desk. She shot a look at Danny and lowered her voice. "If something happens to me and you have to run, use that to pay for whatever you need. Use the ID if anyone has a valid reason to ask for it, like when you check into a hotel or something. There are phone numbers for my teammates programmed into that phone. Call until you reach one of them and tell them where you are and what's going on. They'll take it from there."

Quinn swallowed as dread settled like a rock in his stomach. "Are you... Are you concerned something will happen to you?"

"No," she said. Her voice was firm. She looked Quinn in the eyes with a steely expression that immediately gave him comfort. "But you have to be prepared in case it does."

"Brian Donnelly," he read and then scrunched up his face and eyed her. "Do I look like a Brian to you?"

"You do now," Rene said with an almost imperceptible smile. If it weren't for the hint of a dimple in her right cheek, he probably would have missed it.

She used her keys to unlock her desk drawer and then pulled out a small, portable gun safe. She used another key to unlock the safe, checked the contents without taking anything out, and then locked it again. After looping the strap of her backpack over her shoulder, she focused on Quinn again. "You guys ready? Let's get moving."

Quinn had already suspected that she was more than capable, but now, something in her shifted. While she had deserved respect before, just by the air about her, she now reminded him of one of the characters in those action movies he loved to watch. Rene was in control of this situation. She was in her element. She said she had previously worked with the Witness Security Program. He could see that in the way she was prepared...and not just prepared. She seemed completely consumed with the task ahead. Single-minded, focused, and unerringly calm. His trust in her instantly grew. This was a woman who could, and would, protect Danny.

As they headed toward the back exit, another member of her team rushed their way. Quinn recognized her from the photo. She was the only one he hadn't me, so he thought back over the HEARTS. This must have been the T in the acronym Rene had noted earlier. *Tika,* he recalled as she stopped in front of them.

She held out a bag to Rene. "Are you sure you want to go alone?"

"If Eva and Alexa don't find anything helpful at Quinn's house, I'm going to need you to help Holly find a place for us. Eva and Josh have been scouring the listings for a place to buy or rent. Ask her if she's seen anything remote, someplace we can be ready if anyone approaches. Nothing with close neighbors or a shared driveway. I want to know if someone is coming our way."

"I'll call Eva." Tika smiled at Danny and gestured toward the bag she'd given to Rene. "There are some snacks in there for you. Keep an eye on them. Rene has been known to steal other people's food."

Rene smirked at her teammate. "I didn't steal your slice of cake. I *borrowed* it."

"You can't borrow food," Danny pointed out. "Once you eat it, it's gone."

Holding her hand to her heart, Rene explained, "I replaced the one slice I ate with an entire cake. I more than made up for my mistake."

Danny turned his attention to Tika. "An entire cake is so much more than one slice!"

"You're right there, kiddo. It was a *very* good apology," Rene said pointedly to her co-worker. "If you're done poking fun at me, we are going to head out. I'll check in later."

"Be safe," Tika called as they headed toward the back door.

Before they could exit the office, Quinn's cell phone buzzed. He immediately looked to Rene.

"Who is it?" she asked.

He yanked the phone from his pocket and checked the caller ID. "My brother," he said. His stomach immediately sank. He didn't know whether to pick up the call or let it go to voice mail. If it wasn't urgent, his brother would have texted something simple and curt: *call me, bro,* or *where you at?* But the fact that Keith was calling... "I should get it," Quinn said.

Rene nodded and motioned for Tika to take Danny out of the office.

"Come on, little man," Tika said. "I think I might have a slice of cake someplace in the fridge. Want to see if I can find some for the road for you?"

Danny grabbed his action figures and looked to his dad.

"Go ahead, buddy," Quinn said as the phone call from his brother rang the third time.

As soon as Tika and Danny left the room, Rene whispered, "Put the call on speaker and mute him. Don't tell him where you are." She nodded, and Quinn swiped the touch screen to engage the call.

"Hey, Keith," Quinn asked, trying to keep his voice casual. He tapped the button to activate the speakerphone and then quickly hit mute.

"You busy?" Keith asked, his voice sounding like an uncanny echo of Quinn's.

Quinn looked to Rene, and she nodded her head vigorously. "Tell him yeah," she said. "Ask if you can call him a little later." She sounded serious and stern.

But before Quinn could even answer, Keith offered an invitation.

"Monica's out on a case and won't be home till late. You and Danny up for some company? Thought I'd grab some carry out and stop by."

Rene immediately spoke up. "Tell him Danny threw up and you're dealing with the mess."

Without missing a beat, Quinn unmuted the phone. "Shit, man, that'd be great, but I'm in the middle of a situation here. Danny projectile puked. And you know me, I've been fighting the dry heaves while I clean him and this mess up. Raincheck?"

Rene gave Quinn a thumbs-up, but her face looked anything but pleased.

"Shit, sorry about that. Did he eat something bad? You want help?" Keith pressed.

Quinn frowned and looked quizzically at Rene. That was unlike his brother. Keith and Quinn both had the same sympathetic reaction to vomit. There's no way his twin would volunteer to come help clean kid-puke. Ever.

Rene shook her head once.

"Nah, man, you know how these things go. It could have been too much fast food, or maybe he picked something up. If I call you crying 'cuz I'm puking tomorrow, you'll know it's contagious."

"Shit," Keith said seriously. "Yeah, all right, bro. Give the little man my best." Keith was quiet on the other end for a moment.

Quinn opened his mouth to say something, but Rene held up a finger and motioned for him to wait.

"Check in with me later, okay?" Keith cleared his throat. "Tell D I hope he feels better."

"Will do. Thanks, man."

Quinn ended the call and watched Rene's face.

"What do you think?" she asked.

"Calling last minute to hang out is normal," Quinn confirmed. "Offering to come by and help with puke...not so much."

Rene nodded. "I'm sorry, Quinn. I know it must be hard to question everyone in your life. Especially your twin. But right now, we can't take any chances. Even if Keith doesn't know anything, he could be compromised in some way. It's just too soon to know what's safe to share."

Quinn didn't miss the way she phrased that. *What's safe to share.* What she was really was saying was who they could trust. And for now, it was not at all clear that Keith could be trusted.

"Yeah," Quinn sighed. "I get it."

"Let me get Tika and Danny. I'll come back for you, and then we'll head out." Rene walked past Quinn and gave him a lingering look as she passed. She was gone in a flash, the ponytail poking out of her hat bobbing with her animated steps.

Within seconds, Danny, Tika, and Rene returned. Quinn rested his hands on Danny's shoulders while Rene asked them to wait for her. She carried her bags and gun safe out of the office and returned in less than a minute. Then she wished Tika a hasty goodbye and ushered them out to the car that was unlocked and already running. Once they were in her car, she pulled away from the building.

Quinn looked over at Rene. Their eyes locked, and Quinn sent a silent vow to his boy. He'd do whatever it took to protect his son. No matter who and what that meant protecting him from.

RENE PEERED THROUGH THE BLACKOUT CURTAINS OF the hotel room long enough to scan the parking lot for anything that seemed off. When nothing stood out to her, she let the curtain fall back into place. There were no signs that anyone had followed them. The hotel Sam had picked was nothing anyone who lived in town would have ever picked. It was more of a roadside motel, catering to truckers and travelers passing through on the interstate. With no restaurant or bar, this was the kind of place that considered vending machines an amenity. That didn't make her feel better, though. There were still too many people, too many voices, and too many noises. Every sound made her adrenaline spike.

Almost every sound. There was one that was just so adorable she could hardly stand it. She laughed softly as Danny snorted in a breath followed by a long exhale. The worn-out kid had fallen asleep on the car ride out of town and had managed to stay asleep even when she—not Quinn, since his ribs were too bruised—lifted the little one from his safety seat and carried him into the hotel. They'd checked in using Rene's fake ID to confirm the online reservation that Sam had made for them under their "married" name. On the one hand, the picture they created played to the story they were trying to tell. A family on a road trip. Mama carrying sleeping child, Dad struggling with the bags—although in this case, the struggle was literal since Quinn's ribs still caused him in a ton of pain even as he balanced the relatively light duffel.

Rene was glad Danny slept through opening the hotel room door, juggling their bags, and setting him down on one of the two beds in the room. "Quinn," she whispered. "Let's talk."

He ran a loving hand over the comforter on the queen-sized bed where Rene had tucked in Danny and then joined Rene at the small table near the hotel room door. "Okay," he said. "What now? What do we do?"

She pulled out a notebook from her laptop bag. She gave Quinn a tender look, one which she hoped softened the question she was about to ask. "Quinn," she said, "I'd like you to tell me everything you can about your brother. How long he's been with the department. The name of his girl-friend. His partner. His connection to Eliza. Anything and everything you can think of—whether you think it matters or not."

If Quinn was unnerved by the question, he didn't voice his concerns. He nodded solemnly and swallowed.

"So Keith has been with the force," Quinn paused, "eight years, I think. He was recruited out of community college—we both started there because our folks didn't have money for a four-year university. Keith went the criminal justice route, and I studied economics and accounting."

Rene listened intently, pausing occasionally to take

notes. "Any problems on the force? Enemies? Bad cases? Does he get along with his partner?"

Quinn shook his head. "No, my brother is squeaky clean. Great evaluations, service awards. He works on the tri-county policing initiative, which partners local law enforcement with businesses to foster a sense of openness and safety in our community. He volunteers his time to train citizen on disaster preparedness and first aid." Quinn shrugged. "My brother...a real American hero."

Rene smiled. "Go on. Any enemies?"

"None that I'd know about." Quinn was quiet for a moment. "He has only had two partners in eight years. First guy was an old timer who retired about two years ago. Since then he's been with some guy named Frank...Frank Strickland."

Rene wrote down the name, and Quinn nodded to confirm she'd spelled it correctly. "Anything else?"

"Keith's been dating a detective from a neighboring department for the last two years. Some PDs have rules against relationships within a station or within a department, but as long as partners aren't dating one another, most of the people I've heard about in law enforcement either only date other people in law enforcement or else only date civilians. I'd say it's about fifty-fifty."

"Do you know Keith's girlfriend?" Rene asked.

"Yeah, of course. Not well. I mean, they're serious, but I've been single the whole time they've dated. So other than a few dinners and an obligatory stop on Christmas, I don't really know her." Quinn's face fell a bit. "It's hard for a happy couple to double date with a perpetually single dad hanging around."

Rene sucked in a breath and nodded. "I get that. What's the girlfriend's name?"

"Monica LeBland," Quinn advised. "She's a detective, one county over."

Rene made a note of the name and again confirmed the spelling. "What do you know about Frank Strickland?"

Quinn shrugged. "Keith's partner? Not a whole lot. They're not close; they don't hang out socially. As far as I've heard, he and Keith work really well together, but they've never been the type to like...grab beers after work."

Rene thought for a moment. "And you said your brother's been dating Monica for about as long as Frank has been his partner?"

"Yeah." Quinn nodded, fidgeting a bit in the chair. "Sorry. This is uncomfortable as hell on my ribs. I think that's right on the timing." He looked confused. "Do you think that's related at all? That Frank becoming Keith's partner and Keith dating Monica are in some way connected?"

"I'm not drawing any conclusions at all. Just getting clear on the timeline," Rene explained. "You know, we should get you some food. And some ibuprofen for those ribs. You okay?" She gave him a little smile and looked over at Danny. "Do you think he's out for the night? Or is this just a nap?"

Quinn shook his head. "Regardless, I think we should wake him to eat. He'll be awake at one a.m. asking for pizza if we don't feed him."

"Okay." Rene nodded. "Then I'm going to order a pizza

now and have it delivered." She pulled out her phone and dialed Sam. "Sam? Yeah, can you use a meal service app to order us pizza? And a salad, if you can. Sam," Rene said, keeping her voice low so she didn't wake Danny but also being firm enough so Sam would get the message. "Don't forget to change the delivery address to the hotel where we're staying. And then stand by and let me know when the pizza is arriving so I can go down to the lobby to pick it up."

After Sam confirmed the order and her instructions, Rene ended the call, but her phone lit up with a text alert from Sam.

K, done. I ordered you a six-pack of beer too, so bring your ID for delivery. I know you've got a little one in the room with you, but a little mood juice can't hurt the hunky single dad vibe you've got going on there.

Rene resisted the urge to sigh and instead texted back, *Client, smartass. He's a client. Let me know when the pizza is close.*

Before Rene could finish the thought, Holly's name and number came up on the touchscreen. "Hey," Rene answered.

"Everything good?" The echo in Holly's voice sounded like she must be using a hands-free device in her car.

"So far, yes," Rene confirmed. "Danny passed out on the drive over, and Sam is putting together some dinner so we can eat. How are things on your end?"

Rene could hear traffic noises echoing in the background of their call. Holly continued over the faint sounds of horns honking. "I think we found a place for you. I'm on my way to check it out now. It's one of those vacation house rental things. Fully furnished, two bedrooms, with a partially stocked kitchen. It looks pretty secluded, but I want to see it for myself."

Rene stared back into the room. Quinn was watching her every move as he shifted and adjusted to get comfortable in the wood-back hotel chair. "That sounds perfect, Hol," Rene said. "Thanks."

"If it works out, I'll rent it for two weeks. We'll go from there."

Rene nodded at Quinn to let him know things were looking good. "Have you heard from Eva or Alexa?"

"That was the other reason I was calling," Holly said. "They didn't find signs that anything was stolen or moved. As far as they can tell, the intruder didn't leave a trace."

Rene glanced at Quinn when another loud child-exhalation filled the room. Their eyes met, and they shared an amused grin. While adult snoring could be torture, Danny's deep-sleep sounds were nothing short of precious. "Did they look through the whole house?"

"Yeah. They didn't find anything. But without having a clue what they were looking for, and without really knowing Quinn's house..."

"I know," Rene said. "It was a long shot. Did they get security installed? Cameras?"

"Done and done," Holly confirmed. "I've got old-fashioned timers on the lamps so it will look, at least for the next few days, like Quinn is still here. But we installed cams with an Internet feed so Sam will be monitoring all motion that's recorded inside or outside the house."

"Motion recording?" Rene clarified.

"Yeah," Holly said. "The cameras trip when activated by

movement, and they'll take a still image of whatever set them off. That image will go to an email address Sam set up just for those cameras. She can also log into the live stream and just peek in on the house anytime she wants." Holly's tone changed then. "Rene, I don't think you should mention this to Quinn, but I'm going to send the login credentials to your phone in case you want to periodically look in on the house too."

"Got it," Rene said. She understood, without Holly even explaining, that she was sharing that access for Rene's protection. While she was fairly certain that Quinn had been up front and honest, if this was some type of complicated conspiracy by Quinn to hide any involvement he had in Eliza's murder, then the more access Rene had to objective information, the better. "Hol, I definitely don't want to take advantage of your fiancé, but do you think Jack might know anything about the detective Quinn's brother is dating? I don't have any specific questions, but there may be something useful there."

Holly laughed. "Please. Take advantage of him. It makes him feel good about himself. What is the girlfriend's name?"

Rene pointed to her notes on the table, and Quinn reached for them and held them out to Rene. "Keith's partner is Frank Strickland. Can't hurt to do some asking about him, and then Keith, Quinn's twin brother, is a beat cop dating a detective one county over by the name of Monica LeBland."

"I may need you to confirm the spelling later, but I think I got it. You want to call Jack, or should I ask him?"

"Well, you'll definitely see Jack before I do," Rene chuckled.

"Will do. I'll circle back with you once I'm home. I expect it to be pretty late since I'm heading out to look at that rental, so I may not have anything until tomorrow for you. Rene..." Holly's voice was gentle. "Are you going to get any sleep tonight? Been a while since you protected someone in hiding."

Rene looked toward the window. A thin strip of light made its way through, but for the most part, she was standing in a dim room as the sun started to sink and turn the sky a deep burnt orange. She knew what Holly was asking. And she appreciated that her teammate knew her well enough to ask—even if she wasn't asking the question really on her mind. "Eh, probably not. I think I'll stay awake for the night shift. Can you send someone to relieve me in the morning?"

"I'll come myself. I'll be there early, probably around five."

"Thanks. See you then," she said and ended the call.

"Dad?" The sound of Danny tossing around in the bed drew her attention. He had rolled onto his side and was staring at her with hooded eyes. He wasn't completely awake yet, and he looked scared. "Where are we?" he asked, sounding like he was dangerously close to tears.

She watched Quinn jump with nearly superhuman speed from the chair and join his son on the bed. "Hey, buddy, we're okay. We're in a hotel with Rene. We're going to have some dinner and watch some TV."

The little guy struggled to sit before rubbing his eyes. "I have to go potty."

Quinn groaned almost imperceptibly as he held his ribs while he scooted off the bed. "Come on," he said softly, "I'll take you."

Quinn met Rene's eyes as he climbed out of bed and held his hand to his son. A trace of a grin tugged at his lips. The intimacy of the situation was not lost on Rene. She'd spent many, many years under the same roof with strangers whose lives she held in her hands. But somehow, this felt different. After everything that had happened, this all felt different. But she was still her. Still capable. And no matter the unfamiliar emotions churning up her gut, she had a job to do. And this time, she wasn't going to let anyone die on her watch.

4

QUINN SMILED as a hint of embarrassment lit on his face. "That took longer than expected. Hope you don't mind sharing a bathroom with two guys."

Rene shook her head, her lips twisting into a smile. "It's been a while, but I think I can manage. Everything all right?" She looked at Danny as he trailed from the bathroom with still-wet hands.

"Our hands are clean and we're ready to eat," Quinn confirmed. He couldn't help but watch Rene's movements as he walked through the hotel room with his son. It hadn't been that long since he'd shared a bedroom with a woman, but a bathroom? And looming was the issue of later that night...sleeping in the same room with a woman and his son? This would be a first. Somehow, there was no other woman Quinn could imagine allowing that close to his son...or to him, for that matter.

Danny jumped onto the bed, and Quinn joined him. Danny immediately snuggled up against his dad, so Quinn ruffled his son's hair and pulled him close to his chest. He nudged off his shoes so he could bring his legs onto the bed. Once they were settled, Quinn noticed a look pass over Rene's face. The open, raw expression brought down his reserve, and he asked, "Do you have children, Rene?"

She shook her head. "No kids, never married." She pressed her lips and offered a thin explanation. "Marshal life can make having anything else a challenge."

"I wish I could blame my troubles on being an accountant," Quinn joked, trying to lighten the mood. Rene didn't seem sad or bothered by the question, but there was something underlying her response, something he didn't fully understand. Sadness. Regret, maybe. He wasn't sure.

"Dad, I'm hungry," Danny whined. "Can I have something to drink?"

"I got this," Rene said. Quinn watched as she pulled a bottle of water from her bag. She checked her phone while she walked over to the bed. Their fingers brushed briefly as he took the water bottle from her.

"Thanks," he said. Quinn uncapped the bottle and held it for Danny while he took a tentative sip.

"Okay, guys," Rene said, her voice artificially bright. "I'm going to need to run down and get the pizza in a few minutes, so before I leave, I want to make sure you know how to be safe while I'm gone."

Quinn searched her face. Gone was the glimmer of tenderness he'd seen earlier. She was all business and looked at him intently.

"Have you handled a weapon before, Quinn?" she asked. Quinn frowned. "Yeah."

She seemed to pick up on the discomfort on his face. "Can you protect yourself and Danny with one?"

He nodded. He'd never owned a gun, had never really enjoyed the idea of guns. But when his brother got into law enforcement, he'd spent plenty of time at the range practicing while Keith was a student. He understood the basics. But this would be the first time he'd ever knowingly allowed a gun anywhere near his son. He scanned his brain to see if he'd ever allowed Keith in uniform and armed near Danny—he just didn't think that had ever happened. He warily watched Rene slide the gun safe from where she'd placed it under the bed when they checked in, and then he watched as she unlocked it. She didn't open it, but he knew damn well what was inside. He'd watched her secure a Glock on her hip after she'd carried Danny into the hotel room a couple hours ago. It appeared the gun inside the safe would be for him.

He looked up and saw Rene watching him intently. She seemed to be tracking his unease.

"I'm going to be gone for less than fifteen minutes. I doubt you're going to have to use this, but I need to know you can if you have to."

Quinn tightened an arm around his son. "I can. Keith and I used to go to the range when he was a student. I just..." He trailed off.

Rene nodded and flicked a glance at Danny. "Now might be a good time to give Danny a teeny tiny nibble of a chocolate bar. I need your assistance in the bathroom."

Quinn's breath caught in his chest. "Okay," he said. He looked down at his son and gave him a reassuring smile.

"Danny, you can have a couple bites of the candy bar we brought. It's a treat because we've had a rough day, huh? But don't let it spoil your dinner." He took the candy that Rene offered, carefully unwrapped one end, and broke off a few tiny squares. "I'm going to help Rene for a minute, but I'll be in the bathroom with the door open."

Rene walked into the small bathroom ahead of him and stood behind the door so Danny couldn't see what she was doing. Quinn stood in the entryway where he knew Danny could see his every move. In a low voice, Rene provided a quick refresher to him on the weapon she'd somehow slipped from the gun safe and tucked in an ankle harness she'd been wearing underneath her yoga pants.

She loaded the gun quickly and reviewed turning off the safety and aiming. "Quinn," she said, her voice hard as nails. She looked into his eyes with a steel he didn't quite understand. They were standing close enough together he could feel the heat emanating from her body, and he could smell the soft hints of something tropical and sweet in her hair. "I need to know I can trust you," she said. She waited.

"Rene," he said, "my son is sitting fifteen feet away. You've been armed this entire time. Do you think I'd let that happen if I didn't trust you with both of our lives? I'm not stupid," he said.

"That's not what I mean," she said cryptically. "I just want you to remember something."

Quinn watched the way she drew her lower lip into her mouth.

"You don't put your finger on the trigger unless you plan to shoot."

He nodded and flicked a glance back at Danny. The boy was slurping water, a small ring of melted chocolate over his lip. "I know," he said.

She sighed and extended the gun to him. He took it from her carefully and confirmed that the safety was back on. He tucked it into the waistband of his jeans and tugged his T-shirt over it.

"And Quinn," she continued. "You only aim a gun at someone you intend to kill. Are we clear?"

He cocked his head and nodded. "Yeah, Rene. I understand that."

In that moment, Rene stepped closer to him, and Quinn felt like the air in the bathroom drained away. She put a hand on his chest and gripped the front of his T-shirt in a light fist. She leaned close, and he could literally feel the air that she breathed against his face as she whispered in his ear. "We're a team now," she said. "All of our lives depend on that trust."

Quinn didn't know whether to be pissed off and a little afraid...or turned on. He watched her as she leaned back, released his shirt, and waited for his reaction. She had balls—that he knew. But this was something altogether different. This was a test. Quinn didn't know how he knew, but she was sending him a message. And he intended to respond.

"Rene," he said. "Give me your hand." He extended a hand like he was going to shake hers. She took his without hesitation. Once he had her hand in his, he tugged her close to him and placed her hand over his heart, palm against his chest. He leaned close to her face and lowered his voice. "I swear to you on the soul of that boy's mother."

He let that settle for a moment before leaning back far enough to look her in the face. "You can trust me." He released her hand, but she kept it pressed against his chest for a second or two more. Electricity pulsed through his body at her touch—and then it was clear. That energy he was feeling for her was charged with way more than danger, adrenaline, and fear.

"Good," she said, removing her hand and breaking the tension of the moment. The shroud fell back over her face. "Then we're clear."

Her phone vibrated to alert her that she had a text, and she walked past Quinn and out of the bathroom. He gusted air through his lips—a breath he almost didn't realize he was holding. He immediately felt the absence of her intense, tropics-scented presence, but he followed her back into the room and stood near his son on the bed. With the second gun in his jeans, he intended to remain standing at a safe distance from his son until he could lock the thing back in the safe where it belonged.

He watched Rene brush a hand over the waistband of her yoga pants, and he knew she was checking to be sure her gun was covered by her sweatshirt. Then she grabbed her purse and reminded Quinn to bolt the door behind her. The stairs that would take her from the third floor to the lobby were only two doors down from their room.

"I'll be back with dinner!" she said brightly, no doubt for Danny's benefit.

He followed her to the door and watched as she opened it but scanned the hallway before she stepped out of the room. He didn't see anyone, and she must have seen the same because she stepped into the hallway and turned to face him.

"I'll be right back," she said tensely. "Remember our talk. And check to make sure it's me at the door before you open this to anyone."

He nodded. "I got it."

She started down the hall but stopped a few steps away and raised her brows. He didn't realize he'd been watching her walk away. She'd told him to shut and bolt the door behind her. He immediately lifted his chin to her, closed the door softly, and secured the lock.

Oh shit, he thought, resting his head against the cool door. The last thing he expected when he'd walked into that PI agency was anyone who would literally trigger his heart.

"Oh, hi!" Rene bounced up to the front desk with a friendly but not overly bubbly smile. "Could I trouble you for some extra coffee?"

The annoyed-looking teen at the front desk scratched his head and muttered, "Yeah, lemme call housekeeping."

While she waited, she scanned the lobby. Sam had let her know that the tracking service on the app showed the pizza was five minutes away, so she took her time surveying the guests and employees. Her senses tingled when a man looked away from her before she could catch his eye. She didn't outright stare at him, but she kept him in her peripheral vision until the clerk returned with her coffee. Rene tucked the packets inside her purse and thanked him sweetly

—sweeter than she normally was but just enough to play to the traveling mom act. She checked her phone, pretending to check the food delivery app, but instead opened the camera.

She acted as if she hadn't noticed the tall man dressed in a long-sleeve black sweater and dark jeans. His hair was hidden under a baseball cap, and he wore a pair of sunglasses. He checked his phone, avoiding Rene's eyes, and she focused intently on her phone, moving around from foot to foot and pacing the lobby so she would appear to be impatiently waiting for her delivery.

While she pretended to be absorbed in her phone, she silenced the phone so the camera wouldn't give off the telltale click and snapped several photos of the man in black. Suddenly, a cheap, beat-up sedan pulled to the front of the hotel and the door flew open. The driver left the lights on and the car running, but he had a pizza box in his hand and a brown paper bag on top of it, the contents hidden from view. Rene noticed that her assumed last name was written in black marker on both the pizza box and the bag—large enough to be seen by anyone who happened to be observing. The delivery guy ran up to the door, and Rene confirmed her last name.

"ID?" the guy asked. "Sorry. I gotta check it."

Rene didn't hesitate. She was sure that the fake she'd made would pass a visual check by a rushed delivery driver... and she knew that most handheld apps that allowed delivery drivers to scan IDs when carding customers didn't track against state databases. They were simply a way for a business to record data for a short period of time in case they were audited for compliance by local authorities. There was no way using the fake ID would compromise their safety, so she handed it to him. He scanned it with his phone and handed her the device so she could sign her name with her finger to prove she'd accepted delivery of the beer.

Rene scribbled the fake name on the line, handed the guy a cash tip, and accepted the bag of food with her left hand. She kept her right hand close to her hip in case she needed to pull her weapon. The delivery driver thanked her for the tip and, without ever really looking at her, ran back to his car and pulled away. She scanned the hotel lobby for the man in black. He was still preoccupied with his phone, but he was now speaking into it.

"Hurry up," he urged. "I've been waiting for twenty minutes, for fuck's sake."

His conversation might have eased Rene's mind, but it didn't. He very easily could have been covering his actions and trying to appear as though he were not following her. As soon as she walked past the clerk's desk, she increased her walking pace. She passed the man with her head held high, pretending to be fully engrossed in balancing her food delivery, her purse, and her phone. She snapped as many pictures as she could as she walked up to and then past him. She kept her chin low until she was nearly to the elevators. When she glanced back into the lobby, the man was approaching an annoyed-looking woman who was giving him a hard time for rushing her.

That still didn't ease Rene's nerves. Instead of going to the elevator and risking being trapped inside with anyone who might follow her, she took the stairs that she'd taken down to the lobby back up to the third floor. She examined the stairwells and didn't notice surveillance cameras...which didn't thrill her. But she was alone, and the concrete stairs and fire doors on each floor created an echo that would have alerted her if anyone else was in the stairwell above or below her. Confident she wasn't being followed, she got out on the third floor and headed for the room where Quinn and Danny were waiting for her. She knocked on the door, identified herself, and blew out some of her anxiety on a hard breath as she listened to Quinn disengage the lock.

"Anybody hungry?" she casually asked as she stepped inside. She met Quinn's eyes in silent reassurance that everything on her end was all right. He met her eyes with warmth and an expression that looked like relief.

"I'm going to use the bathroom," Quinn said, which Rene knew meant he was going to secure the gun in the gun safe away from Danny's eyes.

"Make sure you *unload* in there," she said, hoping that the suggestive statement landed the way she intended. She'd wanted to remind him not to just put the gun back but to unload it as well.

Quinn gave her an outright smirk and actually chuckled. "Noted," he said.

"Danny, wanna help me unpack all this food?" Rene asked, distracting the boy so Quinn could slide the gun safe from under the bed and close himself in the bathroom. Danny ran to join Rene at the door, took a bag from her, and carried it to the table. She opened the bag and pulled out the six-pack of beer, a bottle of milk Sam had thoughtfully included for Danny, and the salad. While Danny selected the slice of pizza he wanted and made a big show of getting to eat right out of the box since they didn't have plates, Quinn quietly emerged from the bathroom, slipped the gun safe back under the bed, and then joined them at the table. He sat in the seat next to his son, but his eyes stayed on Rene. She noticed from the lingering grin on Quinn's face, he seemed to still be enjoying their shared joke.

While Quinn mixed the dressing on the salad and shoved half onto one side of the plastic carryout container as a makeshift plate for Rene, she went to the desk where the coffee pot was and pulled the packets of coffee out of her purse. She also took a moment to open the gallery of her images and zoomed in on the various pictures she'd taken of the man in black in the lobby.

He *had* been looking at her. Without a doubt. In three of the shots, he was staring right at her. That didn't mean he was dangerous, though. Men blatantly gawked at women all the time.

"Hey, Quinn," she asked nonchalantly, not wanting to alarm either of them. "Can you look at this?"

He stepped close to her, and she held her phone up for him to look. He grazed the side of her arm with his hand as he took the device and looked at the image. Another small current of electricity traveled through her body at the contact. She shoved the feeling away and focused on the man in black.

"Does he look familiar?" she asked.

Quinn squinted and looked closely at the man and then flipped through the other images in the camera roll until he'd seen all the shots Rene had taken. He shook his head, but when he focused his attention on her face, his eyes had filled with concern. "Maybe...yes? No? Should I know this guy?"

She shook her head and took her phone back from him, careful to avoid contact with Quinn's skin. If he was feeling closer to her, less inhibited from contact, she wasn't sure it would be a good idea to encourage that. "No, not at all. Just wanted to check."

"Rene?" he asked, as if to coax her into sharing.

"He was staring at me, so he set me on edge. I think he was just a creepy guy getting an eyeful while waiting for his date, but I wanted to check. I'll send this to Sam to see if she can find something on him."

Quinn hesitated before nodding, clearly debating if her assessment rang true. Truth was, she was still debating that as well.

"Dad?" Danny called out. "Can I have more pizza?"

Quinn gave Rene a lingering look and joined his son back at the table. She took that opportunity to forward the image to Holly with a text requesting that Sam run facial recognition on the photos and that someone on the team come out and do a quick walk through the hotel lobby and parking lot. If any of them got the sense that there was something more going on, they'd move Quinn and Danny immediately, even in the middle of the night if needed.

Until then, Rene double checked the lock on the door and then joined Quinn and Danny to enjoy their dinner together.

QUINN SWIGGED A HUGE SIP OF WATER AND SWALLOWED down the anti-inflammatories Rene had handed him. He pulled out his toothbrush and got ready for bed, brushing his teeth a lot longer than he normally would. He needed some time to think, some space. He was thrilled that Danny had fallen asleep watching a video on his tablet not long after eating, even if he wasn't thrilled that the disruption to Danny's routine was probably only going to get worse before it got better. Danny had been out of school so much since Eliza's passing. Even though he was only in first grade, he knew routine and consistency were almost more important than anything to his son right now. But Holly had called and spoken to Rene just a few moments ago, which was why he'd excused himself to get ready for bed, even though he was nowhere near close to being able to fall asleep. If the little he'd been able to understand from Rene's half of the conversation was any indication, he and Rene and Danny were going to be hiding out for much more than just the night.

He stared back at his reflection and said a silent prayer to Eliza. He wanted their son safe. He wanted her killer brought to justice. He wanted to face the new normal of their lives and somehow fill the void that Eliza left in Danny's life. At the same time, he was starting to realize that there was more that he wanted. He didn't want to jump to any conclusions or misread any cues. He'd known Rene for basically one day. But their ease with one another—their smiles and jokes and connection during even the most incredibly strange and terrifying time—made him think that maybe he didn't have to spend his life playing the sad, ex-husband role. He wondered if what he was feeling toward

Rene was just a function of their circumstances. How attractive she was, how capable, and yet she had a tenderness toward Danny—and even toward him—that hinted at so much more under the surface.

Quinn slipped his toothbrush back into its travel container and scrubbed his face clean. He didn't know if Rene felt the same spark that he did when they accidentally made contact, but he couldn't stop thinking about the flash in her eyes when she'd fisted his shirt. He roughly dried his face and folded his towel. He couldn't deny how hot that was. As cliché as it made him feel even thinking it, a woman who could be that strong, that passionate...

"You've been single too long, dickhead," he muttered to himself in the mirror. "Stop lusting after your private eye." Rubbing the back of his neck, he rolled his head and quietly opened the bathroom door. He'd changed into his pajamas and felt immediately the intimacy of being ready for bed while Rene stood at the coffee pot, quietly unwrapping a foil pod, still fully dressed and even still wearing her shoes. He had no doubt her gun was still secure at her waist.

"Hey," she greeted. "I'm going to slip past you for some water." She carried the one-cup coffee maker into the bathroom and filled it from the tap at the sink. "I'm on the overnight shift," she explained.

"You're not going to sleep?" Quinn asked. He felt worried for her on the one hand—how safe would they be if she was overtired and exhausted? But on the other, he felt vaguely disappointed that she wouldn't be curled up in the bed across from him. He realized he'd been looking forward to that. A feeling of domesticity and normalcy even amidst all the worry. And maybe too, something about having Rene close to him, closer to him, made him realize he'd been wanting that more than he had even been able to admit.

"I'll keep watch," she said. She motioned toward the laptop on the table and her notes. "I've got some work to do."

Quinn nodded and watched her fix her cup of coffee. She took it black—no condiments to sweeten or soften the bitter brew.

"How long have you been a private detective?" he asked. He followed her back to the table and sat across from her.

She was quiet.

"Sorry," he said, immediately realizing that she'd stiffened up again. "You wanted to get some work done. I'm just nowhere near able to relax and sleep right now." He moved to get up and leave her alone, but she answered him quickly.

"Investigator," she corrected with a smile. "I've been a private *investigator* for about a year." She blew lightly on the paper cup to cool her coffee. "You can sit," she added, inviting him to a chair with her hand.

"And you were with Witness Protection before?" he asked. He watched the dim light from the table lamp illuminate the planes of Rene's face as she spoke.

"Yeah," she confirmed. "Twelve years a marshal with Witness Security, or Witness Protection as most people call it. I'm well trained and highly qualified not only to protect you and Danny but to find out who—if anyone—is after you."

Quinn waited until Rene met his eyes. "What happened?" he asked gently, suspecting he was treading on emotionally shaky ground. "Why did you leave?"

She took a sip before answering. She sighed, and the

sound cut Quinn to the core. It wasn't just sad. Her throat hummed with a low, mournful sound. Her body tensed with unshed pain. "I was the team lead. I lost a team member. She went out on her own and didn't come back."

"Didn't come back?"

Rene leveled her dark eyes at him. The look of sorrow in her eyes magnified. "She was killed in the line of duty."

He could see and hear how haunted she was by the loss. There was clearly more to the story, enough that she blamed herself for the loss, but he didn't know how—or whether—he should press her. He wanted to know her story. He wanted to know everything. But instead he just offered what felt like the only comfort he could. "I'm so sorry, Rene. I can't imagine how hard that was."

Rene frowned. "Thank you." She paused as if debating how much to share but then quickly looked Quinn in the eyes. "I thought I had figured out that a witness was lying. I sensed a trap, but she disagreed with my assessment. She thought I was—"

"Connecting dots that didn't actually connect?" He had meant that to be a joke. He'd sensed she'd suspected him of doing that very thing. He didn't realize the sting his words would have until she visibly winced. "I'm sorry," Quinn said, focusing on his hands. He could only hope that by now she was starting to trust him.

"She went to get more information. To prove me wrong." Rene picked at the curled paper lip of her coffee cup.

"Rene," Quinn said, leaning slightly across the table. He wanted to reach for her, but that seemed like...too much. "Hey," he said gently. "That's not on you."

Rene bit her lower lip. "Maybe not directly, but I should have known she would do that. She was defiant like that, always trying to make a point. I set my instincts aside and trusted that she'd follow protocol. I could have intervened, addressed the elephant in the room. Called her out and made sure there could be no misunderstanding." She paused, and Quinn couldn't help noticing the tone underlying her words. "Instead, I chose to ignore all the signals I was picking up on. And it cost a marshal her life."

Quinn got it then. The undercurrent between Rene and him. The whatever it was...the hint of attraction, the chemistry. Not only was she likely struggling with whether or not she could fully trust Quinn and his story, but if she may have been feeling the same current between them that he was, she was likely not going to let it sit. At some point, one of them would have to address the elephant in their hotel room...

Quinn scooted his chair so close to Rene's that their knees bumped. She watched him intently, her eyes blazing with an unspoken need. "I'm sorry for your agent," he said. "We all make mistakes. But it doesn't sound like the mistake that was made there was yours." There was an energy flowing between them that hit Quinn deep in his body. He wanted to touch her, move the end of her ponytail from where it rested on her shoulder, and stroke the loose tendrils of hair from her face. But before he decided whether she'd appreciate his touch or give him another set of bruised ribs, a blood-curdling wail sent both of them bolting from their chairs.

"Dad!" Danny's shouts were punctuated by an outburst of tears.

"It's okay, buddy. I'm here." Quinn nearly dove into the bed and buried himself under the blankets with his son. "Can you grab me some water?" he called to Rene.

She wordlessly picked up a full bottle. She handed him the water bottle and watched while he encouraged Danny to take a sip of water. While Quinn rocked and soothed his son, he motioned for Rene to join them. She looked torn for a moment but then sat down on the bed beside Quinn in the space he'd made for her.

5

QUINN'S MORNING had been a blur. When he'd awakened just after seven, Rene was gone. Tika had taken her place at the window while Holly skimmed over Rene's notes. As soon as Holly had realized he was awake, a flurry of activities began, and within an hour, he and Danny were in the back seat of Holly's car. As she drove, Tika asked them about food choices and if they needed anything—toothbrushes, deodorant, anything at all—before announcing she'd text Rene and ask her to stop for supplies. Holly explained that Rene would be joining them as soon as she caught up on rest. Quinn had woken several times in the night and found her awake every time. Sometimes looking out the window, going over her notes, or staring at her laptop's screen. Or just watching them—watching him from her seat at the table as father and son slept.

Because he'd opened his eyes so many times during the night, he could attest to the fact that she hadn't slept.

Though he felt bad about that, he didn't feel bad about the amount of sleep he had finally gotten. He was completely worn out, his ribs were still sore, and the rest of his body didn't feel a hell of a lot better after a night of rest. What he didn't completely understand was why he felt so ill at ease without her there this morning. He didn't doubt for a moment that Holly and Tika could protect Danny if needed, but the sense of security he felt at having Rene close by was missing, and his anxiety was slowly increasing with each passing moment that she wasn't there.

"Is Rene getting some rest?" he asked, hoping his question sounded professional and neutral. He was sitting in the back seat of Holly's car, and she met his eyes in the rearview mirror.

"She better be," Holly said with a hint of a grin. She activated her turn signal and turned onto a country road that he would hardly have been able to find if he'd been behind the wheel.

They traveled the road for a few moments, passing unmarked turnoffs and some heavily decorated mailboxes that announced the names and numbers of the residences that broke up the dense woods. Finally, Holly pulled past a small sign that had the street address in clearly marked numbers. He stared down a long driveway that led to the secluded house that sat far enough from the road that the trees blocked his view of the one-lane gravel road. Even if Rene were coming, he wouldn't know until she was practically at the house.

He feared if he asked about her one more time, he'd seem

more like a stalker than a client. Earlier, on the drive, he'd asked if Rene was coming back that day, and Holly reminded him that Rene was stopping by the store for supplies, but that yes, she'd be back. Instead of wondering when he'd see her again, he turned his attention to the whirl of activity that took place once Holly parked the car. After they unloaded the bags from the car, Danny screamed as Tika chased him around the big backyard while Holly added cameras and sensors to the property. Once those were active, any trespassers would set off an alarm, alerting the team to movement anywhere in close proximity to the small house.

Though Holly assured him the property was secure and he could relax a bit more, Quinn wasn't foolish enough to completely let his guard down. He sighed, chastising himself when he inadvertently glanced down the driveway again, checking to see if Rene was on her way. Holly turned and headed toward the house, so Quinn decided to turn his focus to work. He'd set up his laptop and had been skimming the vacation home welcome packet for information about the Wi-Fi password when Holly stopped him.

"Security is almost all set up," Holly said as she closed the back door. "Let me show you." She eyed his laptop. "And I have one request."

Quinn raised a brow and nodded.

"The Wi-Fi is not secure here," Holly explained. "The property owner has provided free Wi-Fi for guests, but there's no password required to access it. That makes sense for most guests staying here." Holly motioned with a hand. "And the house is so remote that it's unlikely any of the neighbors will be able to access the network anyway. But," she continued. "While you're here, I'd prefer that you never use the unsecured Wi-Fi."

Quinn frowned. "That's going to be a problem," he admitted. "I let my office know I was going to work from home with Danny for a few days. I'll need Internet access to work."

"Not a problem," Holly assured him. "I'll have Sam come out to the house later today. We're going to set you up with a VPN. Are you familiar with those?"

"I've heard of it but am not sure what that means for this situation," he said.

"Basically, Sam is going to install a program that will let you access the Internet connection here but will force you to input a password on your device." She gave him a reassuring smile. "You'll be able to work and get on the Internet through the VPN, but anyone who might be monitoring the Internet or have access to the network inside the house shouldn't be able to track your online activity. The VPN provides sort of a secondary layer of protection."

He nodded. "Ah, okay. Got it. When will Sam be coming?"

Holly shook her head. "As soon as possible. I know you need to work. If it's urgent, she can install a VPN on your laptop remotely, but trust me, it's a hell of a lot faster and less complicated if she can jump on your laptop and set it up from here."

"Not a problem," Quinn said. "I'll call the office and let them know Danny's not feeling well and I'll be back online as soon as I can."

"If you can wait, I'd rather you not call," Holly said.

"Hollywood gets some things wrong, Quinn. If you're on your cell phone and your activity is being tracked, the call might be traceable almost instantly. I'd rather you stay out of touch and only use that burner phone until we get your secure Wi-Fi set up. Just remember. We're here because we need to keep you hidden until we know whether or not you're safe. Any contact with anyone outside my team potentially compromises that safety."

"Okay," Quinn said. "I'll wait for Sam."

"She should be here soon," Holly reassured him. "I've got more Internet cameras set up, but they're not activated yet. I want those connected securely as well, but at least they're in position and ready to go." She motioned toward the stairs. "Why don't you check out the upstairs? Pick a room, unpack a little, and settle in. We've got Danny occupied."

"Sounds good," Quinn said. He grabbed his duffel and headed up the stairs. The house had two bedrooms and a large, spacious loft at the top of the stairs with a desk where Holly had unpacked a computer with two monitors. She had written down the username and password as well as directions to log in to view the cameras. On the back side of that was a list of all the numbers where the HEARTS could be reached.

"So this is the surveillance setup?" Quinn called out.

Holly nodded and pointed to the monitors. "The program we have splits the view into several screens, so we'll have eyes on many parts of the property and the house at once. Even inside the house."

He chuckled. "Not a lot of privacy, huh?"

"This is for your safety, Quinn. We won't be watching the bathrooms," Holly assured him.

"I appreciate that," he said.

Sounds coming from outside distracted him from his conversation with Holly. He could hear the sounds of car doors being slammed and footsteps on the gravel path even up in the loft.

"What the heck is in here?" Danny asked, walking into the house right behind Rene.

She set her load down and then reached for the one he was barely able to carry. "Thanks for the help, little man. You might just be carrying a bag full of all the hotdogs I bought for you."

He whooped in a way Quinn didn't think he had in months. "Dad!" he shouted, looking around the entryway of the house. "Dad! Rene got me hotdogs!"

Quinn peered over the loft, an enormous feeling of relief flooding his chest at the sight of Rene. "That's awesome, bud!" he called. "I'll be right down. I'm just putting our stuff away." He stayed in the loft for a moment, making brief eye contact with Rene. Unless he was imagining it, her face lit up with a smile that she quickly suppressed when she saw him.

He watched Sam flounce through the house with her colorful nails and bubbly personality. She rubbed her hands together and said, "Let me at that router!"

Danny trailed behind Rene, asking questions and awkwardly trying to help her unpack the bags full of groceries she'd brought. He liked seeing his son so playful with the HEARTS. He still had a lot of ups and downs, but Quinn couldn't remember Danny being so at ease with someone he barely knew in a long time. Danny had gotten comfortable with every member of the team faster than Quinn had expected. He was glad about that. This would be infinitely more difficult if Danny was nervous around the people Quinn had hired to look out for them.

"Rene," Holly said and then jerked her head in an unspoken request for Rene to follow her. Rene took her duffel bag and headed for the stairs to the loft where Quinn and Holly had been a minute before.

He guessed she needed to be updated on all the things Holly had done since Rene had gone home to sleep. By the time he unloaded his duffel and put everything away, he heard Holly and Rene quietly talking up in the loft. The open concept of the house made it easy for him to watch their muted exchange, but he couldn't hear what they were saying.

Rene glanced his way and flashed a hint of a smile but returned her attention to Holly before he could return her gesture. Instead of standing there awkwardly, he padded downstairs and went to the couch where Danny was explaining something about dinosaurs to Tika. After what seemed like forever, Holly called out to Tika that Sam was done and they were ready to go.

"When will you be back?" Danny asked, following Tika toward the door.

"Maybe tomorrow, little man. We'll see."

"I'll show you the rest of my game then, okay?"

She smiled and held her hand out to get a high-five. "Can't wait."

"Quinn, Sam's got you all set up," Holly said. "She left the log-ins and passwords by your laptop, but she already signed in your laptop and your son's tablet. You should be all set. I'll be in touch." She gave him a wave and then murmured some instructions low under her voice to her team.

Rene followed Holly and Tika to the door and locked it after they left. "I hear this house comes with a super cool hiding spot," she said to Danny once the door was secure. "Did Holly show it to you?"

Quinn followed as Danny led Rene down the hallway. In the space between two doorways, Danny stopped and looked up at her with a little grin. "This is the coolest thing I've ever seen," he said. He pressed on the wall, and it clicked open to reveal a little cubby.

Rene ruffled his hair. "Well, I know this is a new place and you might not always know where to go if you get scared. Anytime you're feeling scared, you hop in there and don't come out until I come to get you."

Questions filled Danny's eyes, and that hint of excitement faded away. Quinn was expecting Danny to ask something like *what if Dad tells me*, but his question shook Quinn to the core.

"What if you die?" Danny whispered.

Quinn was taken aback, but Rene simply responded as if he had asked about the weather.

She nodded. "That's a good question. It's good to be prepared, Danny. The only people you open the door for is me, your dad, or one of my team members. Nobody else. Okay?"

"Okay," he whispered.

"But you don't have to worry about anyone else dying," she said. "You're a brave boy and smart to ask questions. How do you feel about playing on your tablet in your room for a few minutes now that we have the Internet working?"

He held up the game he'd been showing to Tika. "Yay!" Danny darted around her into his room, and Rene finally focused on Quinn.

He blew his breath out. "Sorry about that."

"It's okay," she said.

"He's still—"

"He lost his mom, Quinn. He has a valid reason to ask questions like that."

Even so, the idea that Danny would want a backup plan in case Rene died broke Quinn's heart. His chest burned from the ache, but he also felt sick to his stomach at the thought that whatever they had gotten mixed up with could cause Rene to be hurt. "It's only been a few months. Sometimes we both stumble a little."

She put her hand to his arm and squeezed as she gave him a reassuring smile. Her touch immediately soothed him, and he finally felt like he could breathe again. He must have put more trust in her than he had realized, because simply having her back in his space brought a sense of serenity that eased the tension in his entire body. She calmed him. And he needed that calm more than he had understood.

"No need to apologize," she said. "Why don't you get some work done? It will feel good to do something that feels like normal life for a while. What about Danny? Can you contact the school about his absence?"

"Yeah," he said. What should I tell them? That he's sick? Struggling?

She bit her lips. "I don't want to use Eliza's death—"

"Rene, I'll use whatever means necessary to keep him safe."

She thought for a moment. "I think you should tell them that he's had a setback accepting his mom's loss and will be out of school for the rest of this week while you get him the help he needs. That will play on their sympathies, so hopefully they won't require a doctor's note. If they do, we'll get one, but I'd rather avoid that if possible. The fewer people who know you're in hiding, the better. What about you?" she pressed. "What excuse have you given for missing work?"

"Same. That Danny's sick. I can work from home, so it's not a big deal as long as I keep up with my workload."

"Good. You've kept your phone turned off, right? Holly gave you a burner phone to use in case of emergency?"

"Yeah. But I'm going to need to check it eventually. Make work calls. Check in with my brother." He gave Rene a look. "If I don't, that'll seem...you know. We normally text at least every other day if not every day."

"Okay. Just remember to keep your personal phone turned off unless you talk to me first. I'll have Sam bring a signal jammer tomorrow so you can turn it on and off without worrying that you've compromised our location."

He wanted to protest, but he swallowed the words.

Instead he said, "Do you think all this is necessary?" he asked. "The cameras, the hiding out. Even keeping all this from my brother..."

"Quinn," Rene said. "You came to us because you felt something was off. Eliza is dead and her killer is still at large. Someone was in your house, and that person assaulted you. I absolutely think all of this is necessary. At least until we have a better idea of what's going on. We're never going to regret taking a few extra precautions. At least I hope, if nothing else, you can feel safe here—safer than you would be even at home, right?"

He nodded, wondering if he'd ever feel safe in his own home again.

"Until we have some answers, I'll stay with you. We're in this together," she said.

"Is that a promise?" he asked lamely. He felt like a shit asking after what she'd said about not making promises anymore. He knew his comment landed hard by the pinched look on her face.

"Get some work done, Quinn," she said, turning her back to him.

RENE LAYERED THE EXTRA BEDDING SHE'D FOUND IN A closet into a corner of the loft. Sleeping on the floor wasn't ideal, but she'd slept in worse conditions. The pile of blankets and pillows would do for now. She could have asked Quinn to share a bedroom with Danny, but truth be told, she preferred to station herself between them, out in the open, where any compromise in the security of the home would give her faster access to them. Holly had done a great job of selecting a secluded place and had used a new pseudonym on the rental agreement. Someone would have to dig very deep to find any of them here. But Rene knew better than to ever be lulled into a sense of security. Until the job was done...it wasn't over.

Using a roll of clear tape, she'd found in the desk drawer, Rene stuck some of her notes on the wall of the loft so she could quickly reference them without digging through page after page and trying to decipher her rushed handwriting. She wished she had a white board like the one at the office. While she did her best to keep her notebook in order, she still liked to spread evidence out so she could see everything. She usually copied the most important points onto the white board, but this was going to have to do for now. She'd felt a vague sense of stress around Quinn since he made that promise comment. Over the last few hours, he'd worked quietly in his bedroom while Danny played on his tablet in his new room. Every time Quinn passed through the loft for any reason—a glass of water, to check on Danny—the tension between them was thick. She didn't like the fact that she was becoming emotionally invested in these clients. In her old life as a marshal, that had not happened once. Her job was her job, and she'd done it unfailingly and unflinchingly. Until the day she walked away. In the year since she'd come to HEARTS, she'd had no problem chasing down cheating spouses and tailing people involved in fraud and petty crimes of all sorts. And not once did she feel anything even remotely like this.

Quinn and his son had presented a new and totally unfamiliar experience for her. She huffed a sigh as she realized she was likely just confusing loneliness for something more. Hell, she hadn't been on a date in the year she'd been at HEARTS. When this was all over, she'd blow off some steam, find a nice, no-strings-attached hunk to pass some time with, and she'd go back to feeling normal. But even as Rene had the thought, she knew it wouldn't be that easy. Quinn's chocolate-brown eyes and the puppy-dog look he gave her when she was talking sometimes... He made her pulse skitter in a way that was more about his body, his scent, and his sweetness than her drive to protect him. *Damn it all,* she thought. *Sam's bad influence has finally worn off on me. I'm crushing on a client?* She shook her head to clear the distressing thoughts just as she heard a familiar voice.

"Knock knock." Quinn rapped his knuckles lightly against the wall of the loft. "Sorry," he said with a smile. "Yours is the only room without a door."

"Hey," she said, smiling at the man who had been on her mind. "It's okay. Come on in."

"Can we talk?" He hovered several feet away, looking tentative.

Rene nodded. "What's on your mind?"

"You," he answered directly.

Rene hadn't been expecting that. She took a deep breath and met his eyes. "Anything you care to share?"

Quinn flushed a bit under a light scruff of beard. "I'm sorry for what I said earlier," he said.

"Quinn, don't—" Rene tried to cut him off, but he shook his head and held up a hand.

"Let me finish?" he asked. "Please?"

Rene nodded.

"I'm sorry I asked you for something I know you can't give me. I didn't mean it to be shitty," he said, sincerity infusing his tone. He looked down at his hands. "I—I don't actually know if this is crazy or not to say out loud, but..."

"Quinn..." Rene shook her head. "It's fine. You don't..."

He stepped closer to her. "Am I wrong to feel that there's something between us?" He searched her face, and Rene's stomach flipped as her body responded to his. "If I am, just put my dumb ass in place and I'll tuck my tail between my legs and go back to my room." He looked so open, so vulnerable. "You're a gorgeous and capable woman, and I know I'm a client and your job is to protect me. But if there is any way this feeling is actually something..."

Rene closed the gap in the space between them slowly. She looked into his face. He was a few inches taller than her —tall enough that she had to reach for the front of his T-shirt to tug him closer. "You're not wrong," she whispered. She lifted her face, and Quinn lowered his mouth to hers.

The first press of his lips against hers was tentative, gentle. But then she wrapped her arms around his neck and opened her mouth to his kiss. He tasted exactly like she expected. His lips were warm and strong, and his tongue probing hers was gentle but insistent. He felt right, even if the whole situation was wrong.

"Quinn," she breathed, pulling her mouth from his. "We can't."

Quinn adjusted the front of his tee and nodded. "Right. Shit," he huffed. "Right." He looked toward his son's room and back toward Rene. "We can't. Not here, now." He sighed deeply. "When this is all over and I'm not your client anymore?"

She ran the tip of her tongue over her lower lip. She wanted nothing more than to grab him again and not let go. Pick up where they'd left off, boundaries be damned. But she *knew* better. She *was* better than that. "Yes," she said breathlessly, taking a step away from the man whose musky, minty flavor she could still taste on her lips. "And that's something I *can* promise."

RENE STRUGGLED TO FOCUS ON THE REPORT SHE'D received from Holly. Her eyes were heavy from reading, her stomach was starting to rumble, and her conscience was sending her nasty messages after the steamy kiss she'd shared with Quinn. She sighed and stretched her arms above her head in the loft. Quinn and Danny had gone downstairs to explore the TV options, and she could hear giggles and commotion carrying through the quiet to the loft. The sun had begun to set, and through the small semicircular window in the loft, she could see the muted pink sky and a wispy cluster of clouds over the horizon of the dense trees. This place would have been an ideal vacation getaway if she and Quinn and Danny were a real family on a holiday. But their lives were in Rene's hands, and she was having a hard time focusing on her duty because the fantasy of the house and the promise of that kiss with Quinn was magnetic in its power over her.

The soft sounds of a pair of feet thudding up the stairs pulled her attention from the window.

"Rene?" Quinn stood at the top of the stairs, a tentative smile on his face. As she looked at his mouth, the memory of their kiss rushed back, and she grinned and sighed in spite of herself. "Yeah," he said, a wistful look on his face. "Me too. But what I really came to ask is if you were serious about liking hot dogs or if you were just placating Danny? Because he's asked three times if we can have hot dogs for dinner, and he really wants to know when you're coming down to hang out with us."

Rene grinned. "I was serious about liking hot dogs, but you guys don't have to worry about me, Quinn. I don't want to interfere with your routine more than I have already."

Quinn tilted his head as if he didn't quite understand. "We eat dinner together. That's our rule. If you want to break it, you have to explain that to Danny."

She opened her mouth but couldn't put her finger on what she was supposed to say. "Are you seriously guilting me with disappointing your child if I don't join you for dinner?"

He gave her a greatly exaggerated look of seriousness that she suspected he had mastered on Danny. "We all need to eat."

She gestured toward the desk. "What if I'm working?"

"We don't work through dinner."

"What if I'm sick?"

He shrugged. "I'll need a note from your doctor."

She laughed. "I see. So this dinner thing is very serious business." She very intentionally didn't call it the phrase that popped into her head: *family hour.*

"Are you telling me you don't take hot dogs seriously?" Quinn lowered his voice and gave her a sexy grin. "I made a mixed greens and kale salad on the side. Just for us grown-ups."

Rene laughed at that and stood from the office chair in the loft. "Well, that seals it."

He smiled. "Can you promise us at least one hour?"

"One hour," she agreed with a smile of her own.

RENE HADN'T EATEN A HOT DOG IN AS LONG AS SHE could remember, but tonight they tasted so, so much better than they ever had. Or maybe it was the company. She couldn't help laughing at Danny as he'd made silly faces with his ketchup on his plate, using the end of his hot dog as a paintbrush. And the salad Quinn had prepared was so delicious, she'd eaten seconds. After they finished their meal, Rene and Quinn cleared the table while Danny sat nearby with his dinosaurs, creating a scene of utter havoc between the plastic animals and his metal cars.

"Thank you, Quinn. That was wonderful," Rene said. She slipped her plate into the sink, which Quinn was filling with hot, sudsy water.

He turned to face her, and the moment they shared was too sweet, too domestic. Rene looked away and crossed the kitchen to the coffee machine. When she pressed the button to grind fresh coffee, Quinn turned his attention from rinsing plates to her.

"Isn't it a little late for coffee?" he asked.

"I expect to be up most of the night," she explained.

He wrinkled his brow at her. "Up all night? Rene, when will you sleep?"

She glanced at him as she measured out a full pot's worth of grounds. "I'll take a nap when you're up in the morning."

Concern worried the lines around his mouth. "You've been up all day."

"Not *all* day," she said. "I went home at five this morning and slept. Remember?"

"But just for a few hours."

She finished prepping the coffee before she smiled at him. "I'll be okay, Quinn. I'll rest in the morning."

He did not look satisfied with her answer. "That's not healthy, Rene. You can't treat your body like that."

She lifted her brows. "Aren't you a confessed insomniac?"

"I am, and therefore I speak from experience." He dried his hands on a towel and faced her. "You can't stay up all night after being up most of the day."

"Quinn, if you're worried about your safety—"

"I already sleep in cycles," he said, cutting her off. "Usually I get up and work until I can fall asleep again. How about this. I'll crash at my usual time. When I wake up, I'll come out to the loft and give you a break. You can nap until I'm ready to go back to bed."

"Quinn—"

"You can't protect us if you're too exhausted to function," he stated.

She closed her mouth and considered his words. "Okay.

That's a reasonable plan. We'll sleep in shifts if that will make you feel better."

"It will."

He returned his focus to cleaning up the dishes, but she sensed he wasn't done with the conversation. "Do you think I'm being overbearing?" he asked.

"No," she said. "I appreciate your concern. But I spent twelve years often sleep-deprived because the job demanded it. I can handle this, but I'm willing to compromise. It's a good plan." She couldn't resist the urge to walk up behind him. She breathed deeply and rested her nose lightly against his back. "Now that I've eaten and the dishes are done, may I be excused? I'd like to finish reading the reports from the team."

"Of course," he said. "Anything you're able to share?"

Rene flickered a glance at Danny. "Come see me after you tuck in the little man," she said as she filled the cup she'd found in the cabinet. "We'll talk before you turn in for the night."

Quinn groaned. "Why do I have a feeling I really won't be able to sleep then."

"Come talk to me later," she said. "Danny," she called, interrupting the massacre of a Corvette by a T-Rex. "I'm headed back up to get some work done. Come see me to say good night, okay?"

"Okay!" he shouted distractedly before smashing a whole line of cars with the flick of a brachiosaurus tail.

Though she said she was headed upstairs, Rene first went from window to window, peering out from each and testing the locks. She double=checked that the front door was bolted. And generally walked the house to make sure all the rooms were in order, the cameras securely in place, and that nothing seemed amiss. Only after she had made sure they were secure inside the house did she take her cup and climb the stairs to the loft.

Then the house was quiet.

6

AFTER HE PUT Danny to bed, Quinn jumped into the shower. He took an extra minute under the hot spray, feeling his tense muscles finally relax a little. Then he wrapped a towel around his waist and wandered his temporary bedroom. The house was the kind of unsettling quiet that Quinn had come to hate so much. Some might have called that feeling loneliness, but he wasn't ready to admit that just yet. Instead of dwelling on the stillness and emptiness, he took a T-shirt and flannel pants out of the dresser and very nearly started undressing before recalling the camera Holly had placed in the corner of the room. A little chuckle left him as he glanced up at it. He wasn't sure if Rene was watching him or not, but he offered a weak salute and clenched the towel a bit tighter in his fist before going into the attached bathroom, where he closed the door and changed in privacy. By the time he emerged, his bones ached with exhaustion, but his mind wouldn't slow down. He wasn't even going to pretend that he could fall asleep anytime soon. Instead, he headed over to the loft for his meeting with Rene.

"Knock..." He trailed off, not wanting the joke to go stale.

Rene greeted him with a grin and motioned for him to join her.

"So what has your team found out?" he asked. He sat in a spare kitchen chair that Rene had at some point moved up to the loft for him. She rolled back in the office chair and pointed toward her notes.

"A lot of information. I'll want your thoughts on some of this." She was serious then, the playful, flirtatious woman he'd kissed just a few hours ago hidden deep behind the marshal.

"Hit me with it," he said.

Rene placed a number of printed photos on the desk. "Remember these?"

Quinn looked at the images. Some were blurrier than others, but some had been enlarged to enhance small details. "Yeah." He pointed toward the one he remembered. "You showed me one like this at the hotel the other night."

Rene nodded. "There are a lot more, and some are better than others. Sam didn't get a lot, but I had her run facial recognition on the photos."

Quinn swallowed. "And? What did she find?"

She looked at him and pressed her lips together. "Can you take another look at these? Tell me if you recognize anyone in these photos?"

Quinn picked up the entire stack and flipped through

them one by one. The man was wearing sunglasses. Some of Rene's images were slightly in profile; some were nearly dead center. In one, she captured the side view of his shoulders, and Quinn could tell the guy was fairly big and well-built.

"Rene, I just don't know. I mean, he could be a lot of guys. The hair is dark, the sunglasses... I'd be reaching, and I don't want to reach."

"That's okay," she said. "That's good."

Rene pulled out another printout from a separate file folder. There was a formal photo of a man on it—it was a posed picture. The man in the photo was wearing a police officer's uniform. "Do you recognize this man?" she asked.

Quinn lifted the paper and peered at the official image. "Yeah, of course," he said. "Where did you get this? Why do you have this?"

Rene nodded back at the photos. "We think the man in the photos I took is this man." She watched his reaction.

"Rene." Quinn swallowed hard against the pounding in his chest. "That's Frank. Frank Strickland. My brother's partner." He met Rene's eyes. "Why the hell do you have a picture of him?"

Rene took a deep breath and didn't seem to flinch when he swore.

"Rene," Quinn pressed. "What do you know? Is there a connection between my brother's partner and Eliza?"

Rene shook her head quickly. "We don't know anything for certain." She pointed to a tree she'd drawn on a separate piece of paper. There were small sticky notes with names on them, and she moved each paper as she showed Quinn how each individual on the tree connected. "Right now, I'm figuring out what we know about each person connected to you—" she looked up at him with a concerned expression "—and Danny. And then separately to Eliza." She traced her finger along the tree and explained. "Eliza's connected to all these people, and some of the lines overlap."

Quinn watched as Rene picked up the paper with Frank's name and moved it around.

"Frank is your brother's partner, so he connects to both you and to Eliza, even if the connection to Eliza seems tenuous." She pointed to the blurry images she'd taken with the burner phone. "But why do you suppose Frank Strickland would have been in the same motel we were...on the same night."

She didn't pose it as a question.

"I don't... I can't..." Quinn didn't see how any of this made sense. Or how any of this could possibly be connected to Eliza. "So Frank was at a sleazebag motel. Is that evidence of something? What does it mean?"

"No," Rene said emphatically. "This isn't evidence. We're far from gathering evidence. Right now, we're just gathering information. That's it."

"But it's fucking bizarre." Quinn sank back in his chair and vigorously rubbed his chin. He wished he could clear his head. "The way this looks. Rene... This isn't good."

As the pieces started to fall into place for Quinn, he felt more and more uneasy.

"Do you have any images from the cameras at my house?" he asked quickly.

She shook her head. "No activity has been recorded

except the occasional raccoon running past the sensors since we left."

Quinn felt only marginally better hearing that. "What about the intruder?" he barked but then quickly realized if he were too loud, his voice could carry through the loft and wake Danny. He notched his voice down to a hard whisper, but it was hard to control the emotional toll of this. He'd been concerned about the lack of leads, the suspect trail growing cold so fast...but if this somehow really did not just involve a cop his ex-wife had been dating...

"Rene, I need to know what you know." Quinn faced her, a steely determination on his face. "Could my brother's partner have anything to..." Quinn swallowed hard and racked his brain. He suddenly grew panicked. "What have I missed, Rene? What the fuck is going on!"

Rene looked at him. "Quinn," she said, her voice even and measured. "You need to calm down. All of this..." She motioned toward the pictures fanned out on the desk. "None of this means anything. Yet."

He huffed out an impatient sigh. "Yet." He looked at Rene, frustration raw on his face. "But what if it does? What if Frank Strickland was somehow involved in my wi—" Before the words even left his mouth, he stopped himself. He flicked a glance at Rene, and he was sure he spotted the look on her face as she registered what he'd nearly said.

"Eliza," he corrected. "If Frank Strickland was somehow involved in Eliza's..." He shook his head. "I'm sorry, Rene. This is all—"

"It's okay," she said quickly. "These are emotionally triggering conversations." Her voice was harder than Quinn had ever heard it. "I'd like you to take one more look at the pictures and let me know if you recognize anything or anyone else in any of them. Take your time."

Quinn picked up the pictures again, but instead of studying them, he stared at Rene's face. He couldn't believe he'd slipped—nearly called, or started to call, Eliza his wife. He was worried he'd hurt Rene, that maybe she'd question whether he was really over his ex. Whether he was really able to date her or see her for who she was. But he could deal with that later. Right now, if there was a connection between Frank Strickland and Eliza's death, he owed it to his son to help.

None of the other faces or items in the pictures made any sense to him. He spoke out loud as he touched each picture and identified what he could. "I mean, nothing, Rene. Nothing." He tapped the front desk clerk. "The first time I saw that kid was when we checked in." He glanced up at Rene. "I don't know if I could recognize him again if my life depended on it." There were heads and shoulders and partial faces of others lingering in the lobby, but nothing stood out. "Fuck!" he sighed, tossing the pictures down on the desk. "I feel so useless!"

Rene picked the pictures up and stacked them neatly. "Hey," she said. "Let's take a breather, okay? This is all a lot. There's no need to be so hard on yourself."

Quinn sighed. "That's easy for you to say," he said. His words weren't bitter. Just sad. "If my brother's partner had something to do with Eliza..." He groaned. "My mind won't stop making connections. What could it all mean? Who is involved? Why!"

Rene gave him a thin smile. Gone were the full, almost flirty grins of the woman he'd kissed, the woman whose presence brought him comfort and stability. This was a tolerant smile. One she gave him and probably every other troublesome client she'd ever had. He hated the way that smile made him feel. Like he was as helpless and simple as everyone else. Like she saw him the way she saw everyone else. Not that he could blame her.

"Go to sleep, Quinn," she said simply. Rene took a sip of what was left in her coffee mug. Based on Quinn's memory, that coffee had to be a couple of hours old.

"Can I make you another cup of coffee?" he offered. "Before I try to take my turn sleeping?"

Rene shook her head. "I got it. But thanks."

"Rene..." Quinn stood and gave her an apologetic look. He needed to say something. To erase the emotional chill that seeped in between them the moment he nearly called Eliza his wife.

"Get some sleep, Quinn," she said dismissively.

Before he could say or do anything else, Rene turned away from him and logged into some application on the computer.

Her neck and shoulders were rigid. Stiff. Cold. He wanted to reach a hand out to her, touch the silky ponytail. Anything. Anything to let her know she meant something to him and that no matter how screwed up the circumstances were that nothing had changed for him. That when this was all over… But the set of her back didn't make him feel like a touch of any kind would be welcome.

"Good night, Rene," he said. Then he walked quietly into his room and shut the door.

RENE GLANCED UP AT HOLLY AS SHE ENTERED THE LOFT the following morning. Her boss wasn't the hovering maternal type, so the concern in her eyes gave Rene pause. She sat back in the chair and pushed the file she'd been reviewing aside. She'd spent half the night reviewing the photos and tracing lines from Eliza back to Frank. She knew the two had to be connected. Something in her gut couldn't accept that the very night she hid Quinn and Danny in a hotel that Frank Strickland would be in the lobby of the very same hotel. Another thing nagging at Rene was because of the break-in at Quinn's house. She didn't know why the break-in happened or how it connected back to Frank. She just had to figure out how…why.

"Good morning," Rene said as Holly put a fresh cup of coffee from a local coffee shop on Rene's desk.

"You look like hell," Holly said. "Did you sleep at all last night?"

"Some," Rene admitted. "But not much. Quinn's a bit of an insomniac, so we rotated shifts. I napped out here while he stood watch, but I don't think I actually slept." She stretched her neck to the left and then to the right. "I think all those catnaps might have actually compounded my exhaustion."

"How is he doing?" Holly raised her brows.

"Honestly, I'm not sure." Rene lowered her voice in case he came within earshot of their conversation. Danny was still sound asleep, but she'd heard the sound of the shower coming from Quinn's room earlier. He hadn't come out of his room yet, but Rene suspected he was awake. "He seemed really upset at the possibility that Frank was at the hotel that night."

Holly nodded. "And did his reaction seem genuine?"

Rene sighed. She knew what Holly was getting at. She was still sensitive to any clues that maybe Quinn was in on what had happened to Eliza, that hiring HEARTS and this whole thing were parts of just one massive cover-up.

"Honestly, Holly..." Rene sighed and removed the lid from the coffee so she could deeply inhale the fresh brew, "I'm as sure as I think I can be that the guy is telling the truth. Without evidence, yeah, anything is possible. And I won't let my guard down...but I'm pretty sure the guy is not involved."

"Speaking of being involved..." Holly looked at Rene. "How are you?"

Rene searched her teammate's face. "What are you getting at, Hol?"

Holly sipped her coffee and shoved an envelope toward Rene. "I've got more information for you. But let's talk about you first." She looked down at the envelope as she addressed Rene. "Sam was scanning the feed and spotted...let's just call it a moment...between you and Quinn."

"Oh shit." Rene faced Holly. "Holly, I'm sorry. That was inappropriate—unprofessional."

Holly held up a hand. "Leave the apologies," she said. "I just need to know if you need me to replace you." She looked Rene in the eye. "You know our team policies."

Rene nodded. She did, and she wasn't going to debate them now.

"But," Holly sighed, "you also know that I fell in love with Jack while we were working a case together. Eva and Josh reconnected while working undercover. And shit," she sighed. "Alexa and Dean..." As great as Alexa was in absolutely every way, she'd been the first to admit she fell in love with a client while the case Dean had hired them for was still ongoing. Dean's sister had disappeared, and Alexa—whose sister went missing over a decade ago and had never been found—had gotten too close to the case in almost every way possible. And it had almost cost them all.

Rene shook her head. "Alexa and Dean... What they did doesn't justify my kissing Quinn."

"I don't think that you think it does," Holly clarified. "But Rene, I've known you a long time now. It's not like you to get...involved."

Rene knew what Holly was saying was true. If anything, she was the one on the team who was the least likely to blur an emotional boundary. While Holly had military training and Eva was a former cop, Rene's career had been built on managing the emotional toll of dealing with people. Crimes —both the victims of it and the perpetrators. While protecting witnesses, sometimes she'd been responsible for people who were themselves truly evil, vile people. Keeping her emotions in check and doing the job was ingrained in her. These were more than habits. This was her training.

And she'd gone against everything when she allowed herself to kiss Quinn, a client, in the safehouse she was supposed to protect.

"I know." Rene took a deep breath. "And I should tell you my feelings are compromised, Holly. I'm starting to believe that the police are somehow involved in whatever happened to Eliza." Rene knew what she needed to do at this point. She'd spent half the time she was awake last night running through her mind the way Quinn had nearly referred to Eliza as his wife. If she were Holly, she wouldn't hesitate to make the call. "I don't believe I'll make the same lapse in judgment on this case. But I think you should replace me from on-site protection. I can head back to the office and work with Sam, follow up on some in-person leads. You can bring Tika and Alexa in to stay with Quinn and Danny."

Holly nodded. "I can do that."

"I'm sorry, Holly." Rene stood and paced to the semicircular window, her cup of coffee in hand. The sun was starting to come up over the woods surrounding the house. This place was beautiful. Rene fought against the tugging sensation in her chest. She couldn't believe she had compromised her values. Potentially her client's safety. But she'd make it right. There was still time to make it right.

"You've been on this case for over forty-eight hours. You've barely rested in that time. Go home," Holly said. "Get some sleep. Check in with the office this afternoon."

"No, Holly, I—"

"That was not a suggestion. Go home and rest."

Rene started to tell her that she couldn't rest—there were leads to follow up on. Issues to sort out. She faced Holly.

"Quinn didn't ID Monica," she said in a very low voice. "So either he didn't notice the woman in the picture with Frank was his brother's girlfriend...or he didn't want to tell me."

"Which do you suspect?" Holly asked.

Rene said, "I don't think he knows, Hol. He's reacting entirely from emotion. He's not thinking clearly. I trust that he doesn't know. If there's a connection to be made..." Rene lifted the folder and started gathering her things. "It's going to be us who makes it."

"Leave that here," Holly said.

"You are being one seriously bossy bitch today," Rene said lightly.

"I'm a bitch every day," Holly countered. "And you like it. I don't want to see you anywhere before four this afternoon. Not the office. Not back here. Go home and rest. Understand?"

Rene wanted to argue, but she would lose. Holly didn't back down easily, and Rene was too tired to stand her ground. "Yes, ma'am."

She grabbed her phone and headed downstairs. Tika was brewing a fresh pot of coffee and scanning the fridge for supplies. "Hey, Rene, what time does Danny wake up?"

"Soon," Rene said. "Tell him I said goodbye, will you?"

"Of course. What time you headed back this way?"

Rene shook her head. "Doesn't look like I'll be back. Not anytime soon anyway."

Tika widened her eyes. "Okay." She watched her team-mate carefully. "Something we should talk about?"

Rene shook her head. "I'm going to leave the on-site to you and Alexa for a bit."

"Uh-huh." Tika quirked up the corner of her mouth. "And you're leaving that boy and his father without even saying goodbye?"

"It's not goodbye forever, Tika. I'm just working off-site today." Rene threw her bag over her shoulder. "And Holly is going to find someone to cover tonight for me."

Tika crossed her arms. "What the hell, Rene? Spill it, because you know I—"

Rene sighed. "Nothing to spill."

"Oh please." Tika strode over to Rene and peered into her face. "You're exhausted, so I know your defenses are down. I know I can't torture it out of you, but..." She dangled a bag of home-cooked treats in front of Rene's face. "Holly brought this." Tika let Rene sniff the bag but yanked it back before she could take anything out of it. "*Basbousa* made fresh."

"Jack's mom's been baking for us again." Rene made a grab for the bag of treats, but Tika was ready and snatched them out of Rene's grasp.

"I don't share until you share," Tika sang.

Rene shook her head. "This is not because of the basbousa. This is because you should probably know anyway." Rene snagged the bag from Tika and opened it. She helped herself to one of the slices of syrupy-sweet cake covered in almonds. "I kissed him, okay? I kissed Quinn."

Tika clapped her hands and gave a whoop low under her voice. "Aw shit, no you did not. You? You kissed—"

"All right already. Can you let it go?" Rene flushed and waved her hand at Tika. She popped the whole bite of cake in her mouth and then tried to talk around it. "Good God, keep your voice down."

"Wait. A. Minute!" Alexa joined Tika and Rene in the kitchen. "Did I just hear what I think I just heard?"

Rene shoved her way past her teammates. "Okay, okay, enough."

Alexa clapped her hands softly. "I knew it! I knew it! Those puppy-dog eyes... I knew Rene had a gooey middle underneath that hard-ass marshal exterior! Tell us everything!"

Rene swallowed her cake and shook her head. "There is nothing to tell. I made a critical lapse in judgment."

"And Holly took her *off* on-site..." Tika narrowed her eyes at Alexa.

"Correction," Rene said. "I took myself off on-site protection. I didn't want to put Holly in the position of having to do it." She tossed her purse over her shoulder. "I'm heading out now, okay? Can we all get back to work?"

She grabbed one more piece of cake for the road and dropped the bag on the kitchen counter for her teammates. The she left the kitchen and headed toward the front door.

"Rene." Tika's voice stopped her before she could leave.

Rene turned back to face Tika. "Yeah?"

Tika smiled, a soft, caring smile. "I'm not going to let you leave that man and that boy without saying goodbye. What you do when this case is over is your business. But I'm going to tell them you'll be coming back."

Rene shrugged. "I don't know if that's—"

"Rene." Tika set her jaw and shook her head. "That little boy lost his mother. Quinn and Danny look to you, whether you like it or not, for comfort and stability right now. And I know you. If you kissed Quinn..." Tika giggled. "Well, shit, Rene. That's the first I've heard of you making any decision based on emotion." She grew serious. "Whatever happens after the case, I'll leave that to you and Quinn. But right now, they both need you. Your presence. Go home for a while, but I'm not going to be the one to tell either of them that you're gone for good."

Rene considered that. She appreciated what Tika was trying to do. But Rene knew that what she'd done was wrong. And there was only one way to set it right. "Goodbye, Tika."

Rene left the house and watched while Tika shut the door behind her. She climbed into her car and started the engine. She hated to admit how tired she really was, but as the morning sunlight warmed the car, she had to unroll her window and let the cool autumn air in. The brisk air chilled her, and her droopy eyelids perked back up. She was no longer used to the never-ending hours that she used to work when she was a federal agent. Her body was definitely protesting and was eager to get home where she could collapse onto her bed. Quinn had suggested that she use his bed when it was her turn to sleep, but she'd wanted to be close to the monitors in case he saw something, so she had stretched out on the blankets she'd set up on the floor. And to be fair, the idea of something as intimate as sleeping in Quinn's bed—beneath the sheets where he'd been sleeping... That felt like more than Rene could have handled. That felt like too much. Too close to his skin, too close to his body, even if he wasn't going to be there at the same time she was. Even if she'd been able to rest on her shift in the corner of the loft, every time she opened her eyes, she found him watching her, much like he had at the hotel.

Something about his stare was unsettling, but not in a threatening way. Quite the opposite. She found his presence soothing to her soul. She'd left New York under a cloud of regrets and guilt after her teammate had died. Shame was always lingering in the back of her mind. Even if she wasn't directly responsible for the death, she had a sense of culpability that she couldn't shake. She hadn't realized how much damage she had caused to herself over the last year. Isolation. Blame. Sadness. But for some reason, being around Quinn made her step back and take notice of her self-inflicted wounds. He also—dangerously—helped her feel something else altogether. Something not tied to loss, to regret. To the cost of making a bad choice. He made her feel something promising, hopeful. Something she hadn't felt in a long time. *Home.*

But the problem with that was the home-like feelings were based on a poor foundation. Quinn was a client, and his life could be in danger. For all she knew, his son's was as well. Rene didn't know how she'd survive if she made yet another choice that led to someone—someone she was responsible for——getting hurt. And right now, that needed to be her primary focus. Her responsibilities. Not her heart.

If she did the first well, the second might still be around long after the case was closed and Quinn and Danny were safe. And if she didn't focus first on what she was responsible for... Well, she was not about to allow that.

Her cell phone rang, disrupting her introspection. She glanced at the digital display in her car and saw that the caller ID came up as the HEARTS main line. She pressed the button on the steering wheel to connect the call hands-free. "Sam? I've got you on speaker. I'm alone, but I'm in the car if our connection isn't great. What's up?"

Sam's too-chipper voice came through the speaker. "Where are you exactly?"

"On my way home."

"Cool. I have something for you."

"Send it to my email? I'll see it when I'm home."

"I can do better than that!" Sam nearly squealed, always so happy when she discovered dirt to share with the team. She didn't actively work cases, but she could sniff out a skeleton in the darkest of closets. "Keith drove past Quinn's house this morning."

"This morning?" Rene muttered, a question in her voice. "What time? It's barely morning now."

"About three a.m."

Rene frowned. "How do you know? What did you see?"

Rene could almost hear Sam rubbing her hands together. "Well, it looks like Keith drove by the house in his squad car, parked on the street, and then got out and checked out the house."

"Okay, that was worth the melodrama. Do you have video images? Proof that Keith was there?"

"Sure do. He's clearly in uniform, his face is visible, and I captured both the squad ID and the plate."

"Shit," Rene swore. "And did he let himself into the house, Sam? Did he go inside?"

"He did not," Sam said. "That was the odd part. As far I could tell, he didn't even knock. I set the cameras to record after the initial digital image tracked movement. So I have lots of scurrying raccoon footage and a couple of stray possums and cats wandering by. But it looks like Keith walked up to the house, peered in the front window, and then walked away."

Rene tapped her steering wheel. "He suspects Quinn's not there," she mused. "Sam," she said "I need you to check and see if Keith was alone. Was his partner in the car with him?"

"Hold tight," Sam said. Rene could hear the clicking of Sam's keyboard as she waited. "So the partner is that Frank Strickland guy, right?" Sam asked. "Tall frame, dark hair?"

"That's the one," Rene said. "Is he there? In the car with Keith?"

Sam clucked her tongue. "Hold on to your hat, sister."

Rene rolled her eyes. "Sam, can we cut the theatrics and just..."

She laughed softly. "This is worth it, trust me. Cue the dramatic music."

"Are you out of your mind? Sam, just tell me whether Keith was alone!"

"Oh, he sure as shit was not alone, Rene."

Rene's pulse thudded in her neck as she waited for Sam's intel. "Sam?" she urged.

"Keith parked on the opposite side of the street," Sam explained. "So I don't have a view of the full vehicle. I can see the driver's side door, and there is definitely someone who was moving in and out of the view of the camera. Watching Keith walk up to the house."

"Is it Frank?" Rene asked.

"No," Sam confirmed. "Unless Frank wears bright red lipstick to work, the person in the squad car with Keith is a woman."

7

"Okay, Sam," Rene said, fatigue and frustration seeping into her voice. "That in and of itself isn't news." She rolled the window up to reduce the noise pollution from the growing traffic as she eased back onto the roads. She'd made it through the wooded neighborhood where the safehouse was located, but the morning rush hour was starting to fill in the roads around her, making it nearly impossible to hear the call. "Keith Stanton has a girlfriend. He's been dating Monica LeBland for two years."

Sam clucked her tongue. "Tell me it's not super weird that Keith would bring his girlfriend on a drive past his brother's house? At three in the freaking morning?"

Rene took the last long sip of the cup of coffee she'd taken from the vacation house. "No, Sam. It may not be super weird. In fact, it might be super normal." She thought for a moment about how to reach Quinn and then thought the better of it. "You know what, this is still good. Thanks for the call. I'll see you in the office in a few."

"Wait up," Sam said. "Why aren't you staying with Quinn and Danny?"

"I have other work I need to do today," she said. She knew exactly where this conversation was going. If she knew her teammates, Alexa had dialed Sam to share news about the kiss before Rene even made it to her car. "I gotta go, Sam," Rene said, trying to delay the inevitable.

"Wait, wait! Not so fast!" The laughter in Sam's voice rang out even over the speakerphone. "What's this I hear about a little, how should I say it, canoodling with—"

"Thanks, Sam," Rene huffed. "See you in the office later." She reached for the display in her dash and ended the call before Sam could start in on *the kiss*. Rene knew she'd get hell for that from Sam when she did make it into the office later, but right now, she needed peace and quiet to sort through her thoughts.

What they knew so far was Frank Strickland and Monica LeBland met at the very same hotel where Quinn was hiding out after his home was broken into. That couldn't be just a coincidence, could it? Rene thought through the relationship tree she'd shown Quinn last night. Monica was dating Keith, Frank's partner. She had to assume that Monica and Frank knew each other...but how well did they know each other? What possible reason would they have to see each other at a motel just outside of town? Rene had to consider the possibility that Monica and Frank were having an affair. It wouldn't be the first case of cheating she'd seen. In fact, that was the most logical explanation for why they were together.

But something about that didn't make sense. Why, if

they were sleeping together, would they meet in the lobby? Why risk being seen together if they were hiding some clandestine affair? Why wouldn't they just check into their room and meet there? Rene racked her brain for clues. Was there anything she'd missed that night? She'd been so certain the man in black—who she now knew was Frank Strickland—was watching her, she'd been laser focused on capturing his image while securing her safety. She'd lucked into snapping that picture with the blurry but identifiable female in it as she walked away. So she had some evidence that someone who looked an awful lot like Monica LeBland was there in the lobby meeting Frank...but why?

Rene decided there was only one way to know for sure. She was going to have to ask.

By three o'clock, lack of sleep and a maze of dead ends had Rene all but ready to throw in the towel. She was back in her office after a long nap at home, a shower, and a long-overdue workout in the gym in her garage. After punching the bag a bit, she took a long shower, fearful that if she took a bath, she'd fall asleep under the soothing lavender bubbles. As she scrubbed away the worries and the sweat, she couldn't keep Quinn's chocolate-brown eyes out of her mind. She ran her hands over her body, wondering how Quinn and Danny had been all day without her. She hadn't asked for updates from Tika and Alexa, so she assumed she wouldn't receive any. She half expected them to send her something anyway. The gossips.

They were probably conspiring right now how to set Rene and Quinn up on a fantasy date as soon as this whole case concluded. She couldn't believe they weren't lighting up her phone with updates or at least some kind of information about how their clients were doing. She was disappointed they hadn't.

She pieced together everything she knew about Quinn, and none of it made sense. Why would someone break into his house but not steal anything? If Frank had done it—and so far, he made the most sense as the intruder—what had he hoped to gain? If Frank and Monica were having some kind of affair, why would they involve Quinn? Had he discovered the affair and threatened to tell Keith? Why wouldn't Quinn mention something that important? And worst of all...what did any of it have to do with Eliza's murder? Rene's mind churned in time with her stomach. She realized the last thing she'd eaten all day was the basbousa from Jack's mom, so on the way to the office, she stopped for coffee and a sandwich.

The coffee was long cold and the sandwich wrapper sat in a crumpled heap on the corner of Rene's desk while she again reviewed the coroner's report regarding Eliza's death. She flipped through the familiar report. She'd read it before but hadn't been able to really pour over it. Just as she was tracing the marks on the sketched-out human body, trying to identify the injuries that had been noted on her body, her desk phone buzzed with an announcement from Sam.

"You have a visitor, Rene. Officer Stanton is here to see you."

Rene's head whipped up from her report. She scanned the documents and photos spread out on her desk and, in the blink of eye, opened a desk drawer and slid every last item related to the Stanton murder inside and out of view.

"Okay, Sam," she said through the intercom, calmly buzzing her back. "I'm available. You can send him back."

Rene kept her tone neutral, not wanting to give anything away by the sound of her voice. HEARTS had an office policy around uninvited guests. Prospective clients were always greeted in the lobby by at least two members of the team and escorted to the conference room. That room allowed for surveillance by Sam at her desk as well as any other team member in the office. Each office in HEARTS was equipped with video cameras. Those cameras could be controlled with the touch of a button by either Sam at the front desk or the investigator from her smartphone. Any office could log in and view the meeting taking place in any other office at any time. After a particularly terrifying case, the HEARTS had made a few internal changes to their policies around office and guest safety. By telling Sam she wanted an uninvited and unexpected guest to be sent directly back to her office, she was sending Sam a message that she wanted the room monitored for her safety and that one of the HEARTS should be armed and ready to provide backup if needed.

Rene swiped at the app on her smartphone and enabled the recording of her office. There were signs posted all over the office advising visitors that security cameras were in use, but Rene knew from experience that cameras didn't prevent crime. Especially acts of passion. But they did help later when evidence was needed.

Her office door was open, and a few seconds later a

uniformed figure appeared in the doorway. Rene came around her desk and walked up to Keith Stanton.

"Officer?" she asked, extending her hand. "I'm Rene Schwartz. How can I help you?" Rene searched the planes of Keith Stanton's face, stunned at how exact the resemblance to his twin was.

"Thanks for seeing me," Keith said, a warm smile on his face. He reached for Rene's hand and gave it a firm shake. "We're identical twins," he added.

"Excuse me?" Rene asked.

"You're the third private investigator I stopped in to visit today. Neither of the first two analyzed my face. The others were too busy studying my badge number and uniform. Making sure I was legit, trying to predict what I wanted." Keith pointed to his face. "I figured I'd find the person hiding my brother if I came looking for him myself."

Rene smiled. "I was a marshal for twelve years, Officer," she said. "We could have used eyes like yours on that team."

Keith motioned toward her chairs. "Mind if I close the door? I won't take up much of your time, but the reason for my visit is...private."

Rene nodded and resumed her place behind her desk. She cleared her throat and hoped that Sam had eyes on the office using the surveillance cameras. With the office door closed, any screams would be muted but not totally silenced.

Keith sat across from her and sighed. "How's Quinn? He and Danny all right?"

Rene smiled. "As far as I know, they are."

"When did you last hear from them?" he asked. "Recently?"

Rene leaned back in her office chair. She understood the game Office Stanton was playing. She knew the rules, and she was playing to win. "Why are you here, Officer?" she asked. "If you're concerned about your brother, maybe you should reach out to him and check in."

Keith nodded. "I can and I will." He lifted a brow. "I have, actually. But I'm pretty sure that my brother and nephew aren't staying in their home."

Rene waited. She watched Keith Stanton's face, yet she was always aware of what his hands were doing. He looked so like his brother, with those same chocolate-brown eyes. The same dark hair and angular face. But where Quinn's chin was permanently stubbled and his hair styled longer, Keith looked like a typical police officer. He had a military-style haircut, perfectly clean-shaven face, and his carriage was firm, upright. He looked hard and strong, while Quinn... well, Quinn was strong without the hard edges. Rene wondered if she were seeing the dark side of the twins, when what she'd seen so far in Quinn was most definitely the light.

"Ms. Schwartz," Keith started.

"Call me Rene," she said.

He nodded. "Rene, I came here because I'd like you to give my brother a message for me."

Rene waited, again showing no emotion, no movement.

Keith leaned forward in his chair. He rested his hands on the desk and pushed himself up to his full height. He towered over Rene in what she suspected was a move intended to intimidate her. It didn't. She looked up at him and didn't budge. She didn't blink; she didn't flinch. And she also didn't get up. She met his stare and gave him the tiniest hint of a grin. She was not afraid. She was almost begging him to try something. She'd been on the receiving end of threats by men much bigger, more vicious, and more blood-thirsty than a beat cop who'd possibly had a hand in his former sister-in-law's murder.

Keith glared at Rene then, his demeanor changing in a minute from warm and cordial to icy. "Tell Quinn to stop playing cops and robbers with you and come home. Let the investigation run its course. Everything will be over soon."

Rene sighed. "I'm not sure why you can't tell him that yourself," she said, as though she were bored with this conversation already.

Keith hovered a hand over the service revolver on his belt. "Because I know my brother," he said. He motioned toward Rene with a hand. "And the message will hit home a lot harder and faster coming from his girlfriend."

Without waiting for Rene's reaction to that, Keith turned and started walking back toward the door.

"Rene," he said, hovering his hand at the doorknob.

She didn't bother responding, just set her face in a bored expression and watched him.

"Tell my brother this will all be over soon and he should come home." He nodded to her, opened the door, and walked out.

Rene swiped the app on her phone to make sure it was still recording. She checked the view outside her office, and as soon as she saw Keith leave, she picked up the office line and dialed Holly.

"Hol," she said quickly, not waiting for a proper greeting. "Something's happened. I'm going to need to see Quinn."

QUINN'S HEART DID A STUPID LITTLE FLUTTER WHEN
Rene walked through the door just after five thirty, several
hours later than he'd expected her. His excitement at seeing
her immediately faltered, however. She didn't look like she'd
slept at all. He started to ask why, but Holly beat him to it.

"I thought I told you to get some rest," Holly stated.

Rene cast Quinn a quick glance with bloodshot eyes and
a weak smile before gesturing for Holly to follow her. He
watched them go up to the loft and debated following. If this
was about whatever was going on in his life, he had a right to
know. Clearly something had happened to prevent Rene
from doing whatever it was she'd left to do. He actually took
three long strides toward the loft before stopping. Surely
Rene would tell him whatever he needed to know.

Instead of following them, he sat back on the couch and
attempted to focus on his work. His boss was kind enough to
let him work from home as he "helped Danny cope," but that
wouldn't continue if Quinn slacked on his responsibilities.
However, he couldn't focus. He stared at his laptop, not
seeing a damn thing on the screen, until he heard footfalls on
the stairs. A quick glance in that direction confirmed it was
Holly and she was descending the stairs alone.

She wasn't nearly as open as Rene. Not that Rene was
overly chatty, but she was good company. Holly had alter-
nated between walking the property, checking the security
cameras, and calling to check in on her team all day. Tika
and Alexa had taken turns, keeping Danny busy, making
calls, generally walking through the house whispering with

Holly and acting like he wasn't even there. Quinn had spent far too much of his day hoping Rene was getting the rest she needed, wondering when she was coming back, and thinking about how soon this would all be over.

After Holly went outside without a word to Quinn, he left his laptop open and headed to the loft. He was two steps from reaching his destination when he nearly stumbled to a stop.

Rene was in the middle of changing out of her suit. She turned to face him just as she was stepping into a clean pair of jeans. Her blazer and blouse had been tossed aside, but she hadn't replaced those yet with clothes.

Quinn's stomach dropped to his feet, but he couldn't seem to stop staring at the black sports bra contrasting her pale skin. "Uh. Um."

She grinned as he continued stuttering. "I'm assuming you've seen a woman in this state before, Quinn."

He swallowed hard, trying to find his voice. "It's been a while."

She grinned as she faced him and pulled her hair into a ponytail. She wasn't naked, he reminded himself. Not even close. The black material was basically a crop top. Bikini tops covered less than the bra she was wearing. Yet... He couldn't pull his eyes away. He knew his son was occupied in a loud game downstairs with Tika, but the vision of Rene, topless, standing just feet away, was enough to blot out all rational thought.

With her hair secure, she rested her hands on her hips and cocked her head. "Let me know when you've had enough."

He finally had the sense to look down as heat flooded his cheeks. "Um. S-Sorry. Sorry."

"It's okay," she said lightly.

When he looked up, she had pulled a fitted T-shirt over her chest. He finally managed to walk the rest of the way into the loft as she secured her weapon in a lockbox.

"I wanted to check on you. You clearly didn't get any rest," he said. "And you left this morning. Without saying goodbye." He hadn't intended to say that last bit, but it slipped out. He hadn't been hurt exactly. More confused. After what they'd shared, he didn't understand why she would walk out and leave without so much as a goodbye.

"I got some rest. I'm going to try to catch a few minutes of rest while Holly, Alexa, and Tika are still here." She put the lockbox on the floor next to the pile of pillows and blankets before turning to face him. "Did you get some work done today?"

"Meh."

"A little bit distracted, huh?" she asked. Her question wasn't accusing. She sounded like she'd been distracted in possibly the same way.

"You too?" he asked, hopeful that if he'd been thinking of her all day, maybe she'd give him some clue that she'd been doing the same.

Instead Rene turned and sat in the office chair and motioned for Quinn to join her.

"Quinn," she said, "have you heard from your brother at all?"

He shook his head. "How could I? My phone's been off since we got here. Why? Do you think I should check in with him?" He wondered why she was asking the question.

She dismissed his question with a shrug, which he took to mean that she was on to something, she just hadn't figured out what yet. "Just checking. I'm going to catch a quick nap. We'll talk tonight. After dinner." She gave him a smile that tugged on the walls around his heart. She was planning on joining them for another family dinner.

That was his cue to leave. He caught it, he understood it, but he didn't turn away. He was stuck by a force he couldn't see but could definitely feel. That little inkling of a connection to her suddenly slammed into him like a wrecking ball. The urge to take her to bed—not to love her but to force her to take care of herself—was almost overwhelming.

Instead of leaving, he stepped closer to her. "I was thinking about making spaghetti for dinner. It's one of Danny's favorites, and it looks like we have everything we need. How does that sound?"

"Sounds really good, actually." Rene nuzzled down in her 'bed' on the floor. She rested her head against a pillow and didn't wait for Quinn to leave before closing her eyes.

"Rene," Quinn asked, lowering his voice. "Did you eat lunch?"

"I did," she mumbled. "A sandwich. And I only had two large coffees."

He chuckled. "Good. I was worried you might start going through withdrawal."

"No chance of that."

He didn't realize he was still closing the distance between them until he was directly in front of her.

"Why didn't you sleep?" he asked softly. He kneeled in front of her bedding.

The playful look in her eyes faded, and she immediately diverted her gaze. Uh-oh. That was *not* a good response.

"Rene?" he pressed.

Finally, she lifted her face to him again. The little hint of crow's feet around her eyes suddenly seemed to have deepened, and the crease between her brows was more pronounced. "Work," she said simply.

"What did you find out?"

She looked away as she said, "Nothing you need to worry about right now, Quinn. We're just following every lead we can." When she turned her eyes back to his, the softness had returned. "Please just trust that we're doing everything we can to find out what is going on so you and Danny can go home and feel safe there."

"I do trust you," he whispered. As soon as the words left his lips, the air shifted. That ridiculous connection felt alive and was tugging at him. He thought she must have felt it, too. Her lips parted as if she were going to say something, but the words became lost. He understood that. He couldn't seem to find the right words either.

The spell was broken by the sound of a scream outside. Quinn's heart tripped in his chest and picked up the pace double time as they both rushed toward the window. In the yard below them, Danny yelled one more time, but then he laughed when Tika wrapped him in a big bear hug and spun him around. The two of them seemed to have tapped into some kind of endless energy supply, and Quinn was thankful to Tika for that. He'd get back to being himself soon, he suspected, but right now, he still didn't have it in him to be a playmate to Danny.

"Phew," Quinn sighed. "Just fun and games."

Convinced that Danny was safe, Quinn returned his attention to Rene. Something was bothering her, and he wasn't sure that it was the subtle undercurrent of whatever had just transpired between them. She seemed to be weighed down by the so-called lead she had been following. Something seemed to have left her haunted. He wanted to push the issue, but she appeared to be about to fall asleep on her feet.

"Get some rest," he said, even though the last thing he wanted to do was leave her alone. "I'll call you for dinner."

Just over an hour later, Quinn tiptoed up to the loft. He kneeled in front of Rene and stroked her hip through the blanket. "Rene," he said, hesitant to wake her, but he knew that Holly was on her way out and she wouldn't leave until Rene was downstairs. Quinn watched the planes of Rene's face as she slowly came back to consciousness.

"Mmmm?" she murmured, turning over briefly before shooting to an upright position. "I'm awake," she said quickly. "What is it?"

"Shhh," Quinn urged. "It's all right. Just dinner. Holly is leaving, and dinner is ready. I offered to come wake you, and she said if you weren't downstairs in thirty seconds, she'd wake you herself." Quinn gave Rene a look. "I got the distinct impression that Holly doesn't entirely trust us alone." He tried to make light of it, but he wondered whether Rene had already told her teammates that something had happened between them. He almost didn't want to know.

The thought of Holly mad at him... He shivered. He did not think he wanted to be on the bad side of any of the HEARTS.

"It's okay," Rene reassured him. "I'm up." She yanked the hair tie from her ponytail and smoothed her hair into a clean, fresh bun. "Let's have that spaghetti."

Quinn led the way down the stairs, where they met Eva and Holly.

"Rene," Holly said, giving her a cryptic look. "Eva is going to stay tonight with you and Quinn. Make sure you take shifts sleeping. Got it?"

Rene nodded. "Understood."

Eva padded past Rene with an overnight bag. "I'll set up in the loft, but then I hear there's spaghetti for dinner?"

Danny followed after Eva, peppering her with questions about whether she'd play with him after dinner, if she liked dinosaurs, and what her favorite monster was.

"My favorite monster?" Eva asked, her little shadow close at her heels. "How can I pick just one? I like them all!"

Holly wished Quinn a good night and said she'd be back in the morning.

"Some dinner before you go?" Quinn offered, holding up a slotted pasta spoon.

Holly shook her head and gave Quinn a grin. "My soon-to-be mother-in-law has invited us over for a home-cooked meal."

"Lamb?" Rene asked, looking far more excited about Jack's mother's cooking than Quinn's pasta.

"If I'm lucky," Holly said, giving Rene a look. "And if you're good, maybe there will be leftovers tomorrow."

While Rene walked Holly out and locked up after her, Tika and Alexa went upstairs to say goodbye to Danny. After Eva joined them in the kitchen and Tika and Alexa left, Quinn served up plates of pasta and salad for four.

Quinn settled into his meal and let Eva and Danny chatter about which dinosaur could defeat which monster in a footrace. Eventually, Rene and Quinn joined in the conversation, Rene putting her vote on dragons every time.

"It's a footrace, Rene," Eva said, twirling a spoonful of pasta with her fork. "Dragons are notoriously heavy-footed."

For the first time in a really long time, Quinn enjoyed himself. Even if he was eating dinner in a safehouse, with two women he hardly knew, while Danny's mother was dead and they were both unable to go home, he'd finally been able to relax. He didn't have to worry about Danny. He was safe. Hell, he seemed to be having the time of his life since the HEARTS were so attentive. Even without Alexa to beat at cards or Tika to chase, Danny seemed happy and comfortable chatting up Eva. That eased any guilt Quinn might have felt about taking his son out of school, keeping him away from therapy, his friends, and even his uncle. Quinn knew at some point he'd have to call his brother. He'd have to text, check in, something. And he hoped tonight Rene would share what she'd learned today so they could come up with a plan for getting through this. Getting back to normal. Because if Quinn didn't have a thousand reasons for wanting to get back to normal, the promise of what came next with Rene was enough to make him antsy for this whole thing to be behind them. A date. A real-live date with a woman he couldn't get enough of.

With all the flirtatious glances, moments spent not-so-subtly checking each other out, Quinn could only hope that what he felt for Rene was reciprocated. It seemed she had started using every excuse possible to touch him—brush his arm as she passed him in the kitchen, trailing her fingers along his chest as she asked about how his ribs were feeling. And, though he would never admit it to her, he intentionally gave her plenty of excuses to stand close to him. He wasn't foolish enough to think she'd allow anything more to happen between them when she was working under contract for him. But God, he was getting impatient for more. More of her.

After Danny finished eating, he asked if he could be excused to play with Eva.

"That's entirely up to Eva, bud." Quinn pushed back his chair and started prepping for dish duty. "She may have work or something else she needs to do tonight."

Eva pushed her chair back and crossed her arms. "What time is bedtime around here?" she asked.

Quinn checked his watch. "You've got less than an hour till bath, a book, and then bed."

Eva motioned for Danny to follow her. "I pick playtime over dishes. Come on, Danny," she said. "We don't have much time!"

Eva and Danny ran off to the living room and hunkered down with dinosaurs and cars. Quinn ran the hot water and filled the sink with suds while listening to his son debate which dinosaur could crush a Mustang with one stomp.

Rene walked up behind Quinn and slipped her dish into the sudsy water. "Want some help?" she asked hesitantly.

He handed her a clean, dry dishtowel. "I'll wash, you dry." They worked a few moments in silence until finally Quinn asked, "What were you like as a kid?"

"Me?" Rene sounded surprised. She slowed her hand on a plate that was still dripping wet.

"No, your mother," Quinn teased.

She snorted at his response. "I grew up in New York. The streets were tough. I had to be tougher."

"So...you were a bully? Or the badass who took on the bad kids?"

"Not the bully," she confirmed. Her hand brushed his lightly as she accepted another clean plate to dry. "I was a defender of the meek even then."

He smiled and let his shoulder graze hers as he scrubbed the pasta pot clean. "I could see that."

She set the damp towel down, opened the drawer, and pulled out another dry one. "Once, this kid two grades ahead of me cornered my cousin. He started pulling at her braids and calling her bucktoothed."

"That's not nice," Quinn observed.

Rene glanced back at him as she stacked the plates in the cabinet. "That's what I told him. I told him he had better leave her alone or I was going to kick his ass."

"Did he leave her alone?" Quinn already knew the answer to that.

"Nope," she confirmed. "He looked me right in the eye," she said, leaning forward as she stared into Quinn's eyes, "and pulled her hair again."

He could almost image the child-sized version of the

woman across from him coming unglued. "Oh shit. What'd you do?"

"I kicked his ass," she said. "I went crazy like a spider monkey. I jumped on his back and punched and punched and punched until a teacher pulled me free. I was Danny's age when it happened."

"Did you get suspended?"

She nodded as she accepted the clean pot from Quinn and set to drying it. "But the story has a happy ending. My uncle—my cousin's dad—was so grateful to me for defending his daughter that he enrolled me in martial arts classes. My mother was livid. She always wanted me to be a dancer or take gymnastics. But that wasn't for me. I'm so glad my uncle did what he did. He saw something in me that my mom never understood. She still doesn't," Rene admitted. "But by taking martial arts, I learned how to control my anger instead of..."

"Going spider monkey again," Quinn quipped with a grin.

"Exactly." Rene put the pot on the stovetop, uncertain where it belonged.

Quinn came around behind her and reached for the pot. He let his arms circle her waist as he grabbed for it. She didn't move out of his hold, and he resisted the temptation to plant a kiss on the back of her neck. After he replaced the pot in the cabinet where he'd found it, Rene continued.

"What about you? What were you like?" she asked.

"I was...not the spider monkey type. Keith and I were very different. He was active, and I was more comfortable with books, you know, and numbers. You probably would have enjoyed defending me. I got my ass kicked a fair number of times for being a nerd."

"What about Keith?" she asked. There was a flash of something in her eyes when she asked the question.

"My brother..." Quinn thought back to the many times Keith had called his jock friends off just moments before they beat the tar out of Quinn. "Let's just say I gave the guy enough practice protecting me, he probably would have qualified to be a cop by the seventh grade."

She grinned. "Well, I'm here to defend you now."

Quinn laughed too. A real laugh. A much-needed, genuine laugh. "Keith will be happy he's finally getting a day off."

Rene nodded quietly.

Sensing he'd stepped onto uncomfortable terrain, Quinn dove headfirst into something guaranteed to be more awkward than talking about his elementary school beatings. "So are all of the HEARTS single?" he asked. "You know, the job seems like it would make relationships a challenge."

"No, actually," Rene said, shaking her head.

The dishes were done, and the kitchen was warm and smelled of fragrant soap. The lingering scent of tomatoes and garlic on the air made this place feel homey. Almost like home. Quinn couldn't help it if his thoughts turned to family. To the future.

"Actually, half of us are paired up at the moment." Rene ran through the women on one hand. "Holly, you know." She reminded him that Holly was engaged to Detective Tarek. "Her fiancé has the patience of a saint. And a mother whose cooking has made me wish on more than one occasion that Jack had a brother."

Quinn chuckled. "What's he like?"

"Jack's a cop through and through, but he's laid back. He's not cocky or difficult to deal with. He's really the polar opposite of Holly. He's softened her edges a little, which is nice. They're good together."

Quinn reached to turn out the light above the stove, but he kept his attention on her. The more she spoke of Jack and Holly, the more her eyes seemed haunted. Her smile softened and her voice quieted a little. "Why does that make you look depressed?"

Rene flicked her gaze to him. "Does it?"

"Yes," he said without missing a beat.

She walked over to the coffee pot and filled the carafe with water as she shrugged. "I don't think depressed is the right word."

"What is the right word?" he pressed.

She put far too much effort into setting the glass carafe back down on the machine. She was clearly analyzing the question he'd put before her. "I don't know. I'm happy for them. I'm happy for all of my teammates who've found the right person. Eva is living with her boyfriend, and Alexa is blissfully happy with Dean. So maybe...envious is a better word. No," she quickly said. "That's not right either."

"You're longing for what they have," he said.

She hesitated, but when she finally looked at him, she nodded. "I guess that's it. Which is odd because I've never wanted something like that before. Love, romance... That's not me."

"Wanting to be a part of something special isn't always about the love and romance," Quinn said. "Family is about who you care enough about to make a life with. Home...you know. It really is where the heart is. Most of the time," he added sadly.

Rene stared at him, a bit too long, before she asked, "But was being married good for you?"

Damn. She hit hard even when she wasn't trying. "It could have been. Eliza and I..." He trailed off. "Well, I wasn't what she needed."

"You're enough, Quinn. I think you deserve to know that. To feel that with someone. Even if it couldn't be Danny's mother." She avoided his eyes and focused her efforts on the coffee.

"I think you deserve that too, Rene."

She smiled slightly. "Maybe someday."

"Definitely someday," he said. To himself, he thought, *and that's a promise.*

She checked her watch. "We have about ten minutes until bathtime and about six minutes until this coffee is ready. Can we find something less intense to discuss?"

"Yeah. Sure," he said. "What's the craziest thing you ever saw growing up in a city like New York?"

She laughed loudly. "Oh, Quinn. I think you're far too innocent to hear about that."

Even so, she leaned on the counter and told him all about it anyway.

8

Movement on the monitor drew Rene's attention. Quinn had just walked into the master bedroom after getting Danny settled in for the night. He opened a dresser drawer, pulled out clean pajamas, and then carried them to the bed. The night before, he'd made it that far before remembering the camera above his door. She waited for the light bulb to go off in his head, but he lifted his shirt and tossed it aside. Guilt nipped at her gut as she watched him release his belt and unfasten the button on his jeans. Sitting back at the desk in the loft, she let out a slow breath as he continued to undress.

Look away, she told herself. But of course, she didn't. Couldn't. She watched Quinn push his pants down, tug his socks off, and then slide into a pair of sweatpants and a clean T-shirt. *This is only fair,* she decided, since he'd stared at her when she was half dressed as if he'd never seen a pair of boobs before. She smiled as she recalled the blush on his cheeks when she called him out on his behavior. Even if her little peep show had been earned, since he didn't exactly know she was watching him, she took one last look at the monitor and planned to look away and let him finish whatever it was he was going to do in relative privacy...at least without a thirsty pair of eyes drinking in his lean thighs and the tight cords of his back.

Rene was just about to spin her chair and look away when her breath caught. Quinn turned with the slightest bit of a smirk on his face as he glanced—just for a split second—right into the camera. He knew exactly what he'd done. He'd given Rene a little show. On purpose.

"Fucking men," she muttered, a grin taking over her face. As he walked past her in the loft, Rene pretended to occupy herself in some notes, but she couldn't avoid seeing the tiny bow Quinn gave her.

"Let me know if you need an encore performance sometime," Quinn said softly.

Rene raised her brow and shook her head at him and then went back to her notes. As she listened to him moving around downstairs, she forced her eyes to stay on the relationship tree.

"Give me something," she whispered, moving her sticky notes around.

"Probably not what you are asking the tablet for, but I do have chips and salsa."

Quinn stood at the entry to the loft in his bare feet holding a tray of snacks. He lifted it a bit higher as if to show her his offering. One bowl, a bag of chips, and two glasses of water.

"No coffee?" she asked with a smirk.

He grinned as he walked to the desk. "I will not contribute to the deterioration of your stomach lining. Anything you want to share?"

"Maybe." She leaned over to get a better look at the salsa. "I got mild, right?"

"I think so. I didn't check. You don't like spicy?"

"I *love* spicy," she said reaching into the bag of chips. "Spicy does not love me."

"If you hadn't ruined your digestive system with nearly constant coffee baths, you could probably tolerate seasoning more."

She laughed. "You have a real obsession with my coffee intake, Quinn."

"Well, I'm too scared to tease you about anything else," he said. "You carry a gun, and according to your bio page on the HEARTS website, you're very good at hand-to-hand combat. I'm going to play it safe." His smile spread as he sat in the straight-backed chair beside her. They shared the space without being too crowded, and yet somehow Quinn's knee found its way to lightly resting against Rene's.

"Good plan," she said, lifting a chip with a big scoop of salsa toward her mouth.

"Do you feel like you're making any headway?" Quinn asked after filling a chip with salsa.

Sitting back, Rene brushed salt from her hands and then dragged her fingers over her jeans. She didn't miss the way Quinn frowned as he watched. How many times had he chastised Danny for using his clothing as a napkin? She couldn't count. "Sorry, *Dad*," she said lightly.

He dramatically sighed and handed her a napkin. After

making a show of wiping her hands, she crumpled the napkin and tossed it at him, grinning when he caught it. "I had a visitor at the office today. Your brother." She watched as his eyes widened and his mouth fell open.

"What the hell!" he said, his demeanor changing. "Rene, how? What does he know about me? When were you going to tell me?"

Rene stiffened. Gone was the affectionate man brushing up against her knee like a middle-schooler sitting next to his crush at an assembly. "I would appreciate if you didn't question the manner in which I run my case."

"The manner in which you run your case?" he parroted, a sadness around his mouth. "Rene...why are you being like this?"

She reached for the bag of chips, but he pulled them away and lifted his brows. Though he didn't say a word, she got the meaning. He'd give her chips after she answered his question.

Rene tilted her head at his attempt to lighten the mood. "Quinn, I'm the investigator and you're the client. As much as I know you're personally impacted by every single thing that happens, I really need you to trust that I will share what I can when I can. And if I don't, then you need to trust I have a very good reason."

"You're asking me to trust you? My life and my son's life are in your hands, you withhold information from me that could be relevant to our safety, and you ask me to trust you?" He looked hurt.

"The only way any of this works is if you do." Rene met his gaze. "I couldn't very well blurt out the minute I walked in the door that Keith had come to see me. I had Sam look into a couple of things. And here we are. Discussing it now. At the appropriate time."

"The appropriate time of your choosing." He pushed the bag her way and let her dig in to grab a handful of chips. Quinn nodded toward the notes Rene had been focused on. "All this...fucking sucks."

She couldn't debate his perspective. Rene watched him —stared, really. She didn't like keeping secrets from him, but she'd asked Sam to look into a few things before she left the office, and she'd wanted time to sort through the information before sharing what she expected would be devastating news to Quinn. Shattering the illusions that he had about his ex-wife were one thing. That was going to devastate Quinn enough. But bringing painful, shattering news to him about his twin brother? There was no question that he would understand she was not trying to be cruel. Hurting him before she had information to back up her suspicions would be pointless. Only now that she had something concrete could she sit down and really work through it.

"It fucking sucks," she agreed. "Now can you look at something with me?"

Quinn nodded solemnly and moved his chair closer to Rene. But the welcome warmth of his knee was noticeably absent from hers. She couldn't quite put her finger on why, but her disappointment in that small gesture was almost overwhelming. She didn't want Quinn's anger. Or his disappointment. But she needed his trust. Not just today, to get through this. But if they were going to hope for anything after this...

"What've you got, Rene?" he asked.

"I'm sorry," she said before she could censor her words. As soon as she did, she realized they wouldn't make sense to him. She was sorry for the pain he'd gone through. Sorry for the more that was ahead. Sorry that she had to be the one to bring even more pain to this man's heart.

He creased his brow. "For?"

"For everything you and Danny are going through," she said as a way to cover for her out-of-place sympathy. "And have gone through. I want you to know I really am working hard to fix this."

"I know you are. I've been watching you. You're working *too* hard. I'm concerned you're going to make yourself sick."

"Spoken like a real dad-type," she said, smiling.

"Well, I've had a few years of practice." He sat back and wiped his fingers clean on a napkin. "Can we move on now to what you've got?"

"Sure."

He hesitated before he said, "I can handle it, Rene. Despite what you may think of me, I can handle whatever is coming."

People didn't surprise her often, but she hadn't been expecting that. "I don't doubt that," she said after a few seconds of deliberation. "I don't doubt that you can handle whatever you have to, Quinn."

Quinn was watching her steadily, as if waiting for her to look away. To flinch or reveal that she really didn't think he was strong. That he wasn't as together as she was. But instead, Rene reached for his hand. He slipped his hand in hers, and she held it as she watched their fingers lace together.

"I know you're more than the story you've been telling yourself these last few years," she said softly. "You're terrified you weren't man enough for Eliza. But it's possible that Eliza didn't deserve you, Quinn. That you were the right man with the wrong woman." She released his hand and gave him a thin smile. "Now I need you to look back at a calendar."

She shoved a paper printout toward him.

"When you first came to our office, you told me that a man answered Eliza's phone when you called her. And that a couple of times before the last time, she was late picking up Danny."

He nodded.

"I need you to go back through the calendar and as best you can, pinpoint the dates—or the approximate dates—when you think a man answered Eliza's phone. I also want to know when exactly—if you can remember—Eliza was late to pick up Danny."

"Okay." He nodded. "I need my laptop though. I used to log my visitation hours on my work calendar. I can come close to the dates, at least by month and week, if that will help."

"It will," she assured him.

"Rene," he said, standing from his chair. "What about my brother? Are you going to tell me what happened today?"

All too aware of the man sitting just a few feet away from her, Rene nodded. "Keith stopped into the office today. He apparently has been looking for you and checked the local PI agencies. He said he knew he'd found the right one when he found me."

"Why?" Quinn asked.

Rene smiled. "He suggested that I was your girlfriend, on the one hand. Which I assume was just a comment about the fact that I resemble Eliza and nothing more...informed."

Quinn's mouth dropped open. "Are you suggesting that I told my brother I kissed you?"

Rene shook her head. "No, Quinn. I don't think that. But your brother is a cop. He's been trolling local PI agencies trying to find who's helping you hide out. I know the PIs in town... It doesn't take a rocket scientist to line up me next to Chuck Allison and Falco Carson and assume which firm you'd hire."

"Are those names for real?" Quinn asked.

Rene nodded. "Chuck's a good man, actually. He's got six kids and a wonderful wife. But he's not exactly the cold case kind of investigator. He's more the 'I think my husband is banging the nanny' type."

Quinn nodded. "And Falco?"

"Well," Rene said, "let's just say if you'd met the man in his office, I'd be stunned if you'd have hired him. I hear he lives in his car and takes his work a little *too* seriously." She eyed Quinn. "Tin foil hat seriously."

"Okay." Quinn nodded. "Rene," he said seriously, "other than having dark hair, you don't resemble Eliza. Not at all. You're two totally different women."

His shoulders seemed to droop just a bit more talking about this. Every day he seemed to have a little bit less patience. Every night, he seemed to sleep even less than the night before. She needed to get to the bottom of what was happening so he could find a way to breathe again. However, she couldn't deny that part of her was dreading the end. She liked him and Danny. More than she should. She liked being with them. More than she should. She hadn't spent enough time with them to feel so connected, but she couldn't deny that she did.

She glanced over and caught him watching her again. He did that a lot, but she hadn't called him on it yet. Rene had plenty of experience with men to know there was an undeniable pull between them. But she also had enough experience working with men in high-stress environments to understand how the pressure could be getting to him. Stress hormones had a way of making the idea of sex with someone a person barely knew sound like a really good idea. It rarely was. And if there was any chance that Quinn was gravitating toward Rene simply because she was close and familiar...well, Rene was going to make sure that they were both protected from anything like that happening.

"I know, Quinn," she said, dismissing the concern altogether. There would be plenty of time to deal with the emotions, with the Eliza issues, after they'd put all this to rest. "Keith said he had a message for you. He said to come on home and let the investigation run its course. That this would all be over soon."

He heaved one of those heavy sighs of his. "Same old, same old. That's it?" he asked. "He came all the way to your office, went to the trouble of finding you, just to say what he's already told me a dozen times?" Quinn searched her face. "Is that really it?"

"That's really all he said." Rene didn't waver—her voice, her gaze. She wanted Quinn to believe that she was telling him everything he needed to know.

Finally, he sighed. "I'm going to grab my laptop."

Rene watched Quinn as he walked back to his room. He returned less than a minute later with the device.

"There's that look again," Quinn said softly. "Why do you look so pissed?"

Rene managed a slight smile for Quinn's sake. "Angry? No. I should probably get myself a pair of reading glasses."

"That's wasn't a blurred-vision glare, Rene. That was anger."

Taking a breath, she shook her head. "I should have a lead by now, Quinn. I should be wrapping this up so you and Danny can go home. I'm still driving blind. That's infuriating."

She swallowed hard, waiting to see if he'd bought into her lie. She'd just lied. To Quinn. To cover for Eliza. No. She wasn't covering *for* Eliza. She was protecting Quinn from learning the truth about something she was certain would cause him pain. That was different.

The worry on his face eased, and he gave her that warm smile she'd grown so accustomed to already. "It has only been a few days, Rene. I had no expectation that you could solve this overnight. I have complete faith in you. I know you'll find out what's going on and make sure that Danny is safe in the process. If I didn't believe that, I wouldn't be here."

"Thank you," she said. "Let me know when you have some dates."

While Quinn logged into his laptop, Rene returned to the email she had from Sam.

They worked quietly beside one another, Quinn searching his calendar going back six months, while Rene created a spreadsheet with numbers, times, and dates.

"Can you tell me at least what you're working on?" Quinn asked after a few moments of silence.

She nodded. "Sam was able to hack into Eliza's mobile phone account." She traded looks with Quinn. "We don't ask how, Quinn. We just accept that Sam works her magic, and sometimes, we strike gold."

"Plausible deniability," he sighed.

"When she was able to access the mobile account, we could download and view her cell phone bills. We have contact numbers and dates of activity."

"Rene..." Quinn sat upright in his chair and leaned closer to her. "This is good—great, isn't it? Have the police done this? Do you know if they—"

Rene silenced him with a shake of her head. "We won't have details of what the police have or hadn't done, Quinn. Unless there is a report that's available to the public—a court filing or something—we won't know. We can only look into what makes sense to us and what we can gain access to."

"Okay," he said, clearly trying to tamper down his enthusiasm.

While Rene scrolled through the phone bills, she waited for Quinn to piece together the dates when he believed Eliza was either later picking up Danny or when her phone had been answered by someone she may have been dating. It didn't take long at all for Rene to piece together a pattern.

She'd done it within minutes of Sam sending over the data. There was one number over a period of about six weeks that came up at all hours of the day and night. There were too many messages from that number for the calls and texts to be random. Rene had asked Sam to try to gain access to any cloud storage that might be attached to Eliza's telephone account, and as most people did, Eliza had used the very same password for her phone bill, her cloud storage account, and even her social media accounts. Sam had turned up little to nothing of use on Eliza's social media. She wasn't very active on social media, so other than a few pictures of Eliza and Danny when he was much, much younger, there wasn't much to see.

But the cloud account had backed up all of Eliza's text messages, emails, and other activity on her phone. It had taken some doing, but Rene had a printout of six weeks of text message communications between Eliza and at least one phone number. The majority of the communications between Eliza and the number were in emojis. Smiley faces, kiss emojis, the thumbs up to start, but after about a week, the emojis became increasingly more sexual. Until finally, one day, they just stopped. Clearly there was a secret language that Eliza and the recipient understood that either ended when the texts ended...or that continued elsewhere.

"How are you doing on those dates?" she asked Quinn.

"Here," he said. "I've got the period down to at least to a couple of months. It looks like about two months, July to maybe early September, when Eliza started showing signs of flaking out." He shrugged. "If I go back through my phone, through all the texts I shared with her, I can get the exact days and times. I can find the specifics if you need me to."

"I think what you've done can get us close enough." She pointed to a telephone number that repeated over and over on Eliza's phone bill. "Do you recognize this number?" she asked. "It's very important, Quinn."

Quinn scanned the page and squinted. "No," he said. "I don't have many numbers memorized anymore though. Have you called it?"

Rene checked her watch. The time was closing in on ten p.m. Late but not too late to make a call. Using her burner phone, Rene dialed the number. She dialed and waited for her call to be answered. On the other end, a male voice answered immediately.

"Who the fuck is this," the voice said, menacing and low. "And how did you get this number?"

Rene's stomach dropped. A fist gripped her heart. The voice on the other end of the line was one she knew. One she'd heard before. It was the one she'd expected to answer the burner phone, but hearing it... It sounded exactly like a voice she'd grown used to hearing at her ear. Similar but so very different to Quinn's.

She ended the call.

"Rene," Quinn said. "Who was that? Whose number was that?"

She wasn't ready to answer his question. The implications were too...

"Rene?" Quinn pressed. "Who the fuck was that on the phone?"

"Quinn," she said gently, looking into his eyes. "That was your brother. Keith answered my call."

THE NEXT MORNING, QUINN DIDN'T BOTHER GETTING out of bed. He wasn't surprised to hear Danny stumble out of his room, use the bathroom, and start chatting with Rene in the loft. On the one hand, he felt like an absolute shit for letting the HEARTS take care of his son, but after the night he'd had...he felt certain they would do a better job with Danny than he could. At this point, Quinn was sure a stuffed teddy bear would do a better job parenting his son than he could. He couldn't stop the images from floating through his mind. The questions, the suspicions. He blocked out the early morning sounds of Holly and Tika making coffee and checking in on Rene. He rolled over and jammed a pillow over his head, wishing he could unsee what he'd seen. Unlearn what now he could never not know.

Quinn had to face the reality that his brother had definitely been involved with Eliza in some way. But how? If he and Eliza were trading hundreds of texts over a six-week period from a burner phone—a phone that Keith still had—why? What exactly was going on between them? Quinn didn't want to give up hope that Eliza had been in some kind of trouble—maybe trouble with a case or someone she was dating. Maybe she'd gone to Keith for help and things were far more innocent than they appeared on paper. But then, just as Quinn had that thought, he remembered the text strings of sexually suggestive emojis. That made ignoring the truth nearly impossible.

He stretched out on the blankets and tried to settle the waves of grief washing over his body. Eliza was gone. His son's mother's life had been taken from her cruelly. And why? By whom? Could Keith have somehow been involved in her death? Or was he involved in something else that just coincided with her murder? He tried to tell himself it was just sex. Just a fling. Maybe Eliza and Keith had hooked up. If the time period during which they were texting was any indication, they'd started up slowly, built to a quick frenzy, and then ended all communications about six weeks later.

Regret? he wondered. Maybe they both came to their goddamned senses and realized what a mistake it was—the two of them hooking up. *Keith is my goddamn twin!* Quinn couldn't settle the sick feelings in his gut. No matter how he looked at it, he was disgusted. Disgusted with Eliza for the betrayal. Disgusted with Keith on so, so many levels.

"Jesus," Quinn spat out, figuring the only way to get past this shit feeling would be to get out of bed. He threw his blankets on the floor and headed for the shower. He turned the spray on as hot as it would go and stripped his clothes off. His brother was in a long-term relationship. If he'd cheated on Monica...with Eliza? Then what about Monica? Had she known? The more he thought about it, the more impossible it seemed. He knew his brother. *The real American hero.* Just like he'd told Rene. There had to be another explanation for all of this. There just had to be.

Quinn showered vigorously, scrubbing his skin until it was raw. He scratched his nails against his scalp to clean his hair. He felt dirty, tired. Like he'd never be rid of the feelings of frustration and revulsion. His ex-wife. His twin. He shoved open the shower door and grabbed his toothbrush. He opened his mouth and let the hot water run across his face and teeth and brushed his teeth under the spray until his gums bled. No amount of physical discomfort would ease the pain caused by imagining Eliza with Keith.

He stumbled out of the shower feeling maybe one percent better than he had when he went in. He remembered the cameras in his room but frankly didn't even care. He dropped his wet towel to the floor and shrugged into a T-shirt, fighting the fabric over his still-wet skin. He dredged a pair of boxers from a drawer and slipped on some athletic pants. He left his feet bare and didn't bother even looking at his hair. He needed coffee. He needed his son. He realized too, as he walked out of his bedroom door, he needed to see Rene.

Being near her seemed to keep him grounded as his life continued to spiral out of control. That was an unfair burden to place on her, and he understood that. But they were in this together—whether that was client-investigator or something else. He needed her this morning.

He didn't have to go far. Rene was in the loft, a steaming coffee mug on the desk next to her computer. She gave him a quick look and nodded at her desk. He realized that unless she was lining up refills, she'd brought a cup of coffee up for him. They might have only been a few days into their cohabitation, but he was already familiar with her routine. Just like she seemed to be aware of his and Danny's. That added to the level of comfort he had with her.

"Sit with me?" She posed it as a question.

Quinn crossed the loft to join Rene, listening for the sounds of his son's happy laughter or wild cheering at his game system.

"Where's Danny?" he asked.

"I sent him outside with Tika. I thought we could use a little extra quiet this morning."

"We?" he asked.

Suddenly the gravity in the room seemed to surge. He couldn't stay standing. He didn't have the strength. Dropping down into his chair, he had to remind himself to breathe. Actually, he probably wouldn't have been able to do that if Rene hadn't stroked her hand over his hair and cupped his face as she leaned over to look at him.

"I'm so sorry," she said lightly. "Quinn, I..."

"You did your job," he said. "You're checking into every angle. They were having an affair?"

Rene nodded. "They ended it. Months before she died."

He pulled her hand from his cheek but didn't let go of her. He held tight to her hand. "And you knew? Why didn't you tell me?"

"I only figured it out when Keith came to see me." Rene blinked and pressed her lips together. "I wasn't sure what he was hiding or what he knew, and until I pieced it together with some hard evidence, I didn't want to hurt you."

A bitter laugh left his lips. "That's why you've been acting so strangely, isn't it?"

She tilted her head, and her eyes filled with sympathy again. He pushed her back just enough that he could stand.

His sense of shock wore off, and anger gripped him so tight he thought he might explode.

"You should have told me," he said. "I had a right to know that my brother...and my..."

"They are human beings, Quinn. Just regular people. It looks to me like they figured out pretty quick whatever was going on was a very, very big mistake." She kept her voice even and calm.

He scoffed and glared at her. How dare she stand there and defend Eliza's betrayal? Keith's unbelievably shitty disloyalty. How dare she act like he didn't have the right to be pissed off?

"It's okay to be angry," Rene said, keeping her voice soft. "It's okay to think less of them both right now, in this moment. It's okay to blame me for wanting to spare you from this. Be angry. Be hurt. Be resentful. But when you process all of that, Eliza will still be dead. She will still be the mother of your child. And Keith will still be your blood—your twin."

"Keith is in a relationship," Quinn said. "She had an affair with a man who was committed—practically married."

"But Keith wasn't married, Quinn—"

He laughed bitterly. "We were all family. Even if it wasn't official. She knew I wanted a life with her. She knew how close I was to my brother. And she still..." He raked his hand over his hair and blew out a long breath. "She should have told me. While she was alive and could."

"Yes," Rene agreed, "she should have."

He eyed her. "I need to eat something. As much as I really don't want to, I'm feeling light-headed."

"Quinn," Rene whispered.

"Let's finish this later," he said, standing to head downstairs.

"Quinn, wait." Rene swiveled in her chair to face him. "Your brother and Eliza may have betrayed you, Monica, and God only knows who else. But that doesn't mean that Eliza deserved to have her life taken away. And that doesn't mean that Keith was the one who killed her. Our work isn't done here."

"I think I'm done," Quinn said and quietly padded down the stairs.

9

Instead of heading home when Holly and Alexa showed up to relieve her, Rene headed toward the HEARTS office. She wanted to see what, if anything, Sam had found on Frank Strickland. She didn't know if he was connected to any of this, but her gut told her that if he'd ended up at a hotel with Keith's girlfriend, he was worth looking into. Her gut told her that *any* straw she could grasp at this point was worth looking into.

"Morning, Sam," she said the moment she walked into the HEARTS lobby. She balanced a travel mug of coffee, her laptop bag, and a reusable lunch bag with her breakfast inside. She couldn't believe she had anything edible left at her house, but she'd found an apple and some almond butter that she needed to finish off. "Sam, there are another couple of numbers I want you to try to track down from Eliza's phone records. Do you think you can..." Rene's words faded in her mouth.

"Rene, there is...someone here to see you." Sam lowered

her head, as if she was sorry but she had no choice. She motioned toward the conference room.

Frank Strickland stood in the doorway of the conference room and leveled his gaze at Rene. "Ms. Schwartz? I'm sorry I'm here without an appointment. It's urgent."

She quickly regained her composure. "Of course." She turned her attention to Sam. "I'll see Mr. Strickland in my office." A prickly sensation Rene knew was her intuition sparked the hairs on the back of her neck to stand on end.

"I was hoping I wouldn't have to come and see you this way." Frank stepped aside and waited to follow Rene to wherever she led. This was the second time she was up close to Frank Strickland, and this time he seemed even bigger. Not that his size intimidated her, but she was absolutely not going to let this conversation move forward without her office security in place. She walked into her office and motioned for Frank to sit. She turned on her computer and asked if she could offer him coffee or a drink.

"No, but thanks." He seemed cordial but distracted. He was dressed in his uniform and kept looking at his watch.

"If you can give me a minute..." Rene was trying to open her phone app to start the recording device, but Frank wasn't going to wait for her to settle in before he started talking. She stared him down as she trusted that Sam would be watching the entire encounter and would record the meeting from her end. Frank Strickland looked like every other ambitious man in law enforcement that Rene had ever met. Too clean, too confident. Too...everything. She was put off by him not because of any *one* thing. Everything about him set off warning bells in her mind.

"I'm here because of Keith Stanton," Frank said.

"Okay," Rene said, sipping her coffee and acting casually. She didn't reveal whether she knew him or not, and she sure as hell wasn't going to ask any questions. In this situation, she knew to stand back and let the man in the hot seat reveal what he would.

"What do you know about what's happening to Keith?" Frank asked. "What's been...going on?"

Rene figured there wasn't anything that could have been going on in Keith's life that somehow didn't get back to his partner. She had to wonder exactly how much Frank knew that *she* knew.

"I can't say I know anything about what's happening to Keith."

Frank squinted at her and then let his face morph into a glare. "Can we cut the bullshit, Rene? And is it okay if I call you, Rene? Because we're almost out of time."

"Out of time for what, Frank?" Rene asked, emphasizing the fact that they were on a first-name basis now.

Frank leaned forward in his seat. "In about three hours, it's going to hit the news that Keith has been brought in for questioning in connection with the murder of Eliza Stanton, his former sister-in-law. Quinn's ex-wife."

Rene nodded calmly, refusing to show even the slightest hint of a surprise. "And you're telling me this before it happens because...?"

Frank lifted his hands as if the answer was obvious. "I'll be making a statement to the arresting officer that will provide critical evidence against my own partner. Evidence that will link him to the murder."

"Isn't that your job, Frank?" Rene studied the man's face. She wondered if the conflict she saw in his eyes was stress or grief...or guilt.

"Today it is, yes."

She considered his comment for a few seconds. "So how can I help you?"

"Rene, you and I both know Keith Stanton didn't kill Eliza." Frank let his words linger for dramatic effect. Rene didn't take the bait. She stared, stone-faced, waiting for him to continue. When she didn't respond, he continued in a quiet voice. "I really did come here for your help," he said.

"So tell me how I can help you." Rene crossed her arms over her chest, giving the Glock in her waistband the slightest touch with her fingers as she did so.

"I need you to protect Quinn," he said. "And Danny."

Rene relaxed enough to lean closer to him. "Why exactly do you think Quinn and Danny need protection?"

"Because Keith didn't kill Eliza," Frank said. "And whoever did may want to make sure there is no one left to champion his innocence. We don't know anything for sure, but until the suspect responsible for this is in custody... we can't take chances that more lives will be lost."

"Frank," Rene said, "I'm no police officer, but it seems to me that you can't arrest someone for a crime you know they didn't commit."

"Well," he said, "I'm not going to arrest Keith. I've got an appointment to make a formal sworn statement that will lead to the arrest of Keith Stanton for the murder of Eliza Stanton. Let's just say the evidence I will be providing won't be sufficient to lead to a conviction. But it will get Keith behind bars for a few days, where we can keep him safe until we sort this out."

"This seems like a terrible idea," she said, studying his face.

He nodded. "It wasn't my idea. I'll tell you that much." He rubbed a hand across his scalp, the military-style short haircut making a scraping sound against his skin. "Internal Affairs came to me with some questions. I answered honestly. And now..."

Rene ground her teeth together. "They know Eliza and Keith were having an affair."

Frank released a deep sigh. "Yeah. To be honest, I was shocked. I didn't believe it."

"What kind of proof do you have?" Rene asked.

"He admitted it," Frank said. He cleared his throat and shrugged. "I straight up asked him, Rene."

Rene sat back, not willing to share what little information she had gained, but mindful that if Frank knew about the affair, others did too. And that wouldn't look good for Keith. Or Quinn.

"I know you're protecting Quinn Stanton and Danny," Frank said. "I assume you're also trying to find out why someone broke into their house and why someone would kill Eliza." He frowned when Rene simply stared at him. "I can't tell you much more right now," he said. "But I need you to give me your word that you'll keep Quinn and Danny safe. Things are going to get worse before they get better."

Rene sat taller. "Why?"

"Whoever killed Eliza is going to see Keith taking the fall

for it as either an opportunity to escape." He bit his lip. "Or—"

"An opportunity to finish what he started." Rene nodded. "How did you find me? Did Keith talk to you?"

"Yeah, he did. After IA cornered me, I confronted Keith about his affair with Eliza. He admitted everything. Admitted he'd also broken into his brother's house. He was worried that whoever took out Eliza wanted the whole family gone." He pulled a thumb drive from his pocket and held it up to show her but didn't hand it over. "The night of the break-in at Quinn's, Keith called me. Asked me to drive by and check the place out. He knew he was the one who'd broken in, but he hadn't confided in me yet. He told me he'd been doing periodic drives past the house since Eliza died and asked if I could do the same. He knew Quinn would be spooked after he caught him in his house, but I think Keith expected Quinn to call 9-1-1 first."

Frank looked at Rene with an expression of frustration.

"You know Quinn called Keith the night he found Eliza. Before he called 9-1-1. Keith didn't think Quinn would make that mistake twice. But when Quinn didn't call it a home invasion to dispatch, Keith called me. Told me he'd spoken to his brother and something weird went down at the house and Quinn and Danny were spooked, but they didn't want to make a big deal about it in case it was nothing. We were off duty that night, so I jumped in my car and took a drive. I saw you and your friends swoop into Quinn's house. I ran your license plates."

She frowned. "So you *were* following me. The night I saw you at the hotel."

"Not exactly. But I was there that night and saw you, so I knew you must have had Quinn and Danny secured. I've researched your history, Rene. I felt confident you wouldn't let anything happen to them."

"Why didn't you contact me sooner?"

"No point. I had nothing to share, nothing you could do but what you were already doing," he said simply.

"So it *was* Keith who broke into Quinn's house? Disabled the alarm?" Rene didn't expect him to answer, but the question made sense. She couldn't understand why Keith didn't just tell Quinn that he was in his house. Why break in? Why all the secrecy? But instead of asking Frank questions she suspected he wouldn't answer even if he did know, she redirected him to the risk to Quinn and Danny. "So you're concerned the suspect will take out the whole family?" Rene asked. "Why?"

Frank shrugged. "Keith was afraid of that but never said why. Until I know, I need your help. We won't have much time. I expect Keith to be brought in for questioning and held, but we won't have much time before they have to release him."

"Okay," she suggested.

Rage started to boil in Rene's gut. Quinn and Danny had gone through hell. Because Keith hadn't come clean with his brother. Not about the affair. Not about the break-in. What else was Keith Stanton hiding?

"I think Eliza had proof of something," Frank continued. "I think that's why she's dead. I need to know what she had and who would want her dead because of it."

"And you believe in your gut it wasn't Keith," Rene said.

"Enough to risk his life to try to save it," Frank said softly. "We don't bring in one of our own lightly." He tilted his head and gave her a pointed look. "You know that."

Rene sighed and watched as Frank Strickland stood up in his chair. He looked her over and seemed to stare at the team photo on the shelf behind her desk.

"You remind me of her a little," Frank mused.

"Eliza?" Rene asked, a nagging, sinking feeling twisting in her gut.

"Yeah," Frank said. And with that, he turned and walked out.

Quinn stepped onto the porch as Rene climbed from her car. He hadn't had a chance to see her before she'd left. Actually, he'd avoided seeing her. He had barely slept. Even more than processing Eliza's affair with Keith, he had been kicking himself for lashing out at Rene. He had told Rene everything about their marriage—how losing Eliza made him feel like less of a man, how close to his brother he felt. Rene was right; it would have been heartless of her to blurt accusations and innuendos, to intentionally tarnish his memories until she had evidence to support her suspicions.

He met her at the front of her car. "Hi," he said. "Holly is in the house with Tika and Alexa. Can we take a few minutes alone? Maybe take a walk?"

Rene popped open the truck and left her bags inside. After locking the car, she turned to him. "Let's walk the yard."

With her at his side, Quinn headed down the driveway, past the side of the house, and into the backyard. A light breeze carried a slight chill in the air, but not so much that either of them had worn a coat. Autumn had finally really taken its hold and ushered out the last of the summer warmth but hadn't given into winter yet. The weather was at that perfect in-between—not hot, not cold. Even so, he glanced at her, worried she wasn't dressed for the temperature.

"Are you warm enough?" he asked.

"I am. Are you?"

"Yeah."

She was quiet, clearly waiting for him to start the conversation he had silently indicated they needed to have. Suddenly, though, Quinn was unsure of what to say. He was embarrassed about how he had lashed out and worried that she was going to hand his case over to one of the other investigators on her team. He didn't want that. He wanted Rene there. He *needed* her there.

"I'm sorry about last night," he finally managed to blurt out. "I was taken by surprise. By everything."

"I know," Rene said. "You don't have anything to apologize for, Quinn. I can't imagine how much that hurt you. I'm sorry. I'm sorry it happened and sorry you had to learn about it this way."

Quinn shook his head, his blazing eyes meeting Rene's. "I do need to apologize. I snapped at you like it was somehow your fault that Eliza..." His words trailed off and left a heavy cloud of silence hanging over them. He swallowed as he shoved his hands in his pockets. "Eliza didn't want me the way I wanted her." He had to smile. As stupid as it was, saying the words somehow eased the heaviness in his chest. "Maybe on some level I have been holding on to something that was never going to happen. And honestly, I don't even know why I wanted it to happen. We weren't in love or anything like that. It was easy, I guess. Safe. We had Danny together..."

Rene nodded slowly. "That all makes sense, Quinn. I'm very sorry things didn't work out how you wanted."

"You don't have to apologize for that."

"And you don't have to apologize for getting upset when you found out she messed around with your twin," she said. "You didn't have anyone else to snap at. It's okay. I can take it." She gave him one of her sweet smiles. "I'm very sturdy."

"Yeah," he said, admiration obvious in his tone. "You are."

He appreciated her trying to make him feel better, but anxiety was still a knot in the pit of his stomach. "I know, but you shouldn't have had to take the brunt of my anger, Rene. Will you please accept my apology so I can rid myself of this unbearable guilt?"

Her sweet smile widened into a brilliant one. "Unbearable guilt?"

"It's dragging me into the depths of despair," he said with all the dramatics he'd learned from Danny.

"Well, we can't have that. Of course I accept your apology. And you're not as rough and tumble as you think. I've seen men more pissed off at losing a hand of poker. You were very restrained."

"Thank you. I guess." He started walking again, head

down as he debated if he really wanted to hear any details. However, knowing himself as he did, he had to ask, because if he didn't, he'd just pick every memory of Eliza apart until there was nothing left of her but doubt and anger. That wouldn't be fair to him, to her, or to their son. "How long were they sleeping together?"

"Not long. A few weeks. I'm sure of that."

"Do you think... Do you think they would have stayed together if she hadn't died?"

"No," Rene said quickly. "They made a mistake. I believe she *knew* she made a mistake and was doing what she could to make up for it."

"Is that what got her killed? Her attempt to make up for what she'd done?"

"That we don't know, Quinn. We just don't know whether Eliza's affair with Keith is linked to her death."

Quinn stepped in front of Rene to stop their forward progression. "What do you believe, Rene? You've been doing this your entire career. What do you think happened?"

She lowered her eyes, diverting her gaze as if trying to find the words to say what was on her mind. Finally, she looked up at him. "I have my theories, Quinn. But like with the affair... There's no point in speculating right now. But I did have an interesting conversation with Frank Strickland today."

"My brother's partner."

"Yeah," Rene said. "Turns out Internal Affairs asked Frank about the affair with Eliza after she was killed."

"No wonder the case has gone cold," he said. "They are looking at one of their own. They think Keith did it."

"It looks that way."

"Oh my God," Quinn said as his stomach rolled. "That fucking bastard. You don't think... Rene..."

Rene put her hand on his arm. "Frank seemed pretty adamant that Keith had nothing whatsoever to do with Eliza's death, Quinn."

He closed his eyes and shook his head. "I'll kill my brother myself if he did this. Taking Danny's mother away from him." When he could, he lifted his lids and looked into her eyes. "Over what?" Quinn demanded. "A couple weeks of fucking and a few texts?"

"Maybe there's more to it than that," Rene said.

"What?" Quinn demanded. "What could have happened?" Quinn's throat tightened and his eyes started to burn as tears forced their way to the surface. "Oh my God," he said again.

Rene cupped her hands on the sides of his face and made him look at her. "We don't know what happened. Everything you're thinking is speculation right now."

"But it fits. Doesn't it? One of them wanted to end it; the other didn't. They got into a fight and..."

She nodded. "It fits. But we don't know anything for sure, Quinn."

Without thinking, he pulled her to him and held her tight. An unexpected sob left his chest, and Rene hugged him closer.

"I'm so sorry," she whispered.

Somehow this just kept getting worse. So much worse. Losing Eliza to murder was horrific enough. Losing his ex-wife at the hand of his brother? He didn't know how to process that.

"Hey," Rene said, pulling from his embrace. She put her hands to his face again and used her thumbs to wipe his cheeks as she looked into his eyes. "This is *speculation*. Until we get confirmation, don't let this eat at you."

Like there was any chance of that. But he faked a smile. For Rene's sake. He didn't want guilt sitting in her stomach like it had in his all day. "Okay."

A smile tugged at her lips. "I don't believe for a moment you aren't going overanalyze this."

"I'll do my best not to. That's all I can offer."

"I suppose that's all I can ask," she said. She lowered her hands, but he caught them. She looked at where he was holding on to her.

"Maybe if I had a distraction…" he said.

She lifted her eyes to his, clearly surprised.

"I'm glad you are figuring this out," he said. "As much as I like having you around, I'd really like to get my life back on track."

"I know you would," she said.

A sense of bashfulness tugged at him as he tackled the other insecurity that had been bothering him all day. "I don't mean that just because I want to go home or I want to get Danny back into school. But because I'm ready to have a life again. I really am. So you have to tell me, did I overstep by kissing you the other day?"

"No."

He wished he could believe that, but years of insecurity and being the odd man out made him question her sincerity.

"I don't want things to be awkward between us for however long we're here, but, um...I like you."

A smile spread across her face. "I like you, too."

The setting sun poked through the few remaining leaves on the trees and glistened off her dark hair. If he were a romantic, he'd think that was a sign of things to come.

"Good," he said. Before he could talk himself out of it, he put his hand to the back of her neck and pulled her to him. His pressed his mouth to hers. He wasn't the least bit surprised that her kiss tasted of the coffee she incessantly drank. But the taste fit her. Strong. Bold. Though he wanted to delve in and taste every part of her, he fought the urge and managed to keep the kiss tender.

When he leaned back, resting his forehead to hers, he sighed. "I probably should have waited until after all this to do that."

"Probably," she whispered. But then she leaned up and kissed him.

Heat shot through his entire body, and he wrapped his arms around her, holding her closer. Their bodies felt like two puzzle pieces, snugly fitting together. Quinn threaded his fingers in her hair and deepened the kiss as he'd wanted to do before. Rene clung to him as he discovered her mouth. He would have kissed her forever if she hadn't leaned her head back, breaking the contact. Her cheeks had a tempting blush. He couldn't resist running his thumb across her face.

"You are so beautiful," he whispered.

A little laugh left her. "Thank you." Her smile softened as she sighed. "But I do have to finish your case before we can do this, Quinn. We can't get distracted."

"Too late," he muttered. "I'm having a very hard time not being distracted."

"Yeah, me too," she said. She stepped out of his embrace. "But we have to try."

He grabbed her hand before she could completely move away. There were a hundred things they could have talked about—he wanted to know her favorite food, her favorite movie, what her ideal date would be—but he enjoyed the silence that surrounded them as they strolled along the rest of the yard. When they came around the front of the house, Rene pulled her hand from his and he let her. They walked back in together, the glow of their kiss fading with the setting sun.

10

A SHIVER RAN down Rene's spine. Holly didn't have to voice her displeasure when Rene and Quinn walked into the house. Rene freaking *felt* it. Holly jerked her head toward the loft, and Rene followed without so much as a glance at Quinn. If he hadn't caught on to Holly's irritation, she'd rather he didn't know.

Rene barely reached the landing to the loft before Holly gestured to the monitors. Damn it. She'd set up trail cams to monitor the area around the house. She'd seen Rene and Quinn kissing.

Shit.

"Alexa," Holly said. "Leave us."

Alexa walked by Rene with wide eyes.

"Are you sleeping with Quinn?" Holly asked with a harsh whisper the moment they were alone. Her question was not the girly gossip tone that Sam would have used. Or the suggestive, husky tone that she would have gotten from

Alexa or Eva. Holly's question was stern and unamused. Demanding, if not outright accusatory.

"No," Rene stated firmly.

Holly simply lifted her brow and pressed her lips together.

Rene glanced at the monitors to break the intense stare from her boss and friend. "He told me how he felt. I told him it had to wait until the case was done." Rene was not used to being the center of Holly's scrutiny, and she didn't like it. She and Holly were close. Holly's lectures were usually saved for Sam and her misdeeds.

"Is this going to be a distraction?" Holly asked.

"No."

"Rene, if—"

The slight sense of offense Rene felt surged. "Did I question your competency when you started screwing Jack on a case?"

Holly snapped her lips shut and stared for a few intense heartbeats. "Our lives weren't in immediate danger. Yours could be. That boy's mother was murdered. We can only assume whoever did that is after some kind of evidence that got her killed. I doubt they'll nicely ask you to hand it over if they find you."

Rene scoffed. "I seem to recall there being plenty of immediate danger for you, Hol. You ended up in the hospital, remember? I'm not going to put myself, Quinn, or Danny at risk to get laid."

Holly backed down, but her frown didn't ease. "That's not what I meant."

Narrowing her eyes, Rene asked between gritted teeth, "Then what did you mean?"

Holly looked at the monitors for a few long seconds. When she focused on Rene again, her eyes were softer. "If you need one of us to stay here while you focus on the evidence—"

"I don't."

"What happened today with Frank Strickland?" Holly pressed.

"He gave me a heads-up that Keith is going to be brought in for questioning in connection with Eliza's murder."

"Yeah, well, while you were outside stealing kisses with our client, Keith Stanton was brought in," Holly said with raised brows. "Are you going to be able to handle this?"

"What do you mean...handle this?" Rene glared at Holly.

"It's only going to get worse for Quinn, Rene. I don't want to find you waking up in his bed after you spent the night comforting him. I need to know if you need me to take you off on-site protection. There's plenty you can do from back at the office."

"I'm staying right here," Rene said, leaving no room for argument.

Holly clearly didn't agree with her decision. "Do *not* bring troubles on that man he doesn't need, Rene. This isn't just about us—but if something were to happen..."

Rene opened her mouth to argue, but Holly moved around her and walked down the stairs. Rene shook her head in an attempt to free herself of the disagreement before she followed Holly. By the time she reached the open living area, Holly was going out the front door.

"What was that?" Quinn asked the second the door closed.

Rene drew a deep breath. "She was watching us on the trail cams."

A few seconds passed before Quinn's eyes widened. "Oh, shit. Rene, I'm sorry."

She shook her head. "Don't worry about it. It's fine."

"No, it's not."

"She's worried I'm getting emotionally attached to a client." She smiled a little. "She's not completely wrong, but my attachment to you is *not* clouding my judgment. That's really what she's worried about."

He opened his mouth, likely to apologize once again, but she put her hand to his chest as she stepped around him. Once outside, she took long strides until she stopped at Holly's car. "I like him. And he likes me. But we aren't sleeping together. I only allowed it to happen because this case is all but solved, Holly."

"How so?"

"Frank Strickland warned me that Keith was going to be brought in for his own protection. I think Frank knows who killed Eliza and he was warning me that they're going to nail the killer while Keith is in custody. They know who did it, Hol. They're *this close* to proving it."

"And I gather you think you know who did it, Rene," Holly pointed out.

"I have a theory. But I have no proof, and I need to let the police make their move and play this out until they either screw it up or catch the killer. Whatever is going on between Quinn and me is not going to interfere with keeping him and Danny safe or with finding the proof to nail whoever murdered Eliza to the wall."

Rene watched Danny scream and dramatically throw himself to the ground as Alexa roared like a monster closing in on him. Alexa must have brought him outside to play just in case the confrontation between Rene and Holly got ugly.

"The strangulation, Hol," Rene said. "I've read and re-read the coroner's report. A cop killed Eliza, I'm sure of it. There were no defensive wounds on Eliza's body, which makes me think she knew her attacker. And the small marks on her neck... I suspect someone put her in a police choke-hold. Someone who knew what they were doing could have disabled Eliza in ten seconds, maybe twenty tops."

Holly blew out her breath before facing Rene. "That's a long time for there to be no defensive wounds... Maybe they were getting intimate and it got rough? She didn't expect it to move so fast?"

Rene leaned back slightly. "Could have been... Hard to say. If someone was talking to her, standing behind her trying to talk sense into her, she may have been listening and trying to cooperate. By the time she realized she should be scared and fight back..."

"Frank or Keith?" Holly asked. "You think it was the partner or the ex-brother-in-law lover?"

"I have my suspicions," Rene admitted. "But it's all just theory at this point."

Holly sighed. "You need to be careful, Rene."

"You know I am."

Holly reached for the silver heart at her neck. "I'm not just talking about this case and the cops. I mean with Quinn. With yourself. He's hurting. He's lonely and tired and worried for Danny. And he's probably grasping on to all the comfort he can find...wherever he can find it."

Rene hadn't considered that. She hadn't considered that Quinn might be unintentionally using her, clinging to her, because she was strong when he felt weak. Because she was there when he felt alone. That made sense, and she could see how Holly would be worried that she was setting herself up for a fall.

"I know you can protect them," Holly said. "I'm worried about whether or not you can protect yourself. Don't get attached to him, Rene. You don't know what he's going to feel when this is over and he can finally sit back and think things through. I'm worried about *you*, okay? I don't want to see you hurt."

A lump rose to Rene's throat, and she had to swallow hard to dislodge it. Holly was right. Quinn was in a terrible place right now. And he was probably feeling connected to Rene because she was a beacon in his storm. Disappointment settled over her heart, but she managed to smile at her boss. "Holly Austin, you're such a mama bear under that tough façade."

Holly chuckled and shook her head. "Tell anyone else and I'll fire you for insubordination."

Rene looked to the window where Quinn was watching over the backyard. "I hear what you're saying," she confessed. "You have a valid point. I'll be careful."

"Thank you." Holly took a deep breath and let it out

with a loud sigh. "All right. This is getting way too touchy-feely for me. I'm going to go check the perimeter again. You talk to Quinn. This shit with his twin is going to be all over the evening news. By the way," she said, climbing into her car, "Sam has convinced me to have a so-called *real* wedding. You get to be the maid of honor, which means *you* have to rein her in with all her planning. She's already going over the top, and I just gave in a few hours ago."

Rene opened her mouth, intent on sarcastically countering, but the idea actually appealed to her in a way that she wasn't expecting. She'd spent so much of her life shut down, keeping everyone as far away as she could because of the risks of getting too invested. Suddenly she didn't want that any longer. She wanted to feel the connection she had with her team. She wanted the attraction she felt for Quinn, even if it might just be a phase on his part. He made her feel a kind of belonging that she hadn't felt in a long time. She wanted that. If he changed his mind about them when this was over, then she'd deal with that then.

"Yeah," she said as her smile spread. "Keep pissing me off and see how that goes."

Holly had barely driven away before Alexa stopped chasing Danny and joined Rene at the edge of the yard.

"Everything okay?" Alexa asked.

"Yeah."

A slow smile spread across her face. "Quinn put his tongue in your mouth."

Rene laughed. "Shut. Up. Are you twelve?"

"Thirteen," she countered. "He's super cute. And sweet."

"Yes, he is." Rene's smile faltered. "But Holly is right. He's still processing his loss, and it is very possible I'm just a step on his path to recovery."

"So what if you are?" Alexa asked. "We saw how much you were smiling when you were with him. That's what has Holly so worried. She's afraid you're going to get hurt, and she cares about you. She doesn't want to see that happen. But I think you're a big girl and you can handle a broken heart if it comes to that. I've never seen you look as happy as you did when you were walking with him. You deserve that happiness, even if doesn't last forever."

"Thanks," Rene whispered.

"But you might want to warn him that we will make his life hell until you get over any heartbreak he brings your way."

"I will pass along that warning. Thanks, Alexa."

Danny was halfway up a tree when Quinn walked outside and stopped by Rene's side. He held out a steaming cup of coffee.

"Are you contributing to my addiction?" she teased.

"I thought I probably owed you for the trouble I've caused."

Accepting the cup, she said, "You haven't caused me any trouble."

He scoffed. "Um, your boss just ripped your ass."

"Naw. Not so much. Don't apologize," she warned when he opened his mouth. "She's just concerned."

"About you not thinking clearly," he said.

"That..." Rene met his eyes over the mug of coffee. "And...uh... She's worried you're in a bad place right now with your grief process and that once this is over, you might not be as interested in me."

"She thinks I'm using you as a bandage?"

"Pretty much." Rene smirked at him.

He shook his head. "I'm not."

"The thing is," she said, "she's right to have that concern. You're under a lot of stress."

"Rene."

She continued, despite his attempt to interrupt her. "You have a million things going on."

"Yes, but that doesn't mean I'm not attracted to you." He smiled. "Trust me. I am very attracted to you."

She lowered her face but couldn't stop her own smile from forming. "I don't doubt that." Her lips fell as she looked up at him, though. "I just want you to know that if we come out on the other side of this and you realize you need time to deal with whatever you need to deal with, I won't be upset. I won't be angry. I know you're going through a lot of crazy things, and I know that can mess with your mind and your feelings. I only ask that you are honest with me. If you change your mind, just tell me. Don't feel like you have to keep up some act to make me feel better."

She could see that he wanted to argue, to challenge her assessment of things, but instead he just nodded.

"I'd like you to be honest with me, too. Don't lie to me about how you're feeling."

"I never would," she promised.

"Good. I'm glad we've established our expectations. The other thing you should know is that I fully intend to introduce you to the joys of drinking more water."

"Are you kidding me?" she asked and rolled her eyes, causing him to laugh.

♥

QUINN LOOKED UP FROM HIS LAPTOP AND SIGHED. Again. Rene looked like she was about to lose her mind with anticipation. She had told him as they cleaned up dinner that she wouldn't allow him to turn on the news until Danny went to bed. She knew exactly what he'd see and had made him promise—swear—that he would steer clear of the news until they had Danny down and could process the development together.

Leaning on the desk in the loft, he watched her frown deepen. "Is it time? Danny's been in bed for twenty minutes. If I was going to get the 'Dad, I need a sip of water' call, I would have heard it by now. I think he's out."

"If you're sure..." She sounded disgruntled as she looked at her watch. "I just... I want you to know that what happened today doesn't mean necessarily what it looks like it means."

"Well, I have to face it sometime, Rene." He met her eyes. "Better with you by my side than...well..."

Rene's slow smile caused his heart to do a funny little flutter in his chest. "You got this," she said. "Just promise me you're not going to panic or freak out."

"Promise you?" He gave her as much of a flirty smile as he could muster under the circumstances. "I thought you didn't make promises."

"I don't... I'm asking you to." She smirked at him.

He shrugged. "Ever hear the phrase turnabout's fair play? If I have to make promises..."

"What do you want me to promise you, Quinn?" Rene lowered her eyes.

"All I want is this," he said, taking her hand in his. "That when this is all over, you and me. We'll try. A date, living together... I don't care what together looks like for you, but I don't want to lose this." He motioned between them. "Dinners with Danny, you working an arm's reach away while I put him to bed. Can you promise me we'll try?"

Rene was silent for a moment, staring down at their laced fingers.

"That's a good start, don't you think?" He squeezed her fingers.

"I think it could be," she whispered. "You're a badass dad. Your son adores you."

Quinn grinned. "Well, the feeling is mutual."

"You could be a badass boyfriend."

Quinn chuckled. "Thanks for the vote of confidence. Is that a yes...a *yes, Quinn, I promise*? Because you know I would so love to hear those words come out of your sexy mouth."

He put his hand on her face. His touch was hardly sexual, but he felt the shock roll straight to his groin. He froze, unable to think of anything but the heat of her skin on his. He swallowed, desperate to get his bearings. Being so easily knocked off balance unsettled him. The biggest problem was, he didn't mind feeling unsettled by her. He brushed his thumb over her lips.

"Having you so close is making me crazy," he whispered.

"Shall I leave?" she asked.

"I would just follow you." Quinn's breath came in ragged gasps as he trailed his fingertip along the ridge of Rene's lower lip. "What do you say?"

Rene flicked her tongue against Quinn's fingertip and grabbed his hand with hers. She kissed his fingers and whispered against them, "I promise, Quinn. I promise."

THE NEWS REPORT WAS BRIEF, BUT QUINN HAD watched the two-minute segment at least five times before he had to turn it off.

"He didn't do it, Rene." He scratched a hand against his chin. A shimmer of angry tears brightened his eyes, but his jaw had a new set to it. "Fuck!" The curse came out as a harsh whisper. Quinn stood and paced the loft, mindful to keep his steps light so he wouldn't wake Danny.

Rene had watched quietly as Quinn took in the footage of his brother being brought into the police department for questioning in connection with the murder of his ex-wife. Keith's face had been set in a hard line, and the news reporter confirmed that an internal investigation had confirmed that Keith Stanton, a decorated law enforcement officer with a pristine service record, had engaged in an affair with his former sister-in-law, the ex-wife of his twin brother, Quinn Stanton. The news report included a picture of Quinn, a still they'd pulled down from his accounting website.

"Of course they had to spill it all," Quinn spat angrily.

"The affair, my face." He paced the loft, tugging on his hair until the roots stung. "I need some air," he said.

Rene nodded and let him walk out of the house alone.

Outside in the front yard, Quinn paced, punched the air, and gripped his gut. He thought he was going to be sick. All the dirty laundry aired out on TV. What would happen to his brother's career? His business would suffer. The scandal would decimate their small family, not to mention ruining any relationship Danny could have with his uncle. Despite Rene's assurances that the cops had a lead on the real killer, Quinn wasn't at all sure that he'd survive this. He didn't know where he'd find the strength. He only knew that he had to. For Danny. For Eliza. For himself.

He stormed back into the house and locked the door behind him. He walked quietly up to the loft and put a hand on Rene's shoulder. She was on the phone with someone, and when he touched her, she said, "Sam. I need to go. You know what to do."

When she ended the call, she stood, faced Quinn, and opened her arms to him.

His heart rolled over in his chest as she stared at him with her intentions written plainly on her face. He hesitated, giving her plenty of time to change her mind. When she didn't move away from his hold, he leaned down and put his mouth on hers as everything else around him faded away. He cupped her face, holding her body to his, as he deepened the kiss. He brushed his tongue over hers, nipped at her lip, and then pulled her hips tightly against his.

When she moaned against his lips, he moved his kisses to her jaw and then down to her neck. She slid her fingers into his hair as if to encourage him. In response, he sank his teeth into her neck and suckled at her flesh. The way she pressed against him and inhaled sharply very nearly made him lose what little sense he was clinging to.

Leaning back, she whispered, "Maybe we should..."

She slowly lifted her eyelids. Her eyes were hazy, filled with the same desires he had. "Maybe we should what?" he breathed. "Shit, you're going to kill me."

Stepping back, she rested her hands on his chest. "Do you want to stop?"

The idea was one of the worst he'd ever heard. He wrapped his arms around her back and yanked her against him. Their mouths came together in a heated kiss. This was not sweet teasing or exploration. This was raw passion—a desperate need to satisfy the passion and curiosity that they'd been dancing around for what felt like nearly forever.

"I want you," he said, his voice a tense whisper.

"Me too," she replied.

As he lowered his gaze to hers, the heat in her eyes nearly set him on fire. "Are you sure?"

"Positive."

Taking her hand, Quinn practically ran toward the master bedroom, but she pulled him to a stop.

"There are cameras in the bedroom," she whispered.

"Right. Yeah. Good thinking. Give me a five-second head start and then meet me in the bathroom," he said.

She did exactly as he'd asked.

As soon as they were in the small space, he pulled her into another heated kiss. She let out a soft gasp as he gripped her shoulder-length hair and tugged it aside before delving into her exposed neck. Pressing the palm of his other hand low on her back, he pulled her snug against his groin. He licked, nipped, and sucked at her skin as he pressed his erection against her. She moaned and rotated her hips to meet him every time.

"I am so close to just taking you right now," he whispered before lightly biting her earlobe.

He had barely gotten the words out before she slipped her hands under his T-shirt and dug her fingertips into his bare back. The chill of her hands was like lightning shooting through his body.

"Rene," he whispered, his voice strained, warning her that he was losing control.

"Let go," she whispered. "Stop fighting it."

His breath left him with a tremble in response.

"Please," she added and started to lift his shirt, but he gripped her wrists.

"Let me have my fun," he whispered, "and then I'll let you have yours."

"Trust me," she said, "I'll have my turn..."

"You first," he begged. "I insist, Rene, please."

Rene bit her lip as she looked up at him. "Okay," she said. "Have your fun, Quinn."

He didn't hesitate in lifting her shirt over her head and tossing it aside. She was wearing that same black sports bra he'd seen before. The one that had filled his fantasy as he'd taken a shower and eased his stress. Brushing his fingertips over the material, he took a moment to appreciate her hard nipples. When Rene gasped softly, he worked the peaks beneath his fingertips through the fabric, appreciating every tremor of her body under his hands. Then he explored her ribs, her stomach, kissing and touching every inch of her smooth skin as if it weren't just the first time but the last. He wanted to remember this moment. To sear the feeling of her body into his memory—because he had no idea when they would get to do this again.

He kneeled on the cold tile of the bathroom floor and then chuckled as Rene pointed toward the bathmat with a toe. He yanked the material closer, setting it under his knees for comfort. Then he watched Rene bite her bottom lip and squeeze her eyes shut as he ran his hands along the long, lean muscles of her thighs. She remained still as he slid his hand between her legs. She made a soft whimpering sound as he unbuttoned her jeans and eased her zipper down effortlessly. He tugged her jeans over her hips and down her thighs. He didn't take them off completely, just to her knees. Just to expose what he wanted. And then he pushed her gently but firmly so her body was supported against the bathroom vanity.

She laughed lightly. "Oh, I'm in trouble with you, aren't I?"

"The best kind of trouble," he said as he brushed his hand over the black boy shorts covering her most intimate parts. Goddamn. He could smell her excitement, and like an animal, an untamed beast, he very nearly gave in to the urge to tear what remained of her clothing away and claim her body as his.

Instead, he pressed his fingers against the damp fabric. "Don't move," he growled.

Rene whimpered as Quinn dragged his fingers along

her legs, her thighs, her hips, blowing hot kisses along every inch of her skin. When he lowered his hands, he took that flimsy bit of material with him, exposing her perfect arousal to him. Again, he had to fight the primal urges inside him. She might not appreciate the quick and demanding fuck his body was insisting he give her...and in this circumstance, he was totally unprepared to make love to her the first time in a cramped bathroom standing up. But he was going to enjoy every second of finally, finally making her his.

He slid his hands along her thighs, but this time he traced along the inside of her leg. She tilted her hips, silently begging for him to reach his destination. She muttered something about tickling her, but the words were lost in the sound of the moan that erupted from her when he finally touched her center.

Her body was more than ready as he finally delved into her depths. He slid his fingers in and out of her body as he savored her flesh, nipping along her thighs and squeezing the roundness of her bottom. However, when he firmly stroked her clitoris, she damn near shot off the bathroom vanity. Quinn smirked as he gave her a much firmer bite, a warning about her attempted escape as his hands worked in perfect unison with his mouth, guiding her into an orgasm.

She moaned, writhed, and sighed and then collapsed back against the vanity. As she gasped for breath, Quinn leaned in, taking a moment to slide his tongue along her body, tasting the reward he'd earned.

"Oh, Jesus," she moaned.

Finally, he stood and gave her a light kiss on the lips, the taste of her excitement still on his tongue. "Not how I pictured our first time, but every bit as good."

She faced him. "I can't take my turn when my pants are halfway down, Quinn."

Quinn's breath caught in his chest as he lowered Rene's pants to free her from her clothes. Dressed, she was gorgeous —her body powerful, her face beguiling in its beauty and strength. But seeing her nearly naked...standing before him with no barriers... She was so fucking perfect. He never would have thought himself to be the type of man to push so hard for a woman, but something about her made it impossible for him to resist. He needed to put his claim on her— not that she was property, but damn it, he didn't want anyone else to even think he could have her.

They traded places, and Quinn leaned his ass against the bathroom vanity while Rene lifted his shirt over his head. She shrugged her sports bra off. Seeing her like that, with her legs parted, her breasts free, and her dark hair splayed around her face, he wanted to climb on top of her and make her scream. He had no doubt he could because he wouldn't stop touching, teasing, and tasting her until he did. But he didn't want that right now. Not yet.

She gently pushed his knees apart and grinned as she murmured against the zipper of Quinn's jeans.

"Keep your voice down," he reminded her. "The last thing we need is Danny waking up."

She flashed a vampish smile as she clamped her teeth into her index finger.

"Good girl," he whispered.

Quinn leaned away from the vanity, allowing Rene

enough room to unbuckle his belt, unfasten his jeans, and lower the fabric to the ground. He stepped out of his pants and boxers, and Rene settled herself in front of him, between his open knees. At the first touch of her fingers on his rock-hard excitement, he was lost once more. She maneuvered her mouth over his body, scratching her fingers against the hairs of his thighs, licking, biting, sucking his skin as she explored him. Finally, he felt the sensation he thought would make him lose the last bit of composure. Slick and warm, Rene's mouth drew Quinn's length in, tentatively at first, slowly taking him deeper in torturous, slow measures. She flicked her tongue along his shaft as she sucked him, her fingers just grazing the back of his balls. Quinn tried hard to still the quake of sensations rocketing through his body. He wanted to grab Rene's hair, tug her face to his, and claim every inch of her, but he knew they couldn't do that now. For now, he closed his eyes and let himself give into the feeling of Rene's mouth on his body, the gentle scrape of her teeth against his dick reminding him that he was inside her mouth, his pleasure at the mercy of her every tiny movement.

When he opened his eyes to peek at her, he saw her staring up at him. At the sight of her watching his face, his dick fully in her mouth, he stiffened, let out a muffled groan, and then released. "Rene," he gritted.

When he started breathing again, his thoughts and body stilled enough to be trusted to be quiet, she kissed her way up his body. When she was fully standing in front of him, he took a moment to lightly nibble and touch her breasts before finally finding her mouth. She fisted his hair and pulled him in for a hot, passionate kiss. She groaned, he hissed, and then they started making out again. She was perfect for him. A perfect fit for his mind, his heart, his soul. And most definitely for his body.

As he felt himself getting hard again, he put his forehead to hers and held her gaze. "I think we'd better stop..."

"Don't," she breathed. "Don't you dare." She laughed lightly as she kissed his chest. "Okay," she sighed, "I know you're right. I'm sure we could keep this up all night."

He hugged her close and kissed her head. He wished they could stay like that, but that wasn't possible. However, he held her as long as he could before she stepped out of his embrace and pulled her clothes on.

"I'm going to the loft to work," she whispered. "*Alone.*" The reluctant look she gave him let him know that she was sorry to have to leave the erotic nest they were building in the bathroom. But he got it. The cameras would pick up on her leaving his bathroom, and it would look at least a little less incriminating if she left it fully dressed and alone. "I hope that inspection of your rib injury wasn't too...personal," she teased, quickly putting together a cover story for their time together in the bathroom.

Quinn slipped his boxers back on and turned on the shower. "Thanks for the follow-up, Rene," he said with a smile. He rubbed a hand over his still-hard cock. "If I'm lucky, these ribs will never heal."

11

"Rene? You got eyes?" Sam's voice echoing through the office shook Rene from her fog.

She'd spent the night like she had most nights, alternating sleeping shifts with Quinn. But never had the shifts been so sleepless. She'd then rested back at home for maybe two hours after Alexa and Tika relieved her. Rene rested her head in her hand at her desk, wondering just what the hell Sam wanted. The phone on Rene's desk was beeping, and a little red light let her know that Sam was calling her.

"What's up, Sam?" she asked into the receiver.

"Boss is here. Can you come up front?"

Rene set the receiver back into the cradle of the office phone and grabbed her empty coffee cup. She'd make a fresh pot while she was up out of her seat—as if, she mused, caffeine could satisfy her. Right now, she wanted a month in a secluded cabin with this case solved and nothing but Quinn's body to occupy her time.

Holly lifted her brows at Rene as she joined them at Sam's desk.

"You can't avoid this forever, Holly," Sam stated.

"What are you avoiding?" Rene asked wearily.

Sam smiled and clapped her hands. "Wedding dress shopping!"

Holly closed her eyes and sighed.

Rene felt a little twinge of something in her heart. Not quite jealousy, but maybe a hint of envy. Holly was getting married. Holly was planning a wedding. With a man she loved more than anything. That was definitely something to be envious of. Rene walked around the desk and held her hand out to Holly. "Come on. You have to do this eventually."

They walked into the conference room, where Sam had the screen of her laptop projected onto the wall. She could barely contain herself as she brought up a website. "Okay," she started. "Taking into consideration that Holly is the least feminine female ever, I have already eliminated all the lacy, frilly, and froufrou options available. There are plenty of straight, elegant, and sexy dresses for us to sort through."

"No glitter, sequins, or...anything else sparkly," Holly said, sitting down.

Sam pouted. "No sequins? *Holly*. You have to sparkle so Jack gets enchanted with how the spotlight catches your every move during your first dance."

"Give me a fucking break, Sam," Holly said.

"It's a memory he'll cherish forever." Sam's pout intensified.

"He's a man, Samantha. He'll cherish getting laid when we go home."

Rene laughed as Eva joined them. Glancing at her watch, she decided she'd spend no more than fifteen minutes. She'd give this spectacle fifteen minutes, and then she was going home. No. Not home... She was going back to Quinn and Danny.

"Someone's happy," Eva whispered in her ear.

At first Rene thought she meant Sam, but when Eva nudged her slightly, Rene realized she was talking about *her.*

"Did you get more of that smoochie-smoochie action from Quinn?"

Rene rolled her eyes. "I swear this place is more like a sorority than a business."

Eva giggled and gave Rene another nudge before telling Sam to move on. The dress she had brought up on the screen definitely was not one Holly would want for her wedding. While the cut of the gown was elegant and sensual, the long, mermaid-like train with its intricately embroidered flowers was likely a no-go for Holly. Even for her wedding, she'd want something she could run in—if she needed to. The same as Rene. Sam stuck her lip out before accepting that she had been overruled and moved on to the next option.

This back and forth continued until Rene finally reached the time limit she had allotted. "Okay," she said, standing up. "That's it. I'm out. Good luck, Hol."

"No," Sam cried, "wait! Two more. Rene!"

Rene ignored her pleas. Two more would turn into two more after that, and then she'd lose an hour to this circus. She had no idea why Holly had caved into Sam's need to plan her wedding. This was going to end in a disaster. Either Sam would be crushed that Holly hadn't budged, or Holly would be furious because she allowed her wedding to turn into the fashion show that Sam was dreaming up. Either way, Rene was happy to remove herself from this stage of the process. She rushed to her office to get her bag and headed out before she could get sucked into any other wedding planning.

Even though Sam tended to drive Holly and Rene insane, they would be lost without her. She needed to remind Holly of that before Holly got too fed up with Sam's attempts at giving her the perfect day. Her phone rang just minutes after leaving the office. She recognized the ring tone as Holly's and debated if she wanted to answer.

Finally, she connected. "Hey, did you find a dress?"

"You are a coward."

Rene laughed. "I know when to cut my losses and head for the hills. There were a few very pretty dresses in there, Holly. Pick one and move on to the next thing."

"Easy for you to say."

"Okay. Let me pick one. I promise it will be something you love."

"That's an idea. I think you should take over this entire fiasco before I duct tape Sam to a chair and haul Jack off to the courthouse like I wanted to in the first place. Are you headed back to the house?"

Rene stopped for a light. "Yes, I am." She waited, expecting Holly to say something else, but there was silence.

"I'm sorry about yesterday," Holly said after a long

silence. "Eva gave me hell about it, and she's right. You're smart enough to know what you're getting into with Quinn."

The light changed, and the car in front of her slowly started through the intersection with Rene right behind it. "You were right to point it out. I was ignoring the obvious. Quinn and I talked about it last night. I think we're on solid ground moving forward."

"I hope so. I'm sure we'll know soon enough. Now that the news has broken the story that Keith is being questioned, I'm sure they will have whatever evidence they need soon. The real killer will be arrested, and Quinn can put all this behind him."

A bit of a cloud moved over Rene's heart. "He'll be glad for that."

"You're my friend, Rene. I care about you."

The words were probably as sentimental as Holly Austin would ever get. "I know. I care about you, too, Holly," Rene said with a sad smile. "That's why I'm going to remind you that even if Sam is a pain in the ass sometimes, she's our pain in the ass and we need her. She's a valuable part of our team."

"She's a brat," Holly said. "But...a valuable brat. Be safe." Holly ended the call, and Rene finished her drive, trying to ignore the fact that sooner rather than later, she was going to be going home to her house instead of to the little cabin on the pond that she and Quinn had shared. They hadn't even shared it for that long. Why the hell was she feeling so damn sentimental about it? That was a stupid question. She knew why. She was going to miss having Quinn and Danny around all the time. She was going to miss their company.

And she was absolutely dreading not having them around all the time.

"Idiot," she muttered to herself, knowing that Holly's warning had come too late. She was already attached to them, and she was likely going to get her heart broken if Quinn changed his mind about them.

"Hey, sweetheart," Quinn said as he glanced over from the kitchen. "I was afraid we were going to have to have dinner without you."

"I was told to never miss dinner. I wouldn't dare."

"Good girl."

Rene had a real love-hate relationship with how Quinn's voice rolled through her. She loved how the rich baritone sent a shiver down her spine, bringing every nerve in her body alive, but she hated the power he had over her. She instantly imaged him growling seductive words in her ear as he pinned her to the wall. Maybe he would if she asked him nicely.

"Are you blushing?" Quinn asked as a cocky grin curved his lips.

Denying what he could do to her was a silly game she didn't intend to play. Instead, she set her bag down as she winked at him. "I saw Danny and Tika outside. Does that mean Alexa's upstairs?"

"She is."

She blew him a kiss before heading upstairs. "Hey," she called out to Alexa.

"He cooks. The man is sexy, and he cooks."

Rene laughed at the greeting she received. "Of course he

cooks. He's a single dad. He can't feed Danny peanut butter and jelly sandwiches every night of his life."

"You better snatch him up while you can," Alexa whispered.

She didn't have to wonder if Alexa knew she'd been caught kissing Quinn. Again, her team was more like gossipy college girls on that front. She didn't doubt that *everyone* knew.

"Speaking of good men, how is Dean?"

Alexa's smile spread. "Amazing."

"And his sister?"

She scrunched up her nose and gave a slight shrug. "Still a bit of a mess but getting better."

Dean and Alexa met on a case. His sister had disappeared. She'd been struggling with drug addiction and been trapped in a human trafficking ring until he and Alexa found a way to help her get out. But rehab and recovery didn't come easily. Mandy had yet to find a way to be thankful for the forced sobriety and finding her path.

"She'll get there," Rene reminded her. "This type of thing takes time."

"I know. I just hate watching Dean continue to blame himself. I don't know that he'll ever stop."

"It's hard watching someone you love fall," she said. As soon as the words were out, she had to smile because that was the exact reason Holly had been so upset the day before. She feared Rene was setting herself up to fall. "They'll be okay. Both of them."

"I know. How about Quinn? How is he taking the news about his brother?" Alexa asked.

"As well as can be expected," she said with an exaggerated frown. "But you will be happy to know that he is more certain than ever that his brother misstepped in sleeping with Eliza, but he's damned sure his brother didn't kill her."

Alexa cocked a brow. "If that's true, I just hope the police get the person who did. Soon."

Rene sighed. "We'll see what happens. Thanks for hanging out today."

"No problem. It keeps me from having to listen to Sam whine about Holly's lack of interest in planning a wedding."

"Oh, you missed the online dress shopping fiasco."

Alexa tilted her head and pouted sarcastically. "Oh, darn."

"I'm sure there will be another one soon. Holly is resisting. She's the actual opposite of a bridezilla, unless you can be a bridezilla by not wanting to be a bride."

"Big surprise there," Alexa said as she gathered her things and put them into the tote bag she'd been bringing with her all week.

"Hey, just so you know," Rene said, "I really appreciate you guys helping me carry the weight of this case. I know you have your own cases to work on."

"Don't you worry your pretty little head about it," Alexa said. "If any of us were doing more than research at this point, we would have let you know. Besides, we'll remind you of this someday."

"I'm sure you will," Rene said with a smile. She followed Alexa downstairs and out the front door, where Quinn was calling out to Danny that dinner was about ready. He yelled something to Tika before running into the house at full speed.

Rene watched her teammates leave before going back inside. She headed toward the kitchen as Quinn reached for plates from the cabinet above the sink. Tilting her head, she took a moment to admire the snug fit of his jeans. She couldn't wait to take those off him. "Where's Danny?" she asked.

"Washing up."

Taking the opportunity, since they were alone, she put her hands on his hips and rested her cheek against his back. "You okay today?" she asked.

Turning, Quinn nodded. "I think so. About you—us, yes. I'd like find out the truth about what happened to Eliza and put it behind us."

"I know."

He threaded his fingers into her hair and kissed her lightly. The moment their lips touched, or so it seemed, Danny started running down the hall.

Quinn exhaled audibly and brushed his nose against hers several times before leaning back. "We will finish that later."

"Help me set the table," she said as Danny joined them in the kitchen. The routine was so basic but so familiar already.

As they ate their meal, Rene told herself over and over that she had no business being so damned invested in these nightly dinners. She had no business wanting them to continue. Hoping that this would be their lives after they could leave this house was likely setting herself up for disappointment, but as she sat back, listening to Quinn and Danny banter about video games and dinosaurs, she couldn't help but want to fit into that.

Ever since she had left New York and her old life behind, she'd managed to keep a barrier between herself and the new life she'd created for herself. She didn't want that any longer. She wanted to belong here—here with HEARTS and with Quinn. That need to fit in was a sure sign that she was finally healing and letting go of the guilt she felt about losing a teammate in New York. But it was also a sign that she was making herself vulnerable to that kind of pain and loss again, and she wasn't sure she liked that.

"Hey," Quinn asked when Danny stood from the table to clear his plate. "You okay?"

"Yeah," she said, forcing herself out of her depressing thought pattern. "I'm just tired. It's been a long week."

He reached across the table and took her hand. She watched, mesmerized by the way his thumb brushed over her skin.

"Well, maybe you can actually sleep tonight," he said. "I promise tonight we won't get as...distracted."

"Another promise?" A slow smile curved her lips. "I don't know that I like that one."

Quinn grinned and was about to say something when there was a crash from the living room.

"Dad!" Danny screamed from the other room. "I can't find my T-Rex!"

Quinn closed his eyes and let out a long breath. "Hold that thought. I'll be right back."

She laughed. "Take your time. I'll clean up dinner."

As he took care of Danny, she cleaned the table, put the leftovers in the fridge, and started the dishwasher. Then she checked that the windows and doors were locked. As soon as she confirmed they were safe inside the little house, she followed Quinn's deep voice down the hallway. Leaning against the doorjamb of Danny's bedroom, she felt that heart-swelling warmth wash over her. As they lay stretched on the twin-sized bed, Quinn read the book Danny certainly had to have memorized by now. Even so, Danny was hanging on every word.

Danny noticed her watching from the door and waved her over. She sat on the side of the bed and listened as Quinn expertly read about a cool cat and his crazy adventures. Danny giggled at the voices Quinn was using to tell the story, and Rene had to smile too. Despite everything, he was still such a happy kid. She thought that said a lot about how well Quinn was raising him on his own. Even if Quinn did seem sad and frustrated sometimes, he rarely raised his voice to Danny. They tended to navigate to a truce before it ever got that far. Rene respected that about him. He had a lot of patience for a man going through so much.

When the story ended, she patted Danny's leg. "Did you brush your teeth?"

"Yes."

"Open wide," she directed. She made a show of checking his teeth before nodding her approval. "Did you wash your face?" Again, she examined. "Did you pick your nose?"

"Ew! Rene, that's gross!" The little guy giggled hard and covered his nose with a hand to keep Rene from looking.

She laughed as she ruffled his hair. "See you in the morning, bud."

"Night, Rene."

"Good night, Danny," she said, allowing her eyes to meet Quinn's.

While Quinn finished readying Danny for bed, she went back to the loft to focus on work. On the case. On anything but the heady, secret feelings filling her heart.

QUINN MADE A FINAL PASS OF THE LITTLE HOUSE, checking the doors and windows. He didn't doubt for a moment that Rene had already done the same, but he wouldn't feel comfortable until he'd done it himself. Satisfied that the house was secured, he slipped into the master bedroom, where he knew Rene had gone and closed the door. He didn't care if it made him a cad—he went right into the bathroom, where she paused to look at him.

He entered without an invitation and closed the bathroom door behind him. Yes, he'd known Rene intended to take a shower. And yeah, he crashed her party. That probably did make him a bit of a scoundrel, but he could live with that.

"Are you just going to stand there?" she asked. "Or are you going to help me?"

She didn't need to ask him twice. He kneeled down before her and helped her out of her pants before placing a line of kisses above the elastic band of her underwear. Then, his fingers nearly trembling with excitement, he slid the fabric down her thighs. The moment he maneuvered her out of her pants, he slid one hand between her legs. The other gripped her hip, holding her steady as he leaned in and pressed his mouth to her.

She gasped as his fingers entered her and he used the ball of his hand to press hard against her clitoris, working her into a frenzy with the rhythmic circles and intense pressure.

"Jesus, Quinn," she breathed as she covered his hands with hers, encouraging his assault on her senses. He licked harder at her intimate folds and thrust his fingers faster, deeper, until her knees were trembling. Out of fear of her toppling over, he encouraged her to take a step back against the edge of the bathroom vanity to brace herself as she came hard.

He hushed her when she cried out. He stood, covering her mouth with his as she moaned. When he pulled his hand from between her legs, she breathed a protest and stuck her lips out in a pout.

"If you think it's so easy to be quiet..." she muttered. She reached into her toiletries bag and pulled out a sleeve of condoms she'd packed.

"God love you for thinking ahead," he muttered as he reached behind her back to unhook her bra. The material fell away, revealing all of her to him, and he could have sworn he fell a little bit harder for her. She was so fucking amazing to look at.

Sinking her teeth into his bottom lip, she suckled it as she released the button of his jeans and eased the zipper down. Quinn put on hand to the wall to balance himself as she removed his pants and tossed them aside. She kneeled in front of him again and then looked up at him, a wicked smirk crossing her lips. Goosebumps rose on Quinn's skin as she lightly trailed her fingertips up his thighs and hips before she finally traced the length of his erection.

He closed his eyes as anticipation made him even harder. He wasn't the least bit disappointed as she leaned forward and took the length of him into her mouth. As he let out a long, slow breath to calm himself, he cupped the back of her head. The urge to control her depth and speed was screaming at him, but he somehow managed to control himself and let her work her magic without his input. When she had him panting her name and grinding his teeth, she eased back enough to stand.

She grabbed the condom packet and tore it open. As he sheathed himself, she turned her back to him and leaned forward, folding her arms on the vanity. in silent invitation for him to enter her whenever he was ready. And enter he did. With one solid thrust, he was deep inside her, causing her to gasp with surprise. Rolling her hips, Rene encouraged him to keep going, and within moments, her body tensed around him and he gripped her hips harder. Oh, the things she could do to him. And to think they were still learning each other's bodies.

This was only going to get better.

With his teeth clenched, he set the pace. Hard and frenzied. The sound of their bodies slamming together and their muted panting echoed around the small room. Hearing their sounds bouncing back at him made him call out her name. In response, she pushed back, ground into his thrusts, and moaned out his name.

Quinn gripped her hair and gently pulled her head back. As he did, she opened her eyes. Their eyes locked in the mirror, and he fell over the edge. Seeing the tension on her face, the way she bit her lips, the way her brow furrowed, was more than he could handle. He was doing that to her, making her lose control, and it was the sexiest fucking thing he'd ever witnessed.

Rene rose up to lean against him as her body eased around him. With her back against his chest, he grasped her breasts and held her as he pounded into her. After three hard thrusts, he stilled, grunted, and came so hard he thought he might pass out. But then he started breathing again. She smiled at his reflection as she rested her head back against his chest.

Damn. He'd known they would be good together—perfect together—and they were. In every way. He smiled at her in the mirror before dipping his head down to kiss her neck. "I'm sorry. I interrupted your shower..."

She laughed lightly. "I forgive you."

As he removed the condom, she started the shower to let the water heat. She stepped in first, and he watched the water run over her body. When she was wet from head to toe, he got in behind her. She washed her hair while he watched.

"If they get the proof they need, they'll be arresting the real murderer soon," she said.

"I hope so." He looked up in time to catch a flash of sadness in her eyes before she looked away. He put his hand to her chin and lifted her face. "What's wrong? Something has been bothering you since you got back from the office."

She shrugged. "I'm just going to miss you guys."

"Well, you know where we live. Dinner's at six. Bathtime is seven. Bedtime is eight...eight forty-five by the time I actually get him settled down."

She rolled the bar of soap in her hands until it lathered. "I know the routine."

"Good. I expect you to abide by it."

Putting her soapy hands to his chest, she slowly washed up and down. "Are you sure you're going to want me around once this is over?"

He hated the doubt in her voice. Rene wasn't the type to doubt herself. Grabbing her wrists, he stopped her. "I want you around. Don't ever question that."

Her smile returned. "Good. Because I think I'd like to be around."

"That's settled, then."

"It's settled."

Quinn kissed her forehead. "Now get back to washing me. I'm a very dirty man."

"Yes," she said as her brilliant smile returned. "I've come to like that about you."

She turned him around, and he braced his hands on the shower wall as she washed him much more thoroughly than he would ever wash himself. He didn't complain at all; he loved the feel of her hands on him. And when she was done, he returned the favor. The hot water was running out by the time they finished soaping each other and rinsing off.

After they dried, he put on clean clothes and watched her dress. Her movements fascinated him. Every single one. She was far more graceful than any woman he'd ever known. She had a way of captivating him. He thought she'd even look sexy mopping the floor. The idea quickly turned into a fantasy that was far too cliched to share with her.

"That is one seriously mischievous grin, Mr. Stanton," Rene said when she caught him watching her. "Want to share?"

"I'm pretty sure you know. The gist of it anyway."

She gathered her dirty clothes into a bundle before kissing him lightly. Her breath was minty from the tooth-paste, and he couldn't stop himself from sliding his tongue over her lips to get a taste.

"Despite all that soap I used, you're still a dirty old man," she whispered.

"Might have to try again," he suggested.

He kissed her lightly one more time before she carried her clothes from his room. He followed her into the loft and took his usual seat as she put her laundry in her bag. However, instead of stretching out on the makeshift bed, she took the other chair at the desk.

"You should rest," he said.

"I'm not tired."

"Tell that to the dark circles under your eyes."

She gasped and playfully slapped him. "Hey. A gentleman would ignore such things."

He pulled her hand to him and kissed her knuckles. "I'm no gentleman."

"I just want to review a few things."

Standing, he pulled her with him and guided her to the pile of blankets. "Rest. For ten minutes, and then you can review whatever you need. Please," he said when she started to protest. "For me."

"Okay. For you," she agreed. She eased down and curled onto her side. "Ten minutes and not a moment more."

Quinn went back to his chair and tried to focus on his laptop. However, not even three minutes later, the soft snoring that he'd become familiar with sounded from the corner. Looking over, he confirmed that she'd already dozed off. He closed his laptop, giving up on even attempting to work. Instead, he moved to the corner, eased down beside her, and stared at the ceiling as he listened to her breathing. She wasn't the only one who was going to miss how things had changed since their paths had crossed. He'd come to depend on these nights, these quiet moments when the sound of her breathing was like a guided meditation, a soothing sound that calmed the fears inside him.

Closing his eyes, he listened, curling up with her and letting her lull him into that peaceful place where only she could take him.

12

THE SUN WAS BARELY UP when Quinn felt Rene rouse from sleep. She stared at the ceiling for several long moments, watching the reflection of the sun dance on the ceiling as it bounced off the pond outside. Slowly her mind seemed to snap to, and she gasped as she sat up.

Quinn looked at her and smiled. "Good morning, sunshine."

"Morning? It's morning?"

"According to the position of the sun in the sky." He grinned, but she wasn't amused.

"You let me sleep all night?" She knew her voice was accusatory, and she wouldn't apologize for that.

"You needed it," he answered.

"When did you sleep?"

"I dozed off a little here and there."

Rene raked her hand over her hair as she looked at him. "We are supposed to sleep in shifts."

"I'll sleep today while you're at work and one of the other HEARTS is here."

That made sense, and she hated him for it. "We're supposed to sleep in shifts," she repeated when her phone rang. She patted along the floor until she found it. Squinting his eyes, he was able to read the name on the screen.

Jack Tarek.

Holly's Jack. Quinn's heart lurched in his chest before picking up its pace. He waited while she answered and put the phone to her ear. "What happened?"

"Sorry to call so early."

Panic gripped Quinn so hard he could barely breathe. It wasn't that long ago that Holly had been hurt working a case. He guessed Rene was feeling the same heightened feelings as her voice was tight. "Is Holly okay?" she asked.

Quinn couldn't hear Jack's side of the conversation, but he watched Rene close her eyes and let out her breath. "Okay."

Anxiety washed over Quinn as in a sudden rush as he watched Rene sigh. "Let me guess."

"What is it?" Quinn asked.

She ran a hand over her face, ignoring Quinn and his questions. "Thanks, Jack." She turned to Quinn. "That was Jack—Holly's Jack. Things are happening."

He practically jumped up from the floor. "What? What happened?"

"Nothing yet." She tossed the covers off her legs and pushed herself up. "I have to get dressed, Quinn. I want you to stay with Danny today. Don't let him out of your sight."

"Rene, Jesus. Don't hold back on me. What did Jack say?"

"Nothing. He didn't need to," she muttered as she grabbed her bag.

"Is Holly coming over? Or someone else? What should I do?"

"Just be alert. Stay with Danny. You know where the gun is."

Within ten minutes, Rene was dressed and armed and Quinn had Danny out of bed and downstairs. Quinn leaned on the table with his hands wrapped around a cup of coffee as he listened to Danny slowly practicing letters in a notebook. Reading wasn't Danny's strongest area. He was more of a dinosaur–science fact kid. He had just leaned closer, ready to help him sound out a word that he'd gotten stuck on, when they heard a car approaching. The crunching of gravel was a sound Quinn had learned well since hiding out at the house. He walked to the window, expecting to see one of the HEARTS approaching for their daily shift. His stomach dropped at the sight of Monica LeBland easing her car door shut.

"Danny, hide!"

And just like that, Danny dashed off. The cubby door closed just as Quinn ran toward the bedroom to get the gun safe from under the bed. He used the key that he'd put on the nightstand to unlock the case and then pulled out the Glock Rene had put there.

While he held the gun in one hand, he grabbed his phone with the other. Rene was upstairs in the loft, monitoring Monica's movements on the video feed.

"What should I do?" he asked.

"Answer the door," she said. "I'm going to go around the back of the house. And Quinn," she said, "dial 9-1-1. Keep your phone in your pocket and put it on speaker. Tell the operator the address and tell her not to ask any questions, that you're tracking an intruder and you have a minor in the home."

Moving down the hall, he did what he was asked and held his breath at the sound of footsteps on the porch. A moment later, someone knocked. Quinn listened to the intense silence. Other than his heartbeat pounding in his ears, there was no sound.

He jolted when the woman knocked again.

"Quinn," Monica called from the other side of the door. "It's Monica. I need to speak to you. It's about your brother."

Quinn closed his eyes and exhaled.

"Quinn?" Monica said again. "Something has happened that you need to know about."

"Just a minute," Quinn called out. By the time he crossed the living room to the door, he was able to stop his hands from trembling. He opened the door and smiled. "Good morning, Monica. How the hell are you, sweetheart?"

The woman smiled. "Oh Quinn!"

He stepped aside and gestured for Monica to enter. He mentally prayed that the phone in the pocket of his athletic pants could pick up the conversation. He gave Monica a half hug, making sure that the gun in his waistband didn't touch her clothes. He didn't want her to suspect he was armed and prepared for her.

"Where's Danny?" she asked. "I've been worried sick about you two, with everything going on!"

"Danny's not here," he said calmly. "He's out for a walk. The poor kid's getting a little stir crazy."

Monica's smile fell as she became solemn. "Yes, God. I can't believe everything that little guy has been through. I've been trying to reach you. Thank God Keith told me about the investigators you hired before all this shit went down. I came over as soon as I could. I wanted to check on you guys in person."

Quinn's gut twinged. Something about what Monica was saying didn't seem quite right. He knew that Keith knew about HEARTS, but as far as he knew, his brother had no idea where the safehouse was. Where Rene had been hiding them out. "Well, thank you, Monica. I bet you've been a wreck too. You want some coffee?" Anxious to put a little distance between them, Quinn took a step toward the kitchen.

Monica looked around. "I'm surprised that you're here alone. Is there anyone else here? Any of the PIs you're working with?"

The twinge in his gut turned into a sucker punch. "We're being looked after," he said without directly answering. "Very closely. You don't have to worry about our safety, Monica." At least he hoped to hell someone at HEARTS was monitoring the cameras. Please, just let one of them take a peek and realize something was wrong. "I think you can go. We're okay," Quinn said, wondering if there was any chance she'd turn and walk out that door. "Unless you want to catch up? I'm anxious to know everything you can tell me. About Keith—" he looked at Monica "—and Eliza."

"I think it's best if I stay here with you and Danny. I would hate for something to happen to you. Where is Danny?"

Quinn's heart sunk. He pieced together the facts that he had. The police knew that Keith didn't kill Eliza. He knew that Monica had met with Frank Strickland at the very same hotel where he and Rene hid out that first night. Now Monica was here... "You leave Danny out of this," Quinn whispered.

Monica smiled. "I'm not here to hurt you or Eliza's son. I want to protect you."

"I'm sure you do."

"Keith killed Eliza, Quinn. I'm sure of it. I just need to make sure that you're sure of it too."

Quinn's stomach started to burn. "I don't know anything."

"You must know they fucked, Quinn." Monica's painted red lips turned down. "You two were close. Did your brother compare notes with you? Did he show you the pictures he took of her?"

"Monica, you need to stop." Quinn held up a hand. "I don't know what you're talking about. My brother didn't kill anyone."

"That's why I'm here, Quinn. I suspected you'd never believe your perfect twin would do anything wrong. I didn't think he'd betray me, but look what happened. People do things like that, you know." She ran a hand along her hip, where Quinn presumed her gun was holstered.

Quinn shook his head. "Keith didn't kill Eliza, Monica."

Monica took a step closer. "The police seem to think he did." She looked down the hallway. "And unless I'm sure you think so too, I'm not leaving. At least not without Danny."

Quinn stepped in front of her, blocking his view of the hallway. As he did, Monica pulled the gun from her hip. "Monica, stop," he said, his hands in the air. "Danny and I don't need to be involved in this."

"Really, Quinn? Isn't it a little late for you to worry about being involved in this?" She pointed her gun at Quinn's chest. "When the police run Keith's phone records, they are going to find that on the night of Eliza's murder, his cell phone was in her house." She grinned. "My phone, however, was right beside my bed all night." She advanced on Quinn. "That should be the last little bit of evidence to tie Keith to the murder. Means, motive, opportunity...looks pretty simple to me." She scowled. "At least it was. Until you hired a PI to protect you."

"Monica, please..." Quinn held up his hands. "I didn't know about the affair. You know how much I loved Eliza."

"And you know how much I loved Keith!" she spat. "But loving someone doesn't keep them safe, does it, Quinn!"

Just then, the front door flew open and Rene burst in, her gun drawn.

Monica immediately lifted her hands and smiled, as if to show she was no harm. The gun in her hand told a different story. She slowly turned. "Rene, I presume? What's going on?"

"Quinn, get Danny and get out of here," Rene ordered, holding her weapon on Monica.

Quinn ran, just like he'd told Danny not to do a hundred times, down the hallway and threw the door open. "Come with me."

Danny took his dad's hand. As they neared the living room, Quinn picked him up. "Close your eyes and hang on tight."

Rene held the gun steady on Monica. "Put down your weapon, Monica. Let Quinn and Danny walk out of here."

She smirked. "Really, Rene?"

"Monica," she said, using the firm tone she'd learned when dealing with criminals as a federal agent. "It's over. The police are on their way. Keith has already been released from custody. He's already given them his official statement. That he suspected you confronted Eliza about the affair and murdered her when things got out of hand."

"There's no evidence," Monica laughed. "If there were, I'd already be done for. No forensics, nothing. Keith is going to pay for what he did to me. He betrayed me! With that stupid, fucking bitch!"

"Dad," Danny whimpered.

The sound of Danny calling Quinn "dad" set something on fire inside of Rene. He was terrified. And that made rage surge through Rene like she had never felt before.

Fuck this woman for threatening them in front of a kid. For insulting his mother. The mother she'd stolen from him forever. "Monica," she stated, her final warning. "Lower your gun."

"I don't think so," she said, bracing to pull the trigger.

"Danny, don't!" Quinn yelled from behind her.

And then, running as fast as he could, Danny darted

toward Monica. Rene took two big steps and grabbed the back of his shirt just as Danny tackled the woman with the gun.

"Leave us alone!" Danny screamed. "Don't hurt Rene like you hurt my mommy!"

Rene pushed Danny into Quinn and pivoted to one side as she pulled her trigger. She wasn't fast enough. Pain burned her right arm as a bullet grazed her.

She fired again and heard the distinct sound of Danny screaming. She managed to get two more shots off, but as she did, another burning sensation hit her and spread throughout her stomach. Quinn had turned, grabbed Danny, and curled into a ball to protect him. Rene put herself in front of them, firing until her gun emptied.

She had to save them. She had to protect them.

Even though her gun was empty, she pulled the trigger until Monica collapsed in front of her. As soon as the woman hit the ground, she turned. Her head was spinning, and the pain was radiating throughout her torso. But Quinn and Danny were safe. That's all that mattered she told herself as she closed her eyes and fell to her knees, no longer able to stand. The pain was too much.

"Rene," Quinn called, but he sounded a million miles away.

Opening her eyes, she attempted a smile for him but didn't succeed before falling forward.

Danny screamed and screamed. She tried to tell him she was okay, but the words didn't form. Quinn hovered beside her, touching her, moving her hair from her face like he loved to do. Danny grabbed her arm and begged her not to die.

Then the world spun out of control and everything went dark.

QUINN HELD DANNY TIGHT ON HIS LAP. THE LITTLE guy was sound asleep now, but it had taken Quinn a long time to calm him down. He had never seen Danny cry so hard as he had as they'd watched Rene being lifted into an ambulance. Her eyes had fluttered a few times, but she hadn't come to. Danny had asked over and over if she was going to die like his mom had.

He had been strong when Eliza died. But he hadn't seen the trauma unfold before him like he'd seen with Rene.

Quinn did what he could to reassure him, but Danny was bordering on hysteria by the time the ambulance left. He had finally stopped crying once they arrived at the hospital and sat quietly as they waited for Rene to emerge from surgery. Now they sat waiting for her to wake up. Several hours after she had been taken to a room, she still was out. But she was going to be okay. The doctor said she was strong and the bullets hadn't done any serious damage. She was lucky—very lucky. And would be fine. Quinn wished he could say the same about Danny. As if he hadn't already been traumatized enough, he'd seen Rene take two bullets and fall to the ground.

He had refused to leave her side, even when Tika offered to take him to get a snack, and had finally drifted off to sleep as he and Quinn sat by her bed. The last few months had been hell on his mind, his body, and his sleeping habits. Now that this nightmare seemed to be ending, he was starting to feel the exhaustion down to his bones.

Resting his chin on Danny's head, Quinn closed his eyes to let them rest. He jolted at the feel of someone shaking his shoulder. He blinked several times before he could focus on Danny's irritated face.

"You're snoring, Dad," he stated sleepily. "*Loud.*"

Quinn checked his watch. Two hours had passed since he'd last looked at the time. The few minutes of resting his eyes had turned into a long nap. "Sorry," he said and cleared his throat. He shifted and winced. His legs were aching from the weight on his lap. "Can you stand up for a bit?"

Danny climbed down and went right to the bed. "Why is she still sleeping?"

"Because I'm pretty darned tired," Rene muttered.

Danny gasped loudly as he turned to Quinn. "She's awake!"

"Shh," Quinn hushed. "I bet other people are still sleeping."

"She's awake," Danny repeated but with a whisper.

Leaning over the bed, Quinn stroked her hair. "Rene?"

"Danny's right. You were snoring loud," she said.

He chuckled as a smile tugged at her lips and her eyes fluttered before she was able to open the lids and look at him. "You're okay," he said before she even asked. "They removed the bullet, and no major damage was done. You'll be fine."

"How are you?" she asked weakly.

"I'm okay. So is Danny, thanks to you."

Rene lifted her hand, and Danny took it. She smiled at him. "You were so brave."

"I'm sorry I got you shot," he said quietly.

"You didn't," she told him. "You didn't do anything wrong." She tugged at his hand. "You were scared, and you acted to protect me. I know that. It's okay."

Quinn stroked her hair again.

"What happened to Monica?"

"Dead. You killed her." Leaning forward, he kissed her head, reminding himself that none of that mattered now. What mattered was that they had all come out of this mess alive. "Don't worry about this right now, sweetheart. The 9-1-1 operator got it all on the call. The police showed up just minutes after you went down. For now, you need to rest."

She smiled slightly. Her face was still too pale. She had lost so much blood. He didn't know how she'd survived. He was just so thankful that she had. He brushed his hand over her hair for probably the millionth time as she lazily looked up at him.

"You're so bossy," she said.

"Someone has to take care of you."

"Come here, buddy," Rene said when Danny sniffled.

Quinn lifted him up so he could sit on her bed. "Just be careful of her boo-boo."

Rene laughed dryly. "My boo-boo?"

He cocked a brow but didn't chastise her for picking on his choice of words. Danny crawled up the bed and put his head on Rene's left shoulder. She hugged him close and rested her head against his.

"You got shot twice," he said. He pointed to her right arm and the bandage that had been placed there. "You have stitches. I saw them."

"Is it gross?"

"Not too bad."

She kissed his little head, and he snuggled closer to her.

"There was a lot of blood," he said softly.

"I'm sorry you had to see that. I bet it was scary. I'm going to be okay."

Quinn ruffled Danny's hair as he realized just how much of a setback the boy had likely suffered in his recovery. But Rene was right. She didn't die. She was going to be okay. And that would hopefully help Danny realize that even when bad things happen, sometimes they don't end the way his mother's life had.

He would make it a point, however, to call their grief counselor as soon as he could to make an appointment. They were both going to need to work through what they had witnessed today. What they'd been through this week. As he watched Rene and Danny cuddle, Quinn damn near started crying. The relief that filled him was overwhelming.

Something bad had happened, but they were okay. He had to remind himself of that as much as he was going to have to remind Danny.

Leaning down, he kissed her head again, silently thanking whatever force had been looking out for them today.

"Oh my God," Tika said as she walked into the room. "You guys are so cute!"

Quinn laughed as he sat back. However, when he looked at her, he realized that Tika hadn't come in to tell them that they were adorable. "What is it?"

Her face sagged and sadness touched her eyes. "Hey,

Danny. Alexa is right outside. Can you sit with her for a few minutes?"

"Go ahead," Quinn said when Danny looked at him, silently questioning if he had to.

Tika walked to the bed and took Rene's hand. "Damn good to see you with your eyes open."

"Yeah. Apparently I needed a nap or something," Rene said with a slight smile.

"Do you have an update?" Quinn asked.

"Eva called," Tika said once Danny was gone. "All of the evidence IA had gathered put the final nail in the case. From the sounds of it, Keith had figured out almost immediately that Monica killed Eliza. What he didn't count on was that she'd want to make sure he took the fall for it."

"Payback," Rene said.

Quinn nodded. "But what I don't understand is why hurt Danny and me?"

"She realized that Keith was onto her once he started watching your house," Tika continued, "Monica was probably afraid that if you suspected Keith was innocent, you'd do everything in your power to make sure your brother's name was cleared."

"So what?" Quinn said. "She was going to kill us too? Or just make sure we believed her side of the story?"

"It's not clear which one," Tika said softly. "But we're pretty sure she had no plans to kill you and Danny. I guess that's for the police to sort out. All we know is she did kill Eliza, she tried to frame Keith for it, and she worked pretty damn hard tailing Holly and stalking Jack to make sure she could get to you and Danny. What she planned to do..." Tika shrugged. "Let's just be grateful this ended the way it did." She squeezed Rene's hand before she looked at Quinn. "I'm going to see if I can convince Danny to go to the cafeteria with me to get some dinner. Should I bring you back something?"

"No," he said.

"Yes," Rene countered. "Make him eat something."

Tika grinned. "So cute," she whispered before leaving them alone.

Quinn sat beside Rene, resuming his vigil. His heart ached at seeing how weak she appeared. "Don't ever scare me like that again."

"I'm sorry."

"I thought you were going to leave me."

"Shh," she hissed softly. "I'm okay."

He cupped her face and leaned forward until he could put a light kiss on her lips. "You better be. I think I'd be lost without you." That was the truth. Even if they hadn't spent years, or even months, together. He needed her. He needed her strength and her smile and her kindness. He needed to be able to lean on her and to be there for her to lean on. And he didn't give a damn if it was too soon to feel that way.

"Stop looking so worried," she said. "I'm tired, that's all."

"Well..." He smiled. "It may have taken two gunshot wounds and a massive loss of blood, but at least you're finally resting."

She laughed and then winced. "Oh. Don't do that. Don't make me laugh."

"Sorry," he whispered.

She looked up at him, her eyelids already growing heavy. "We're supposed to sleep in shifts," she said. "It's your turn."

Quinn nodded. "I'll take my turn, but you take yours first."

"Promise?" Rene asked.

The words were barely out of her mouth before her eyes closed. Settling back in his chair, Quinn listened to her breathing. The steady rhythm that he had come to know. The soft sound that lulled him into that peaceful place. This, time, however, he didn't close his eyes and let it soothe him to sleep. This time, he silently thanked the universe he was still able to listen to that sweet sound. "I promise, baby," he whispered. "I promise you forever."

EPILOGUE

RENE WONDERED if Holly had been this annoyed by the amount of hovering that the HEARTS did when she'd been injured. Rene could barely move without one of them rushing to her side to see what she needed.

Quinn and Danny weren't much better.

Over two weeks had passed since she'd been released from the hospital. Today was her first day back to work, and her teammates would not stop popping in to check on her.

"I'm fine," she said as Alexa peered into her office for the third time since Rene had arrived at work two hours earlier.

"Isn't it too soon for you to be here?" Alexa asked. "Shouldn't you be home—"

"Resting?" Rene sat back and shook her head as she finished Alexa's thought. She was so damn tired of being told to rest. After being released from the hospital, Quinn had insisted that she was staying with him. No way, no how was she going home alone. He and Danny had been bigger mother hens than all the HEARTS combined, and that was no small feat. "No. My doctor cleared me to return to work. He said I just have to take it easy and go home when I get tired. Which I will do. *When* I get tired."

Dropping into a chair, Alexa stared at her as if she'd get Rene to crack. "Are you sure you're okay?" she asked after a long time.

"I'm fine, Lex. My doctor—"

"To hell with the doctor. I'm asking *you*. Are you sure you aren't overdoing it?"

"I am perfectly fine," she said. "It's almost time for the morning meeting. Come on. Tika just wrapped up a case on an insurance scammer. She's been so excited to tell everyone about it."

Alexa put her hand to her heart. "I'm so proud of her. She's growing up so fast."

Rene chuckled. She also knew how happy Tika was to be in a position to share updates on a case she worked alone. Since Rene couldn't work full-time, she had been Tika's go-to for questions and suggestions. Rene was very impressed with her. Holly was right when she said Tika was ready to take on more than just legal aspects at HEARTS. She was going to be a great investigator, too.

"Go on," Rene said. "I'll be there in a few minutes. I want to wrap this up."

Alexa left her alone, and Rene sighed. The real reason she wanted to be left alone was because standing hurt like a bitch, and she didn't want to alarm her co-worker and friend. Placing her hands on her desk, she held her breath, closed her eyes, and pushed through the pain with only the slightest of grunts and a few choice words.

"That was graceful," Holly said.

Rene opened her eyes to the woman standing in the doorway. "That's me. I could start a new dance trend with these moves," Rene joked as she slowly moved around her desk and toward the hall.

"Speaking of dancing," Holly said. "Sam has it in her head that Jack and I need to take lessons for our reception. Didn't I say you should rein in her planning?"

Rene grinned. "I was a little busy. I'll get on that."

"Thank you."

"You should do it, though," Rene said.

"Dance lessons?"

"You're not exactly a natural on the dance floor."

Holly snorted a laugh. "This is getting out of control. I need a justice of the peace and a chocolate cake. That's it. I don't need dances and champagne fountains and whatever the hell else she is dreaming up."

Stopping outside the conference room, Rene eyed her. "It's one day, Holly. One day that you will remember forever. Sam wants to make it special for you. We all do. Have you set a date?"

"No, she hasn't," Sam yelled from the other room. "But I think December is perfect."

"December is cold and slushy," Holly countered. "I'm not getting married in December."

"I found the perfect dress for a Christmas wedding," Sam explained as they walked into the room.

"I'm not wearing that froufrou mess of lace and ribbon that you found," Holly said. "Do you even care that this is *my* wedding?"

"You're not getting married in a courthouse," Sam stated.

Rene eased into the chair she always occupied during team meetings. She glanced around at how everyone stopped fussing to watch her. "I'm fine."

"I don't believe her," Alexa said.

"Start the meeting," Rene said to Holly.

As soon as the women around her started chattering, Rene's mind faded. She tried to stay in the present, but she couldn't help wondering what Quinn and Danny were doing. She glanced at her phone. Danny had been struggling getting back into the routine of school. Quinn had to leave work several times to meet with the principal. Apparently the grief counselor had also talked to the school and they were all working together to give the boy a sense of stability that had been lost when his mother died and completely re-shaken when he'd seen Rene shot.

He had become clingy with her and Quinn since the incident. That was normal, Quinn had been told. They had to ride it out until he felt safe and comfortable on his own. They had continued their routine, the one that had been established at the little house. Rene hadn't spent a night at her home since being released from the hospital.

She was healing, though. And Danny would heal too.

As soon as she convinced herself of that, those same doubts would start nagging at the back of her mind. What was going to happen to them when this was all over? When Danny no longer needed to see and touch Rene to know she was okay, would things be the same between them all? Or would Quinn realize that maybe they had jumped into all this too fast and ask Rene to go home? To *her* home.

Rene jolted when someone gripped her hand. Looking at Tika, she blinked a few times.

"Are you okay?" Tika asked.

Rene nodded. "Yeah. Sorry." She forced a smile. "I faded a little."

"You faded a lot," Sam said.

Rene frowned and tucked her hair behind her ear. After giving her head a hard shake, she cleared her throat. "I'm sorry. Maybe I did come back too soon. You guys don't need me for this. I'm going to go home. And yes, Alexa, I will rest."

"Good plan," Alexa said softly, clearly worried.

Rene wasn't surprised when Holly followed her from the conference room. "Do you need me to take you home?"

"No. I'll be fine."

"Where was your mind in there?"

Rene sighed. "Nowhere. I just need a bit more time to clear my head."

"Take all the time you need."

Holly started to turn away, but Rene called to her. "Pick a date. Buy a dress. And marry that man before he gets away."

Holly tilted her head, clearly seeing through Rene's suggestion. "You think Quinn will leave when the dust finishes settling?"

"Don't read my mind. I hate that."

She smiled. "Don't be such an open book."

Rene didn't want to voice her fears, but they rushed from her throat before she could stop them. "Everything about us centers on Eliza. We met because of Eliza. He's scarred because of Eliza. Danny's trauma is running so deep because of Eliza. At some point, Quinn is going to realize that too."

"And you think that will make him change his mind?"

"Maybe."

Holly shook her head. "And maybe he won't, Rene. Maybe he's smart enough to know when he's got something really good going. Don't question why you're together. Just know that you are and let that be enough."

"You sound really smart sometimes," Rene said.

"That's because I am really smart." Holly smiled. "Go home. Don't come back until you're ready."

Rene didn't need to be told again. She gathered her things and left the office. Though she wasn't particularly thrilled about the idea of going back to the quiet house Quinn and Danny had invited her into, she didn't have anywhere else to go. It was too early to ask Quinn to meet her for lunch somewhere. Danny was in school. Her team was probably sitting around the conference room table analyzing her life.

She didn't need to be there for that.

Rene slowed as she neared the driveway to Quinn's home. His silver sedan was in the driveway. Beside it was a moving truck loaded with empty moving boxes.

Parking in front of his vehicle, she rushed as fast as she could toward the door.

"You're home!" Danny screamed as he ran across the room. "Dad, Rene's home!"

Rene opened her arms to catch the little guy in a hug. He had figured out to hug her to the side so he didn't hurt her stomach. Pulling him against her, she squeezed him tight.

Her heart melted a little bit every time he showed her affection like this.

Chuckling, she eased her hold on him. "What are you doing home so early?"

"Dad said I could stay home to help him move you in. He let me skip school. Isn't that awesome?"

"Yeah," she said, ruffling his hair. "Awesome." But she didn't really think so. What happened to working to get him back on his routine? "Wait. What? You're moving me in?"

"Oops," he said. Then he giggled and darted off.

She lifted her brows and opened her mouth when Quinn approached her, but no words seemed to form.

Quinn shrugged. "So, first off. Surprise. I rented a truck and got boxes."

"I see that."

"How are you?"

Rene bit her lips, imagining that her smile was as big and goofy as a schoolgirl with a crush. "Better now that I'm here. How are you?"

"Pretty amazing, actually."

"What's going on?" she whispered.

"Well, since you are starting to get more mobile, I thought you might start getting the idea that you were going to go home. And since this is your home now, I'm going to move you in."

Rene lifted her brows. "Just like that?"

"Just like that," he said as doubt shadowed his eyes.

"Without even asking me?"

Fear and doubt played across his face, but he forced them away and gave her a curt nod. "I'm asking now. But I won't take no for an answer. Because this is what we need. All us."

Resting her hands on his chest, she held his gaze. "This is awfully sudden, Quinn."

"We've been living together for over a month."

"We've only known each other over a month."

"And in that time, I've come to care about you and I almost lost you. I know what it means to lose someone, Rene. To wish you could go back and take all the chances and say all the things you didn't say. I don't want to feel that way anymore. I don't want to regret not jumping in and living life. I want you here. Danny wants you here. So be here. With us. Please. If it doesn't work out, leave. But give us a chance first. Okay?"

She closed her eyes, took a deep breath, and then nodded. Looking at him again, she smiled. "Okay. Move me in."

"Yes," Danny said as he worked his way into their hug.

Rene laughed as she put her hand to the boy's head and looked up at Quinn. "I never thought I'd be so happy to be living in sin."

"What does that mean?" Danny asked.

Rene ruffled his hair. "We'll have that talk later."

"Much later," Quinn said as he pulled Rene closer.

Danny beamed up at them as he put his arm around each of them. "We get to be a family now, right?"

"Yeah," Rene said. "We get to be a family now."

MORE MARCI BOLDEN PLEASE!

Here is a sneak peek of Marci Bolden's The Road Leads Back, Book#1 of the Stonehill Series.

STONEHILL
BOOK ONE

the road leads back

MARCI
BOLDEN

CHAPTER 1

Kara Martinson squeezed her way toward the crowded bar, nudging between two kids she couldn't quite believe were old enough to be legally drinking in public. They should have been funneling cheap beer in a college dorm somewhere. Or sneaking shots from Daddy's liquor cabinet.

Art gallery openings used to be much more sophisticated than this. When she was a young artist, openings were about appreciating the art and the artist, not the free booze.

Shit.

Had she really gone there? Kara shook her head at her bitter thoughts.

The bartender, a walking tattoo with spiked black hair, leaned over the counter. "What'll it be?"

She realized all she wanted was wine. And quiet. The kids around her were acting more like preteens jacked up on sugar than art aficionados. One made a face, squished and reddened, as he held up an empty shot glass as proof of his triumph.

Kara wondered when she had gotten so damned old. She never used to snub her nose at a good drink. Actually, she completely understood what her problem was, and it had nothing to do with age. She'd conformed. She'd fallen in line. She'd done what she was supposed to do.

Agent? *Check*. Gallery opening? *Check*. Interviews with all the fancy-pants art magazines? *Check*.

But this wasn't her. None of this was her.

Frowning, she leaned toward the bartender to make sure he heard her over the jeering kids. "Tequila."

Within seconds he set a glass in front of her and filled it with amber liquid. He started to walk away, but she held up one hand and lifted the glass with the other. She downed the drink, slammed the glass onto the counter, and gestured for another. One shot wouldn't be nearly enough to numb the misery of this evening. She motioned for him to fill the glass again.

The young man raised his brows and smirked as he poured. "I can't do this all night, lady."

"One more."

"Some of the crap in here costs more than my car. No puking. Got it?"

Kara chuckled. Clearly he didn't recognize her as the artist responsible for the crap. "Honey, I was doing tequila shots before your daddy dropped his pants and made you."

The barkeep threw his head back, laughed, then filled her glass one more time. "Nice one, babe."

Babe? Kara snorted, the shot almost to her lips, when someone squeezed her shoulder.

"Kara?" asked a deep, smooth voice, as if the man wasn't certain.

She turned and her eyes bulged as she looked into the intense, dark gaze she hadn't seen since the night she'd lost her virginity.

The music had been loud, the beer lukewarm, and everybody who was anybody—and several nobodies like Kara and Harry—in their senior class of Stonehill High was at the graduation party. The only person she had cared about, though, didn't care about her. Or so she'd thought. Until she somehow ended up on Shannon Blake's disgustingly pink and ruffle-covered bed with Harry Canton, book club president and algebra superstar, who clumsily removed her clothes and left slobbery kisses in their wake.

Kara swallowed hard as the flash of a memory faded and the man standing before her, looking as shocked as she felt, came back into view.

She downed the liquor, slammed the glass against the bar, and sighed before she announced, "I've been looking for you for twenty-seven years."

He sank onto the vacant stool next to her and lifted his hands as if he were at a loss for words. Something that appeared to be guilt filled his eyes and made his full lips sag into a frown. She'd be damned if temptation didn't hit her as hard as it had when she was a hormonal teen.

"I wanted to tell you I was leaving," he said, "but I didn't know how."

"You should have tried something like, 'Kara, I'm leaving.'"

"You're right. But I was a kid. I didn't have a lot of

common sense. All I could think about was how I finally had my freedom."

She tilted her head and narrowed her eyes at him. "You had your freedom? You selfish prick."

His eyes widened. "Well, that might be a little harsh. I was just a kid, Kara. Yes, I should have told you I had no intention of staying with you, but I was a little overwhelmed by what had happened. I'm sorry."

"You're sorry?"

Harry's shoulders slumped, as if he had given up justifying sneaking out on her in the middle of the night. "Look, I saw a flier for your gallery opening, and I wanted to say hello. I thought maybe... I don't know what I was thinking." He sounded hurt—dejected, even. "I didn't mean to upset you."

Harry stood and Kara put her hand to his chest and shoved him back onto the barstool. The move instantly reminded of her their one night together. All of seventeen and totally inexperienced, she'd fancied herself a seductress and pushed him onto the bed before straddling his hips like she had a clue what she was doing.

As she touched his chest now, warmth radiated through her entire body.

She glared, pulling her hand away and squeezing her fingers into a fist. "Do you live in Seattle?"

He shook his head. "I had a conference in town. There were fliers at the hotel. As soon as I saw your picture, I knew I had to come." His smile returned and excitement lit his face. "I can't believe you have a gallery opening. This is amazing, Kare."

She wasn't nearly as thrilled by her accomplishment as he seemed to be. She felt like she was selling her soul instead of her art. She'd always preferred the indie route, but that crap agent had cornered her at a particularly vulnerable moment and convinced her she needed him...just like he'd convinced her she needed to be in a gallery. Although, now she was glad she'd conceded on the open bar.

The tequila swirled through her, making her muscles tingle and preventing her from fully engaging the nearly three decades of anger she'd been harboring. She had spent an awfully long time wanting to give Harry Canton a piece of her mind.

Even so, hearing him say she'd done something amazing warmed her in a way very little ever had. If he had come looking for another one-night stand, she hated to admit that she would consider reliving that night again—only this time with more sexual experience and less expectation of him sticking around.

He might be almost three decades older, but his face was still handsome and his brown eyes were just as inviting as they had been when he was a high school prodigy and she was a wallflower.

She smirked at a realization: he was in a suit, probably having just left a corporate meeting, while she was wearing a red sari-inspired dress at her gallery opening.

He was still the straight arrow. She was still the eccentric artist.

"Did you hear what I said, Harry? About looking for you for the last twenty-seven years."

His shoulders sagged. "I never meant to sleep with you

that night. I mean"—he quickly lifted his hands—"I was leaving and should have told you before taking you upstairs. I shouldn't have just left like that, but I didn't think you wanted to see me again anyway. If it's any consolation," he said, giving her a smile that softened the rough edges of her anger, "I'd been working up the courage to kiss you since junior year when you squeezed a tube of red paint in Mitch Friedman's hair after he made jokes about Frida Kahlo's eyebrows in art class."

Kara frowned at him. That hadn't been her finest hour. Then again, neither was waking up thinking she was starting a new life as a high school graduate and the girlfriend of the cutest boy she'd ever met, only to find the other side of the homecoming queen's bed empty. "There's nothing wrong with a woman embracing her natural beauty."

His smile faded quickly. "I'm sorry," he said, sounding sincere. "I shouldn't have left you like I did. I hope you believe that I regret it. Not being with you," he amended, "but leaving without explaining."

He'd had that same nervous habit in high school. He'd say what was on his mind and then instantly try to recover, afraid his words had come out wrong. Usually they had. For as awkward as she'd been, at least she'd always been able to say what she meant and stand behind it. Of course, that ability got her in trouble more often than not.

She'd told herself a million times that Harry didn't owe her an explanation. They hadn't been in any kind of relationship. She'd drooled over him from afar, but he'd barely acknowledged her existence in high school. Even if he hadn't gone off to start his Ivy League college career the day after graduation, he likely never would have looked at her again. Well, at least not until she could no longer hide the truth of their one-night stand from the world.

"I expected so much more from you, Harry," she said sadly, the sting of what he'd done back then numbed slightly by the tequila.

"I know."

"Why didn't you ever write me back?" She thought her voice sounded hurt and pathetic. She was surprised that after so many years of being angry, there was still pain hiding beneath her fury. "I must have sent you a hundred letters."

He creased his brow. "Letters? I didn't get any letters."

Kara searched his eyes.

He looked genuinely confused.

"I sent them to..." Her words faded. Suddenly the tequila-induced haze wasn't so welcome. "Your mother said if I wrote to you..."

"My mother? I never got any letters."

"But you sent money."

Harry shook his head slightly. "What the hell are you talking about? Why would I send you money?"

She stared at him as realization started to weave its way through her oncoming buzz. He hadn't responded to her letters because he hadn't received her letters. And if he hadn't received the letters, he hadn't sent her money. And if he hadn't sent her money, he hadn't known that she needed it. Sighing, she let some of her decades-old anger slip. Her head spun, either from the alcohol or the blurry dots she was trying to mentally connect. Leaning onto the bar, she exhaled slowly. "They never told you, did they?"

"Who? Told me what? What are you talking about?"

Kara couldn't speak. Her words wouldn't form.

Someone wrapped an arm around Kara's shoulder, startling her and making her gasp quietly. She turned and blinked several times at the man who had just slid next to her.

"Sorry to interrupt," he said, "but I need to get home." Leaning in, he kissed her head. "Congratulations on the opening, Mom. It was great."

"Um..." She swallowed, desperate to find her voice. "Thank you, sweetheart." She flicked her gaze at the man sitting next to her. The longer Harry looked at her son, the wider Harry's eyes became.

Phil cast a disapproving glance at Harry, the way he always did when assessing a man who might distract her from her responsibilities, and then focused on her again. "Don't forget that Jess is expecting you to make pancakes in the morning. You promised."

"I haven't forgotten." Kara returned her attention to Harry. His jaw was slack and his cheeks had grown pale.

Phil nodded at Harry, as if he were satisfied that he'd made the point that his mother didn't need to stay out all night, and walked away. Harry watched him leave while Kara waved down the bartender and pointed at her glass. The tattooed kid hesitated, likely debating the ethics of giving her another shot. She pointed again, cocking a brow for emphasis, and he finally filled her glass.

"Kara..." Harry's voice was breathless, like he'd been kicked in the gut. "Was...was that my...son?"

No. His mother definitely hadn't given him the letters

Kara had written. She lifted her shot, toasting him. "Congratulations, Harry. It's a boy."

Harry couldn't deny Phil was his if he tried. The picture on
Kara's phone might as well have been a picture of himself
from twenty years ago. The man had Harry's dark—almost
black—hair and his dark brown eyes. He had the same oval
face and long nose. Phil had Kara's smile, though. Wide and
inviting. Or at least that's how Harry remembered it. She
hadn't exactly smiled at him since he surprised her.

When he walked into the gallery and saw her, she'd
looked as beautiful as she had back in high school. His heart
had nearly exploded. Her long, strawberry blond hair hung
in waves down her back, and when she'd turned to him, he
could easily make out the spatter of freckles across her nose
he remembered from so many years ago. The lines caressing
her mouth reminded him how he'd once traced his thumbs
over her cheeks before delving in for their first kiss. He'd
seen that in a movie and had played it over and over in his
mind, imagining Kara instead of Molly Ringwald.

If only he'd stuck around to give Kara a happy ending
like the movies promised.

Almost thirty years may have passed, but he felt like he
was instantly transformed back into that awkward teenager
who wanted nothing more than to profess his undying love
and promise her forever—if only she'd want him, too. She
never had. Whenever he'd smiled at her in the hallways at
school, she'd always looked away. He'd tried talking to her

several times in art class. She'd blown him off each time, muttering responses, too focused on her work to give him the time of day.

But he wasn't that awkward teenager anymore. He was confident and successful. He took life by the balls and dragged it where he wanted it to go, not the other way around. Not anymore. So when he'd spotted her as he walked toward the bar, he had taken a breath and headed straight for her.

He'd expected her to be a little miffed by his disappearing act all those years ago, but he'd thought they'd talk it out and move on. He'd even had a little light of hope that she'd forgive him. He'd wanted to ask her to dinner, catch up on her life, find out if she was as fascinating to him now as she'd been all those years ago.

What he hadn't expected was for his life to be turned on its ear.

He had a son. He was a father. A real father. Not a stepfather who had never been quite good enough for his ex-wife's kids.

He had a kid. His own kid.

Not that Phil was a child anymore.

"I still can't believe this," Harry said.

Now, sitting in a diner down the street from the gallery, Kara ate pecan waffles and drank coffee, while Harry stared at the picture of his son. The sounds of her coffee cup and silverware clinked in the empty diner as they put together the pieces of how their parents had sealed their fates.

Kara's parents had kicked her out without a second thought. She had run to Harry's house, desperate for help.

His mother had assured her all would be well. She fed Kara and tucked her away in Harry's bedroom while discussing the issue with Harry's father. Then, Elaine sent Kara away with false promises and never, not once in twenty-seven years, said so much as a word to him about his child.

While Harry was in college, Kara had lived in a community that not only supported but embraced girls like her—single mothers with no one else in the world. They'd both lived lives they'd seemed destined for—Harry with corporate friends and family and Kara with likeminded artsy types who embraced a bohemian lifestyle.

Harry had married the woman he was supposed to, and Kara had moved from place to place with Phil in tow. She'd lived all along the West Coast, only settling in Seattle after Phil had asked for help raising his daughter. Harry had returned to Iowa after college and took over his father's marketing firm. Kara hadn't set foot in her home state since the day she left it.

"Phil?" he asked. "Why Phil?"

"Why not?"

Harry wasn't sure if her clipped tone was from sarcasm or frustration or something in between—she never had been black and white like that—but her meaning was clear. He had no business questioning decisions she'd had to make without him.

He lowered her phone. He didn't blame her for being angry, but he couldn't help that his mother had deceived him.

If anyone other than their respective parents knew that Phil existed, they had kept it a tight-lipped secret. In all the years since Harry had come home from college, his mother never even hinted that she had a grandson. How many times had he told her how disappointed he was that his ex-wife hadn't wanted children with him? How many times had he said he wanted a family of his own? Elaine could have given him the one thing he'd been missing all his adult life. Instead, she had stolen his one chance to be a father.

He was angry, too, damn it.

He clenched his jaw. "I was robbed of my son as much as he was of a father. I would have stood by you, Kara."

She narrowed her eyes. "The only standing by me you ever did, Harrison, was to sneak out while I was sleeping."

"I'm not proud of that, but if I'd known about our son, I would have been there."

She looked out the window at the deserted street. "Your mother was so sweet when I went to her. So understanding. She let me stay at your house that night. The next morning she fixed me breakfast. She said she'd talked to you and you wanted to finish school, which was the most logical thing because you couldn't support a family without a job. She said she'd help me out until you could. I was so relieved. I remember wishing I knew her well enough to hug her because I'd been so scared she'd turn me away, too. And then she put me on a bus, and I never heard from her again. Other than receiving a check once a month."

"I'm sorry," he whispered.

She blinked, but the sheen of unshed tears in her eyes caught the light as she focused on him again. "I sent you letters every week. Stupid, stupid letters, thinking you were reading them. That you cared about us. But you never responded. Finally, I stopped writing. It took five years," she said with a bitter laugh, "but I finally caught on that you weren't coming for us. Even so, I felt obligated to let you know where we were. Every time we moved, I'd send a note with nothing but an address inside. I kept you...*your mother* up to date on our whereabouts until about seven years ago."

"What happened seven years ago?"

She hesitated, as if she didn't want to share the next bit of information. "Phil became a father himself. I figured at that point, if you hadn't opted to be a part of our life, I wasn't going to invite you to be a part of hers."

Harry's heart leaped in his chest, and he sat a bit taller. "I'm a grandpa?"

Kara actually smiled, and it was as dazzling as he remembered. "Her name is Jessica. Scroll through the photos. There are plenty on there. She, um..."

Harry paused on a picture, and his smile dropped a bit. The girl had Phil's dark hair and dark brown eyes. Her eyes, however, were set wide apart and slanted, and her face was flat and broad.

"She has Down syndrome," Kara said.

Harry stared at the photo. The girl wore a long sundress and yellow rain boots. A pink bandanna kept her braids away from her face and she held up dirty hands. He looked at the next photo and the one after that. Jessica was smiling in all of them. Not just smiling. Beaming.

"Is she always this happy?"

"No." Kara laughed. "She's as moody as any other seven-year-old girl. But I don't take pictures of sulking."

Harry chuckled. "She's beautiful." He looked up and

saw doubt playing on Kara's face. "She's beautiful," he said more firmly.

"Yes, she is," she whispered. "Do you, um... Do you remember what song was playing when we were together?"

He creased his brow as he thought back. It may have been a lifetime ago, but he still had a clear memory of that night. He'd wanted to be alone with her, to tell her what he'd been wanting to say for two years—that he thought she was amazing. Wonderful. That he wished he'd been braver and had asked her out. That he was sorry he'd blown their high school years being a chicken shit.

While everyone else was getting drunk, he'd taken her hand and led her upstairs so they could talk. It turned out the only empty room they could find was Shannon Blake's bedroom. He hadn't planned to have sex with Kara that night, but before he could work up the nerve to say anything, her curious gray eyes lured him in. He kissed her—his first real kiss. And then somehow they were on the bed, and he was pulling at her clothes. In true virgin nerd fashion, he was inside her and both of their first sexual experiences ended before they even knew what they were doing. Their time together couldn't have lasted more than five minutes, but being with Kara had changed everything for him. From that moment forward, every woman in his life was judged on his own personal Kara scale. And none of them had ever measured up to the memory he'd cherished, and probably embellished, over the years.

He could remember that. All of that. But he couldn't recall any music playing.

"'One More Night,'" she said. "Phil Collins."

Harry stared at her for a moment before he finally realized why she was telling him this. He had asked why she'd named his son Phil. "You named our son after the artist singing the song he was conceived to?"

She shrugged. "I had asked for permission to name him after you, but you didn't answer my letter. I didn't want to name him after my father. He'd disowned me. I was at a loss. Phil was all I had."

"What's his middle name?"

Kara gawked, as if he'd just asked the dumbest question she'd ever heard. "Collins."

He let her admission process for a moment before he laughed outright. She threw a wadded-up napkin at him.

"I'm sorry, but...Phil Collins Canton?"

"Martinson," she corrected. "He has my name."

His smile faded at the sting in his heart. His only son didn't have his name? But why would he? Harry hadn't been there. He hadn't married her. He hadn't raised his son. "Right. Of course he has your name."

Tension rolled between them for a moment before she grinned. "If you'd been able to figure out how to get me out of my clothes faster, I would have had to name him Starship."

Harry laughed, but it wasn't as heartfelt. "That's better than calling him Mr. Mister, I suppose."

"Oh, I considered it."

He chuckled as he scanned the diner, not really seeing the booths and bored waitresses. He couldn't fully grasp how the night had turned out like this. The one girl he'd never been able to get out of his head was sitting across from him, and she was the mother of his child.

"You said you've been looking for me for twenty-seven years." He scoffed. "You couldn't have looked very hard, Kara. I moved home after I graduated college. I never left. I'm on social media. I own a business. I'm not exactly living under a rock. And my mother still lives in the same house. If you sent me letters back then, you knew how to find me."

"Yeah. 'Looking' might have been a stretch. Like I said, I stopped writing to you on Phil's fifth birthday. I always kept you—or so I thought—up-to-date on where we were living. I figured if you were so inclined, you'd reach out to us."

Harry frowned. "I know it doesn't mean anything now, but I would have been there. I would have given up everything to be there."

"I guess your mother knew that, huh?"

He nodded. "I guess."

"I've never been back." She focused on her coffee mug, but before she looked away he glimpsed the hurt she must have felt at being shunned by her family. "Not for class reunions or birthdays or Christmas. I don't even know if my parents are still alive. I've thought about contacting them, but...what would I say? What could they say? Sorry doesn't cover it. And I don't know if I could forgive them. Every time I think about how they threw me out, I just get so angry. I could never be so cold to Phil."

Guilt tugged at him. She shouldn't have had to face that alone.

"The last time I saw my father, he was shutting the door behind him after shoving me out. He told me I was never welcome in his home again." She worked her lip between her teeth as she blinked rapidly. The sheen of tears returned. "I sat on the swing for what seemed like hours, thinking they'd calm down and let me back in, but they didn't. I didn't know where else to go. I didn't exactly have friends back then. So I went to the closest phone booth and looked up your address. Thankfully you were named after your father. It made narrowing down which Canton household to go to much easier."

Harry lowered his face as her voice quivered. He figured these were memories she didn't dredge up too often. "This place that my mother sent you. What was it like?"

"It was nice, actually. I don't think she could have found a better place. There were women there who had been through similar situations. When Phil was born, they taught me how to change diapers and nurse him and all those things that...that my mother should have shown me. They taught me how to garden and sew and barter for the things I couldn't make. We left there when Phil was five and landed in another place like that. It kind of started a trend. I moved a lot, learning and growing. Phil resents not having a regular childhood, but we saw so much and did so much. I think he'll appreciate it someday."

"I bet you were—are—a great mother."

She scoffed, and Harry thought the pain in her eyes deepened. "He's like you, Harry. He's just like you. He needed a stability that I couldn't provide for him. I couldn't stand to be in one place for too long. I still can't. Whenever roots start to grow, I get twitchy. I need to keep moving. I've only stayed in Seattle this long because of Jess."

"Running," he offered.

She looked offended, but he suspected he was more right than wrong. She was still hurting from her parents' rejection. She was still angry over raising a son on her own. She was still feeling alone, even if she had Phil and Jessica.

"It's called *running*," he said. "And I hope you'll stop now, Kara."

She held his gaze. "But I so enjoy it, Harry," she responded with the sarcastic bite she'd had since he'd met her.

He was tempted to call her on it, but they had more pressing matters to discuss. "I'd like to meet them. My son and my granddaughter."

She frowned and drew a slow breath. "Well, I'm sure they'd like to meet you, too."

CHAPTER 2

Kara smacked at Phil's hand as he tugged his tie. "Stop it," she snapped. "You're making me crazy." She tugged the knot loose only to retighten it at the base of his neck. "You don't even need this, you know. He's your dad, for crying out loud."

"I want this night to be perfect."

"It is going to be perfect. Now stop fidgeting."

He skimmed his gaze over her outfit—a green and gold tunic over matching pants. "Is that what you're wearing?"

"What's wrong with what I'm wearing?"

"It's very..."

"What?"

"Buddhist. Are you Buddhist now?"

Kara stopped straightening his jacket and cocked a brow at him.

"For the better part of my life, I thought you were Janis Joplin reincarnate. Lately you look more like...Maya Devi."

"Mrs. Prasad brought these for me from India. They

were made by—"

"Single mothers trying to survive the caste system. I know." He grinned at her frown. "Mom, I appreciate you being here tonight, but can you please tone down the eccentricities? Just for one night?"

"I have no need to impress your father, Phil. I already know him. *Intimately*."

He furrowed his brows. "I don't want to hear about anything you know intimately. I just want things to go smoothly tonight."

"And my clothes are going to cause waves? I'm not naked."

"Mom. Please."

"Fine." She sighed. "I'll put on something more Eleanor Roosevelt."

He widened his eyes. "Please, for the love of all that is good and holy, Mother, do not talk politics, feminism, sex, religion, Indian caste, or any other topic that could possibly be construed as controversial."

"Don't call me Mother. I hate that. It sounds so chastising. And do you really think I don't have enough common sense to get through one evening with your sperm donor? Just because I shirk the conventional doesn't mean I don't know how to act like one of them."

He moaned. "I don't know why I thought having you around would make tonight easier."

She laughed as he walked away, readjusting his suit coat. She'd never understand how she ended up with a conformist for a son. She'd never colored within the lines, but Phil was born that way. While she'd lived life wandering and changing from day to day, he'd clung to normalcy like it could save him.

And maybe it had.

If he hadn't gone to college like society told him he should, he wouldn't have married and had Jess. Even if the marriage had failed miserably, he was left with the most amazing daughter who gave him a reason to be stable, which was what he'd longed for all his life. He definitely was Harrison Canton's son. In this particular battle of nature versus nurture, nature had won tenfold.

Less than twenty minutes later, dressed in black slacks and a white blouse with her long hair swept into a loose bun, Kara bowed before Phil. "Better?"

"You look perfect. Thank you."

Kara crossed her eyes and stuck out her tongue at Jess.

She giggled. "You look so normal, Grandma."

"That's what I was afraid of." Winking, she poked the girl's stomach. "Aren't you supposed to be in bed?"

"She's headed that way now," Phil said.

Jess stuck her lip out in a pout. "I want to stay up."

"Not tonight, Punky." Phil swooped his daughter up and kissed her head as he hugged her tight. "It's a school night. You need to get to bed."

Jess's face melted a bit. "But, Daddy…"

"Hey, it's already past bedtime. Now, go brush your teeth and wash up. I'll be right up to tuck you in."

The girl wriggled down and hugged Kara around the waist. "Good night, Grandma."

Kara ran her hand over Jess's head. "Good night, love. I'll see you in the morning."

"You said you're going to teach me to paint horses, remember?"

"I remember."

Jess grinned and darted off.

Once her footfalls were far enough away that she couldn't hear, Kara asked, "Why aren't you letting her meet him?"

"I want to meet him first." He stopped messing with his cuffs and met her gaze. "No, it's not because I'm hiding her."

"I didn't say you were."

"You were thinking it."

She smirked. "Since when can you read minds?"

"You aren't exactly difficult to understand, Mother."

She opened her mouth to challenge him, but he continued.

"There's no point in my hiding her, even if I wanted to—which I don't. You already told Harry Jess has Down syndrome." Leaning over, Phil kissed her cheek. "I know you feel like you have to protect her from the world, but you don't have to save her from me. I'm her dad, remember?"

Kara exhaled as a sense of shame caused her cheeks to heat. She was fiercely overprotective of her grandbaby. She couldn't help herself. People had a tendency to feel uncomfortable around Jess. Other people's bad reactions to a perfectly normal little girl pissed Kara off.

"Yes, I remember."

"I just don't want her to get excited at the thought of having a grandfather, only to have him disappear for another twenty-seven years. That wouldn't be fair to her. She wouldn't understand."

"You're right." She nodded. "Of course you're right. But I don't think he'll disappear again. He honestly didn't know about you."

Phil returned his focus to tugging his sleeves down. "I can't believe his mother sent you away like that."

She smiled slightly. Phil rarely came to her defense. "Well. At least she found a place for us and sent money every month. Mine just washed her hands of us. We were better off anyway."

"Easy for you to say," he muttered. "You enjoyed living in a commune."

"Yes, I know." Her sentimental feeling deflated as his lifelong resentment spilled from his mouth. "Your childhood was filled with *so much* disappointment."

He stopped fussing over his jacket and looked at her. "All I wanted was to go to a normal school and have a normal life like normal kids."

The doorbell rang, and Kara lifted her brows. "Oh, shoot." Her voice oozed with sarcasm. "I was so enjoying this conversation." Her smirk softened when Phil's shoulders sank and his dark eyes, so much like his father's, widened.

"He's here," he managed to say.

Kara waited, but Phil didn't move. She couldn't blame him. Her nerves were wound so tight she felt a little queasy herself. Undoubtedly, Phil was a thousand times more anxious. She squeezed his arm, giving him a supportive smile, and stepped around him. Taking several breaths as she crossed the small living room, she opened the front door. Her heart tripped when she found Harry looking nearly as fearful as his son had moments before. Kara gave him that same weak smile she'd given Phil—a silent offering of support in a moment that was far too stressful for all of them. Stepping aside, she gestured for Harry to enter. He didn't move from the doorstep.

"I didn't know you'd be here. Not that it's a problem," he quickly amended.

"Phil's a little bit nervous."

Harry grinned. "Yeah. Me, too." He looked down at the teddy bear in his hand. "I didn't know what...but I thought..." He thrust the stuffed animal at Kara. "For Jessica."

She took the gift. "She's already in bed, but I'm sure she'll love it. Would you like to come in?"

He blinked several times, as if surprised that he was still standing outside. He crossed the threshold and looked around the small home. Kara couldn't afford much on her artist's wage, but it was enough. She taught classes and some one-on-one lessons, but her income was iffy most times. She was much better at bartering for her needs than earning money. Unfortunately, the utility companies didn't trade services.

Phil had been laid off four months before and moved in with Kara to save money, making the tiny home seem even smaller. She didn't mind, though. She loved having Jess there day and night. It had taken some time getting used to having Phil under her roof again, however. He didn't appreciate her carefree life any more now than he had as a teenager.

Harry stopped in front of a painting of the sun setting over the ocean and smiled. "Is this yours?"

"Yeah. I tried my hand at landscapes for a while. It didn't

stick."

"Why not? It's great, Kare."

He turned his smile on her, and she had to look away. He made her stomach tighten and her heart trip over itself even now. He always had, but she wasn't a stupid girl anymore. She refused to swoon just because he gave her a compliment.

"I always envied your talent," he said.

"Oh, yeah? Well, I always envied your..."

He grinned at her. "My ability to avoid getting my ass kicked by the cool kids?"

She snorted. He could talk his way out of any situation then, and she suspected he still could. Whereas she would resort to sarcastic commentary that got her in more trouble than not, Harry could always soothe the most ruffled of feathers. The day she'd squirted paint all over the most popular boy in school, Harry convinced Mitch Friedman not to retaliate even as he aimed tubes of paint in her direction.

"Yeah." Kara pushed the memory aside. "Something like that."

He focused on her painting again. She realized he was stalling.

"Are you ready to meet your son? He's in the next room."

He looked at her, and the fear in his eyes made her heart ache for him.

"Is he angry?" Harry whispered.

"No. I told him you didn't know."

"I'm sorry. For everything you both went through."

She frowned at the misery in his voice. "It wasn't so bad. We had a good support system."

"You should have had me." Guilt tinted his eyes.

She drew a deep breath. "Harry—"

"I didn't sleep at all last night. I just kept thinking back on how selfish I was to leave like I did. How idiotic it was of me to never even call you and tell you why. I know we were just kids, but I hate that I was so scared of my parents, of you...of everything."

She creased her brow. "Me? Why the hell were you scared of me?"

He stared at her for a moment. "Because I was a nerdy boy and you were a beautiful girl."

"Right."

"I wasn't lying last night," he said softly. "It took me two years to work up the courage to kiss you graduation night."

She laughed. "I hate to remind you, buddy, but you did a little more than just kiss me."

He grinned. "The rest was just icing on the cake."

"It was something," she muttered. Taking a breath, she wiped the smile from her face and nodded her head toward the other room. "He's in there. And he's just as terrified as you."

Harry exhaled harshly. "I doubt that."

"Come on."

She nudged him toward the living room. After a moment, he took a few hesitant steps toward the doorway. Phil stared at them, his mouth open slightly and his eyes wide.

"Phil," she said when the men remained silent. "Say hello to your father."

Harry looked across the room at this man who was his son. He wanted to laugh and cry and hug him all at once, but he was frozen. He thought the look on Phil's face—one of shock and confusion—must have mirrored his own. Yesterday he woke up without a family, other than his mother. In what seemed like the blink of an eye, he had a son. A granddaughter. He hadn't even said a word to Phil, hadn't seen Jessica, but somehow his world seemed fuller, more complete.

Kara was standing at his side, but she seemed miles away. His son was a younger version of himself staring back at him. Phil was a full-grown man with short-cut hair and a close-shaved face. He was wearing a suit and tie. There was nothing about his son that was a child anymore.

As quickly as Harry felt joy, remorse took its place. He'd missed Phil's life. He'd missed everything. Every milestone, every chance to teach his son how to throw a ball, every scraped knee, every birthday, every Christmas, every Halloween.

He'd missed his entire life. Almost.

A sob choked out of him, and Kara put her hand on his arm, snapping him back to reality.

"I'm sorry," he said. "I, uh..."

Phil stepped forward, closing the gap between them. "It's-It's good to...meet you..."

Harry looked at the hand being held out and bypassed it. He pulled his son to him and hugged Phil like he was a kid. Harry was hugging his son. How the hell had that happened?

After a long time, Harry leaned back and put his hands on Phil's face. Harry blinked away the tears blurring his vision. He didn't know why he was crying. He wasn't a crier, damn it. But he couldn't seem to control whatever it was that was rolling through him.

He already felt so much love for this stranger that the sensation was overwhelming him. He searched Phil's eyes, wishing he could have seen them look up at him like he'd seen so many other little boys looking at their fathers.

"Please, Dad." He imagined his child saying the words. "Just one more..." One more book, candy, ball toss... One more whatever it was that was so important.

He'd never hear those words from Phil. He'd never run down the street holding the back of a bicycle seat shouting encouraging words to his son. He'd never read him a bedtime story or ground him for staying out too late. He'd never fight with him about doing his homework or make up with him by taking him fishing. He'd never build him a tree house or help with a science fair.

That damn sob welled in his chest again, but he swallowed it down this time. "I would have been there," he managed to say around the brick of emotion in his chest. "I wouldn't have abandoned you or your mother."

Phil nodded. "I believe you."

Harry felt a bit of the restriction around him ease. He had worried all day that Phil would hate him, blame him. But his son's eyes were sincere and welcoming. He didn't seem to have the same underlying grudge that Kara had. Harry had a long way to go to make things right with her, but relief surged through him with the first indication that Phil was giving him a level playing field. He could never get back all the moments of his son's childhood, but he could be there now and without the resentment he saw when Kara looked at him.

She may have understood that it wasn't his fault he hadn't been there for her, but she still harbored anger. And he didn't blame her. He just hoped they could move beyond it. He already felt more optimistic about Phil.

"I'd better check on Jess," Kara said.

She left them alone, and Harry finally released his hold on Phil.

Harry took a deep breath and let it out slowly. "I apologize for being emotional."

Phil shook his head and gestured toward the couch. "No. It's good. It's... I wasn't sure how you'd feel about having a kid you never knew."

"How do you feel about having a father who never knew about you?"

He gave a lopsided smile. "It's better than thinking you didn't care about us."

Harry sighed. "I'm sorry you thought that."

"Mom always said you were just working far away. She never said you didn't care, but as I grew up I kinda came to that conclusion. When I was younger, I'd ask where you were. She'd tell me stories about what she thought you were doing. When I was convinced I'd grow up to be an astronaut, she pointed to the moon one night and said, 'I bet your dad is up there building the first city in space. Maybe we'll live on the moon someday.' I talked to the moon every night until I was eight and one of my friends told me how stupid that was. When I asked her if she really thought you were on the moon, she said probably not. She thought you were probably in New York, working at a top-secret pizza factory. I think we had some form of pizza for dinner every night after that for months."

Harry laughed gently, but his amusement faded quickly as he imagined a young Kara lying to protect her little boy from the truth. He could see it in his mind as clearly as if he had been there. He pictured her putting a hand on Phil's small head, smiling that warm smile that had won Harry over the first time she'd offered it to him, and using that soft, soothing voice to reassure Phil that his father—who had never acknowledged his existence—was out in the world doing something wonderful. The fake memory tugged at his heart and made breathing difficult.

Harry had clearly seen the blame and resentment in Kara's eyes the night before. Yet, she'd risen above painting an ugly portrait of Harry to his son—a son she presumed he had abandoned. He'd have to thank her for that. She could have easily twisted Phil around and made him hate his father. It seemed that despite her own feelings, she'd never said a negative word about Harry.

Looking down at his hands, he rubbed his palms roughly together in an attempt to stop the emotions from surging through him again, but he couldn't stop shame from settling in his gut. He could hardly look Phil in the eye. "I wish...I wish she wouldn't have had to do that. She shouldn't have had to lie to protect you. I should have been there."

"Well," Phil said, shrugging slightly, "like you said. You would have been. If you'd known." Phil gestured to the books on the coffee table. "Um, Mom thought you might want to look at pictures."

"Yeah. That'd be great."

"She has about a million," he said, moving to the sofa. "Some guy gave her a camera before I was born. She was obsessed with taking pictures. She still takes photos for people sometimes, but mostly she paints and sculpts." He reached for an old tattered album. "Start with this one, I think. Yeah," he confirmed after flipping the cover back. "This one."

Harry hesitated before moving to the couch. He nearly laughed. He was about to sit down and go through his son's baby pictures. Easing down next to Phil, he sighed when he looked at a picture of Kara pulling a shirt tight against her stomach. She was wearing clothes that were obviously home-made, and guilt tugged at him again. She hadn't even had proper maternity clothes.

Harry pushed the sense of responsibly from his shoulders and focused on the image. Her heart-shaped face was the same as he remembered. Her hair was different, though. Instead of the feathered look she had sported in high school, it was un-styled save for the braids that kept the front from hanging in her face. Her stomach was bulging to the point that it looked like she could topple over at any moment.

Though she wasn't much older than she had been the last time he'd seen her—sleeping soundly in Shannon Blake's bed—she somehow looked wiser and more aware of life. She looked like a woman in the photo, like someone who had realized that the world wasn't as cut and dry as teenagers tended to believe.

She'd matured. It showed in the shadows in her eyes.

Harry imagined if he looked at a photo of himself taken

at the same time, he'd still look like a kid. He'd been carrying on in college, not exactly living it up, but he certainly hadn't been facing the hard truths that Kara had.

There were several photos of her showing off her stomach, but on the next page, she had an infant in her arms. The blanket he was in was old and ragged, definitely used, but Kara was smiling brightly. However, Harry was certain he saw fear in her eyes. He traced his finger on her face, trying to imagine how terrifying it must have been. She'd given birth to their son without him. She'd pushed and screamed and cried as Phil came into the world, and Harry was hundreds of miles away, living his life as though it was just another day.

In one photo, a woman with dark hair leaned in close to Kara. She looked protective of the new mother and child, but that did little to ease the ache growing in Harry's chest. As he once again skimmed the first photo of Kara holding a newborn, he noticed more than her pale face and timid smile. The sheets had a paint spatter scheme, something that was on trend back in the day. The room around her was a far cry from a clinical hospital setting.

Harry tried to age the image, but it was clear this was taken right after Phil had been born. He was still red and wrinkled. Kara still had a sheen of sweat on her cheeks. "What hospital were you born in?"

"Hospital? This is Mom we're talking about. I was born in a birthing pool at some midwife's house. Mom tilled and seeded her garden that spring to repay her. There are a few pictures of her gardening with me on her back."

Harry frowned. He never would have allowed his baby to be born in a pool.

There were two pages of photos of newborn Phil. Most of the photos showed women supporting Kara. In some, girls not much older than Kara held Phil in well-worn blankets. In others, a woman held Kara's hand, looking as though she were doling out motherly advice.

Page by page, Phil grew. First, he was a tiny red bundle tied to Kara's back by a long wrap of material while she peeled a huge pile of potatoes. Then a chunky little boy grinned up from the same papoose-type wrap while she leaned on a hoe, apparently taking a break from tearing up the ground. That must have been the midwife's garden. Harry chuckled as he looked at a close-up of Phil's face. His cheeks were round and full. He hadn't wanted for food as a baby, that was for sure.

Kara, however, lost the pregnancy weight fast. She was thin, possibly thinner than she'd been in school. Her simple handmade clothes never seemed to fit properly.

As Phil grew bigger, Kara's hair grew longer and more ragged. Sometimes she wore long skirts and baggy shirts or bohemian sundresses with her long, wavy hair in braids or pulled back. He smiled at one picture of a tiny Phil sticking flowers in her hair. She was smiling in all the photos, even the candid ones, though in the close-ups Harry thought her eyes reflected buried pain. The setting around them changed constantly—farms, deserts, the ocean, mountains. They must have moved more frequently than Harry had imagined.

"She said you guys had a good life," Harry commented, more an observation than an expectation at conversation.

Phil scoffed. "She had a good life."

Harry stopped looking at the album and turned to his son. "What do you mean?"

Phil shrugged. "I just wanted to be in one place, have a house, go to school. Mom moved us around a lot. She's never held down a real job. She was always bartering for things. She'd paint murals on someone's wall, and they'd let us crash there for a while. She'd tend to someone's garden, and they'd give us food. We never stayed anywhere long."

Harry remembered Kara's off-the-cuff comment about Phil resenting his childhood. "Sounds like an adventure," he offered.

"I was in eighth grade before I convinced her to put me in public school. She'd homeschooled me all that time. Sometimes with other kids. That bartering thing again. 'I'll teach your kid if you feed mine.'"

"Well, that sounds like a job to me."

Phil ignored Harry's defense of Kara. "I was thirteen when we finally settled in a little town on the Oregon coast. She got an apartment, an actual apartment." He smiled. "It was the first time I had a bedroom I didn't have to share with her or other people's kids. I still remember what it looked like. Mom convinced the manager to let her paint the rest of the apartment, but I refused to let her touch my room. For the first time in my life, I finally had plain white walls. We stayed there until I graduated high school, but as soon as I left for college, Mom was off again. She didn't settle down until Jess came along. She wanted to be close to help out— and it's a good thing she did. My ex-wife left when Jess was just a baby. We've been in Seattle since."

Harry looked around the living room. It was the color of rust. The entryway had been a lemongrass color. He had not seen a single white wall, not that he'd ventured far into the house. "You got over your dislike of colors, huh?"

Phil glanced at him. "Oh, no. This is Mom's house. Jess and I moved in a few months ago. The marketing firm I was working for merged with another company. They laid off most of us from the business that got swallowed. I haven't found a new job yet, and I didn't want to blow through my savings. Jess and I moved in here to save money while I get back on my feet."

Harry heard all of what Phil had said, but he was hung up on two words: marketing firm. "What did you do? At the firm?"

"I designed print ads, banners, things like that."

"I own a marketing firm, Phil." Harry's son eyed him suspiciously. "The Canton Company. Not very original, I know, but my father started it when I was just a kid. He was content with it being local, but I've been working on gaining some national accounts. I was out here for a convention, hoping to network. I took a lot of résumés, but if you need a job, you've got one."

Phil stared at him for several heartbeats. "Really?"

"Yeah. Insurance. 401k. Paid vacation. The works."

"What's the catch?"

Harrison shrugged. "No catch. I mean, not really. You'd have to relocate to Iowa, but you guys can stay with me."

"The hell they will." Kara stood in the doorway, her eyes narrowed angrily as she glared at Harry.

CHAPTER 3

Kara tried to calm her fury, tried to bite her tongue, but she'd never been good at impulse control. "I leave you alone with my son for ten minutes, and you're already trying to convince him to leave?"

"Mom," Phil warned.

She ignored her son. "What the hell gives you the right to try to take my family from me?"

Harry sighed. "I'm not trying to take anyone away from you."

She cocked a brow. She'd heard enough to know otherwise.

"I own a marketing firm," Harry said. "It just so happens my son works in marketing."

"Isn't that beautiful? Must have been all the time you spent with him when he was a kid."

"Mother!"

Harry lowered his face, and Kara mentally kicked herself. She wanted to apologize, but the anger she felt ran too deep. Phil and Jess were all she had. Sure, she'd made friends over the years. Sure, she'd been in Seattle for the last seven years. Sure, Phil was an adult with his own mind and his own life to think about, but Harry had no right to drop in out of nowhere and try to be Father of the Goddamned Year.

Phil stood and walked around the coffee table. He stopped in front of Kara, giving her the disapproving look that came so naturally to him. "He's offering to help me. In case you forgot, I'm unemployed at the moment."

"You don't need to go to..." She poked her head around him. "Where are you living these days, Hare?"

"I'm still in Stonehill, but the office is in Des Moines."

She refocused on her son. "You don't have to go to Iowa for a job, Phil. This is Seattle. You will find a job here, like you planned. You just have to keep looking."

"Do you know how many résumés I've submitted?"

"Four months ago, when you were laid off and I suggested moving, you had a laundry list of reasons why we couldn't relocate. It was important to keep Jess in her school, keep her where she is familiar and comfortable. What about that?"

"Christ, Mother," he seethed. "He didn't even finish offering me a position. I haven't had a chance to think about it, let alone accept. But you know what? Maybe you were right, for once. Maybe Jess will adjust. Maybe it would be good for her to try something new and meet new people. Maybe I should expand her world and show her different things."

His words took the wind from her. When she'd argued the logic of relocating, it was just the three of them. She'd pictured them living in a small town like the ones that she and Phil had passed through during the years Phil was growing up.

Kara had tossed out the idea, the logic, the hope of relocating, but not to the Midwest. Not to Iowa. And definitely not Stonehill.

"I have a big house. More than I need. You could stay with me." Harry walked to where Phil was staring down Kara. "All of you could. If you wanted."

Kara's heart dropped to her stomach. She turned and stepped nose-to-nose with Harry. "How dare you show up after thirty years and try to turn my life upside down all over again!"

"Goddamn it." Harry raked his hand through his hair. "I would have been there. I wouldn't have left you alone."

"But you did," she spat. "You got to live your life while I was sent away like some kind of leper."

"I didn't know you were pregnant!"

"Of course you didn't, Harry! How could you when you barely took the time to pull your dick from between my legs before abandoning me?"

"Jesus," Phil said, reminding his parents he was in the room. "I did *not* need to hear that."

Both Kara and Harry sagged a bit. Tears bit at her eyes. *Damn it.* She didn't want to cry. She refused to cry.

"Look," Harry said gently. "I'm not trying to take them away from you, but this is my son. My granddaughter. And I deserve to know them. I deserve to be in their lives as much as you do. I didn't choose to leave them. I know," he cut in before she could speak, "I walked away from you, and I sincerely apologize for that. But I didn't leave Phil. I want to know my son. I want to know his daughter."

"Then come *here*." Kara hated how her voice trembled with a crazy mix of anger, fear, and desperation.

"I can't. I have a business to run, and I can't do that from here. Phil needs a job. He needs insurance and security for his daughter. I can give that to him. For the first time in his life, I can give him something. I can take care of him. But I can't do that with him here." He turned to Phil. "Come to Iowa. Bring Jessica." He focused on Kara again. "You can come as well. Des Moines has changed so much. You can find a place to show your art there."

Returning to Iowa was not an option. Going home had never been an option. It was never going to be an option. She had been forced to leave, and she'd never looked back. She would *never* look back.

Heavy silence hung in the air until Harry said, "You don't have to decide now, Phil. You can come whenever you want. The offer is open-ended. If you choose to stay here, I'll help out as much as I can. It shouldn't all be on your mom. And I'll visit, if that's okay. I'd like us to have a relationship, even if it is long distance."

Phil smiled, and Kara despised the way he looked at Harry. Like Harry was so wonderful, so wise, so parental. She didn't think she'd seen that expression on Phil's face since he was six years old. Phil's clear admiration for Harrison tore at her heart, and she wanted to cry and scream and take back the moment she'd admitted they were father and son.

"Thanks, Harry," Phil said. "I'll think about it."

Harry shifted when Kara rotated her jaw and turned away. "Do you think I could talk to your mom for a few minutes?"

Phil lifted his brows at Kara, and she completely understood what he was trying to convey to her.

Be nice.

"I was thinking a beer sounded good. Would anyone else like one?" Phil didn't actually wait for anyone to answer. He stepped around his parents and left the room.

Kara rolled her head back and exhaled. "You are unbelievable," she whispered.

"Because I want to know my son?"

"He doesn't need you to fix things for him, Harrison."

"This isn't about fixing things, Kara. Damn it. That's my kid. He's an adult now. A father. He's twenty-six years old. He's been married and divorced. He's graduated high school and college. I missed all that. I didn't get to help him with any of that, but I can help him now. And I do have a right. I'm his father."

"You don't even know him."

"That wasn't my choice. I wasn't given a choice." He lowered his voice. "Look..."

She knew that trick from his teenage days. On one hand, it pissed her off even more. On the other, she couldn't help but be soothed a bit.

"We both got screwed over, okay? But we're here now. All of us. Together. I'm not trying to take Phil and Jess away from you. But they're my family, too, and I want my chance."

He put his hand over his heart, and hers broke a little.

"I want to get close to him," Harry said. "I want him to

see me as his father. Not because I had unprotected sex with his mother when we were both stupid kids but because I *am* his father. A father who is there, who he can rely on. Who *you* can rely on when you need someone to help you out. I want to make this up to you as much as I do to him. I know we aren't technically a family, but you're the mother of my child—my only child. That makes us family in my eyes, Kara. And I need a second chance with my family. All of my family."

She sighed and looked away. "I can't go back there. I can't. Not there."

"I can't leave. Not when my business is growing. And it isn't just my business anymore. It's Phil's, too. It's his future. His and Jess's."

"I can't."

He put his hands on her shoulders and held her gaze when she looked at him. "I know it hurts. I have to face my mother, too. I'm terrified. I'm furious with her. Part of me wants to cut her off, never speak to her again. But I have to know why. I have to know if she and my father even cared that their grandson was out there, growing up without me. I have to face the past, Kara. And so do you."

She couldn't breathe. Could barely hear his voice over the pounding of her heart as the truth she'd been ignoring for almost thirty years crashed down on her.

She had wanted to confront her parents so many times. She wanted to demand an apology. She wanted to shame them the way they shamed her when she told them she was pregnant.

But more than anything, she wanted to know why they

hadn't loved her enough to help her when she needed them most.

The thought of following through, however, was worse than any other fear she'd ever faced over the years. "Harry...I can't."

He caressed her cheeks, reminding her of the way he'd touched her that night. "Yes, you can. I'll help you. It's time to stop running, Kara."

Continue The Road Leads Back...

ALSO BY MARCI BOLDEN

A Life Without Water Series:

A Life Without Water

A Life Without Flowers

(Coming 9/29/2020)

Stonehill Series:

The Road Leads Back

Friends Without Benefits

The Forgotten Path

Jessica's Wish

This Old Cafe

Forever Yours

The Women of HEARTS Series:

Hidden Hearts

Burning Hearts

Stolen Hearts

Other Titles:

CPSIA information can be obtained
at www.ICGtesting.com
Printed in the USA
BVHW081334120820
586208BV00001B/30